P9-APV-346

DATE DUE			

Crush
WORTHY

For Charlotte Ross-Parkinson, who was there at the start, read every chapter as it was written and didn't complain once about marathon 'Jinx talks'; for Binny and Tim Wookey, who remain endlessly interested—and generous with their spare room; and for Niki Robinson, who not only opened a restaurant but gave me the Russians and a hell of a lot of laughs besides.

Crush
WORTHY

SARA LAWRENCE

razor
bill

Crushworthy

RAZORBILL

Published by the Penguin Group
Penguin Young Readers Group
345 Hudson Street, New York, New York 10014, U.S.A.
Penguin Group (USA) Inc., 375 Hudson Street, New York, New York 10014, U.S.A.
Penguin Group (Canada), 90 Eglinton Avenue East, Suite 700, Toronto,
Ontario, Canada M4P 2Y3 (a division of Pearson Penguin Canada Inc.)
Penguin Books Ltd, 80 Strand, London WC2R 0RL, England
Penguin Ireland, 25 St Stephen's Green, Dublin 2, Ireland
(a division of Penguin Books Ltd)
Penguin Group (Australia), 250 Camberwell Road, Camberwell,
Victoria 3124, Australia (a division of Pearson Australia Group Pty Ltd)
Penguin Books India Pvt Ltd, 11 Community Centre, Panchsheel Park,
New Delhi – 110 017, India
Penguin Group (NZ), 67 Apollo Drive, Rosedale, North Shore 0632,
New Zealand (a division of Pearson New Zealand Ltd.)
Penguin Books (South Africa) (Pty) Ltd, 24 Sturdee Avenue, Rosebank, Johannesburg 2196,
South Africa

Penguin Books Ltd, Registered Offices: 80 Strand, London WC2R 0RL, England

10 9 8 7 6 5 4 3 2 1

Library of Congress Cataloging-in-Publication Data

Lawrence, Sara, 1979–
  Crushworthy : a Those girls novel / by Sara Lawrence.
    p. cm.
  Summary: What started as potentially the best term ever at the exclusive Stagmount School for
Girls turns sour for wealthy seventeen-year-old Jinx as her best friend Liberty grows mysteriously
distant, boy problems erupt, and Daisy Finnegan always seems to spoil the fun.
  ISBN 978-1-59514-173-6
  [1. Dating (Social customs)—Fiction. 2. Best friends—Fiction. 3. Friendship—Fiction.
4. Conduct of life—Fiction. 5. Boarding schools—Fiction. 6. Schools—Fiction. 7. England—
Fiction.] I. Title.
  PZ7.L4377Cru 2008
  [Fic]—dc22
                                                          2007031140

Printed in the United States of America

1

Hampshire, A Few Days before New Year's Eve 2007

Jinx Slater sat at the kitchen table of her parents' house in Hampshire, flicking moodily through the papers and giving her elder brothers, George and Damian, the occasional death stare. She was in the grip of a fierce bad mood. Damian had just finished an epic bout of complaining about his monumental hangover, and was now slumped in the corner with a pillow over his face. George was engrossed in sorting out the massive pile of mail that no one had looked at for days. Even the dogs looked bored as hell. They were ranged by the back door and didn't even look up when one of the farm cats jumped through the cat flap, landing on the mat in front of their noses with a thump.

Jinx sighed loudly as she thought about a spat she'd had with her mum earlier that day over the shocking state of her bedroom. She hadn't meant to upset her mum, but most of the Slaters were suffering from a severe case of cabin fever following an excessively boozy Christmas; she had to think about packing and getting herself ready to go back to Stagmount—the exclusive girls' boarding school perched high atop Brighton's cliff face where Jinx was in the lower sixth—for the start of the spring term. But worst of all, as far as she was concerned anyway, for the first time since she was fourteen years old and allowed out to party with her friends, she had a grand total of zero options for New Year's Eve.

Jinx wouldn't even allow herself to think about Liberty, her best friend and partner in crime since they'd met on their very first day at Stagmount. She missed her terribly—and the absolute last thing she fancied was a boring night in with her parents when everyone else in the world would be living it up at some fabulous event complete with rivers of vodka, uber-cool DJs, hot boys, and probably bloody rock stars as well, knowing her luck.

"Right...then I guess it's just me and Jinx who will be RSVP-ing yes to," George said, looking up from the letter he'd just ripped open and winking slyly at his sister, "Tarquin Stone-Hall's super glamorous party."

Damian sat bolt upright, looking more alive than he had all morning.

"Tarquin's invited us to his party? Well," he said skittishly, "since it's *him* I guess I can make an exception to my usual no going out on New Year's Eve rule."

"You're such a terrible snob, Gaym," Jinx snorted, secretly pleased that she'd be spending the evening with her brothers at Tarquin's gorgeous country pile—his parties were legendary but she'd never been allowed to go to one before. And since all of her school friends were out of action—Liberty was probably hanging out with a bunch of hippies in California by now; Chastity had gone skiing in Austria with her mother and her mother's new fiancé, Ian; and Liv and Charlie were going to a party hosted by some friend of theirs in London—this was the best, and only, invitation she'd so far received.

"Oh Jinx," smirked George, "don't be so naïve. I don't think it's Tarquin's *ancestry* our dear brother is interested in. I think he's more taken with his *ass*."

"Well," said Jinx, her eyes bright with delicious anticipation, "I can't say I've ever heard you use the words 'super glamorous' to describe any event. Are you sure you're not taking a leaf out of Gaymian's big gay book?"

"Shut up!" George blushed. "I only said 'super glamorous' because *super glamorous* is the THEME of the bloody party. It's printed on the invitation." He squinted as he held what looked like a cardboard cutout of a cocktail glass up to the light. "Alongside such gems as 'champagne on arrival, Viagra on departure,' 'dress to impress' and 'leave your inhibitions at the door.'"

Yes, Jinx reflected two days later as she looked vaguely around the room she was chilling out in, thank God for brothers with friends who have parties. She was lounging on a chaise lounge covered with a pale silk embroidery and—even if she did say so herself—she looked pretty damn hot-to-trot in her black silk dress and vintage purple Biba platforms with dramatic makeup. It had taken her at *least* an hour to get ready before they'd left. She drew in a massive, self-satisfied toke from the bong that was hovering in front of her; belatedly realizing it wasn't simply hanging in the air but rather being proffered by a tall giggling man wearing a red trilby hat, and tried to focus. And even though her current viewpoint was decidedly impressionistic, Jinx realized as she looked around that she was in an extraordinary room.

The ceilings seemed miles away and the antique coffee table was covered with glasses and ashtrays. Jinx shuddered as she clocked a huge stag's head mounted on the wall above the fireplace that was framed on either side by two very gloomy-looking oil portraits of fat men dressed all in black. The remnants of a fire were dying in the grate and the stag's horns had a straggly piece of red tinsel looped from one to the other and back round. A man stood in the corner wearing what appeared to be a suit made of metal. He was stock still and the rest of the party seemed to be completely ignoring him. As Jinx peered over at him she could have sworn she saw him sway slightly.

"Hey dude," Jinx said, tapping his arm in a friendly way as she walked past on her way to the door, "is everything okay?" She waited for an answer, but whoever was inside the thing was clearly in a vicious bad mood and refusing to talk to anyone.

"Ok," she huffed, cross that he'd ignored her when she'd made such an effort to include him, "have it your own way. I was just trying to be nice. Fuck you!"

Jinx stuck her middle finger in front of his visor and staggered towards the door. She was about to sway through it when George flew round the corner, hotly pursued by a naked girl with long blonde hair astride a chestnut brown pony. Jinx drew back and stared in awe after the three of them as they clattered down the corridor. She was sure she'd recognized the girl…and a horse in the house? Maybe she would like to live here!

Standing in the wide door frame, Jinx suddenly felt rather short. She looked down at her feet and groaned. "Fuck it," she muttered, miserably contemplating her dirty bare toes, "I've lost Mum's favourite shoes."

Clutching her head in her hands, Jinx vaguely recalled that she'd been chatting to a couple of girls on the grand marble steps at the front of the house for a good hour or two at some point earlier on. She also recalled—more sharply this time—that she had neglected to mention the borrowing of the purple suede platforms to their rightful owner who had, incidentally, managed to keep them clean and safe since the freaking sixties or something. Shit. She *had* to find the fuckers. Jinx purposefully turned left and made her way in the direction of what she was sure was the front entrance.

Five minutes later she was delighted to find herself standing at the foot of a stunning Jacobean staircase that wound its way through four floors to the top of the house and was lined with yet more gloomy portraits of ancient fat people, some of whom were astride noticeably thinner horses.

She spotted the man in the silver suit standing to the side of one of the impressively shiny—considering the layers of filth that seemed to cover the rest of the place—dark wooden steps. "Oi," she yelled, pointing an accusatory finger at him, "you! Are you following me?"

She was incensed when he ignored her again and stomped up the few steps to the half landing above her to confront him. "Hey!" she shouted. "I'm talking to you! It's *beyond* rude of you to ignore me like this!"

Jinx was in full flow when a gaggle of older girls, enjoying a good old bitch about some poor soul, stopped to look at the commotion going on halfway up the stairs and started pointing and laughing in her direction.

"Christ," she muttered under her breath, thinking she recognized one of them as Not So Lovely Lydia. She was one of George's more terrifying exes. "What now?"

"Is that you, Jinx?" asked the most impeccably groomed, blondest one, who Jinx sadly realized was definitely Lydia. "Jinx Slater?"

"Um," Jinx managed to squeeze out before Lydia interrupted her.

"Girls," Lydia practically screamed, "*this* is Gorgeous George's little sister. Can you believe it?" Her acolytes giggled and shook their heads. Jinx wanted the ground to open up and swallow her whole, shoes or no bloody shoes.

"Jinx," Lydia said, raising a perfectly shaped eyebrow and gesturing at Jinx's filthy feet, "are you aware that you've got no shoes on, there's a humungous rip in the back of your dress, and you're standing on your own, shouting obscenities at a suit of armour?"

"Um," Jinx said again, the shock of this unexpected and highly undesirable encounter temporarily removing most of her powers of speech. "Well, yes actually, I *am* aware—"

Anything else Jinx might have had to say on the subject of saving her dignity was lost when the girls turned as one and began screaming with ear-splitting delight as a tall, bronzed, surf-god type made a very belated entrance clutching carrier bags filled to bursting with bottles of vodka, beers, and mixers.

Her fury at Lydia's bitchy comments meant that Jinx momentarily forgot her current shoeless state. She aimed a vicious kick at the suit of armour. As her right foot connected with the suit's iron leg, Jinx felt an unimaginable pain in her big toe. She screamed a hell of a lot louder than the girls in the hall combined, stumbled, skidded, and fell backwards down the very shiny stairs. She closed her eyes and waited for the inevitable thud, hoping she'd knock herself out and therefore not have to endure the look on Lydia's smug face.

She felt a thud all right, but it wasn't the kind she'd been expecting. Whatever she'd landed on was pretty soft…but sort of hard at the same time. She decided she wasn't going to open her eyes just yet but enjoy this unfamiliar swooning sensation for a little bit longer. She was making a confused mental note to explore other falling-down-staircase possibilities when she realized that the arms circling her waist were not her own. She kept her eyes tightly closed as she registered that they were strong, muscular arms, warm and definitely belonging to a man. She surreptitiously sniffed the air and was rewarded with the incredibly sexy combination of smoke, beer, surf wax, and chewing gum.

"She's mucking about. Look at the state of her." Lydia's voice echoed into Jinx's head from farther away than it had been a second ago, "She's absolutely trashed. She was shouting at that suit of armour a second ago like a proper nutcase."

"Hey," George's best friend Jamie said softly in what seemed to Jinx an impossibly sexy voice. Gosh, she thought dreamily, how one word can spark a zillion thoughts!

She cautiously opened one eye and gave Jamie a quick once-over.

She was so overwhelmed by what she saw that she rapidly shut it again and felt a hot flush begin to spread across her face. Dammit! She hadn't seen him since George and Gaymian had taken her, Chastity, Liberty, and—Jinx almost had a total gross-out just thinking about the bitch's *name*—fucking Stella Fox to his party last term. Trust her to—oh my God, she thought, nearly hyperventilating at her most recent unedifying memory—land on top of him from a great height looking her absolute freaking worst.

Jamie, George's pal from school and now the richest art student in Brighton, was a lovely boy. He had a huge trust fund, which he was charmingly embarrassed about, and had used some of it to buy his incredible seafront apartment about ten minutes west of Stagmount. He'd always felt slightly shady about his vast wealth, so he rented rooms out for practically nothing to his mates, most of whom were amazing surfers. He was constantly throwing parties for the rest of his scruffy student chums, and Jinx knew him to be an extremely genial host.

Nor did it hurt that he was totally hot. Jamie was six-foot-four with brownish blond hair, complete with golden highlights courtesy of the hours, days, and weeks he spent surfing in

Brighton and Cornwall. All the salt and sea air had left him with a permanent honey-coloured tan, and his blue eyes were shot with flecks of green. He looked like the lovechild of David Beckham and Matthew McConaughey wearing just one of Diddy's gold chains. Even his clothes were so damned sexy. He was wearing Diesel jeans with a pale-green faded T-shirt and navy-and-silver Onitsuka Tigers trainers in the cool, understated way that was made for beach boys like him.

The last time Jinx had seen him she was so preoccupied with Stella's evil plans for Liberty that when she'd finally managed to get Liberty on her own outside she'd jumped at the chance to find out what was going on. Although the more she thought about it, the more she recalled a distinctly hot-and-bothered feeling when he'd met them at the door. She prayed its repeat wasn't spreading across her chest in the manner of a livid rash at this very moment.

Jinx really liked him; she always had. Since the beginning of last summer holidays in fact, she'd begun to feel a bit hot under the collar every time she saw him. And, if she really thought about it, she had to admit that it hadn't taken long for that same feeling to take hold even when she only *thought* about him.

"Hey," Jamie said again, slightly louder this time, "*are* you okay, Jinx? You've been lying there not saying anything with your eyes closed for ages. Talk to me, Slater!"

"Oh my God," Jinx spluttered, realizing she'd been lying in his arms and daydreaming for probably like ten minutes already and opening her eyes wide in horror. "I'm totally fine, Jamie, I'm sorry! You can put me down."

Jinx struggled in his arms. Ooo, she thought with a shiver, he really was the fittest guy she'd ever seen.

"Easy, tiger." Jamie laughed and gently placed Jinx on her feet. "You'd better start watching your step. I might not be so handily placed the next time you decide to take a flying leap."

"Um…" Jinx stood in front of him, but since she couldn't bring herself to look into his eyes she found herself staring determinedly at the top of his right ear as she tried to speak. "I—"

She didn't manage to finish her sentence because Jamie tenderly cupped her face with one hand, licked the forefinger of the other and used it to wipe a smudge of dirt from her cheek.

"There you go," he said, standing back and appraising his handiwork with a wide smile. "Now you look like the million-dollar babe we all know and love."

Jinx felt like she'd been struck by lightning and also struck dumb in the process. She very much doubted she was capable of saying another word even if she wanted to.

Jamie put an arm around her shoulder, pulled her in close and gestured at her feet. "Something tells me," he said, before turning to wink at her, "that someone needs to find her shoes."

"Yes," Jinx agreed, finally finding her nerve and twinkling up at him from where she was squidged deliciously into the crook of his armpit. "I do."

As the pair of them made their way outside they ran straight into George and Damian. At the same time Jamie relinquished his hold on Jinx's shoulder, Damian grabbed her arm.

"We've looked bloody everywhere for you," he said, clearly

very cross about it, "and we want to go home. NOW!"

"Yeah," George agreed. "Come on, Sis, Mum and Dad will take it out on *us* if we don't get you home soon."

Jinx was furious inside, but knew from past experience there was no point in defying the Slater boys when they'd already made up their minds to go home after a party. She knew they couldn't wait to get home and raid the fridge—there was literally nothing she could say to dissuade them at this point, however much she might have pleaded. Her stomach clenched as Jamie leant over, kissed her cheek and softly whispered a goodbye into her ear, but she had no time to think about anything as the boys clasped each other's shoulders before she was practically frog-marched away from the crowd by the door.

"Jinx!" hissed Damian suddenly. The trio had slipped past the crowd towards the winding drive that would take them on the road to home, but Damian had stopped to point in horror at a pair of beautiful shoes discarded by the fountain, and was now giving his sister a fright. "Please tell me those aren't Mum's Biba shoes perched precariously on the edge of that fountain!"

"Thank God!" Jinx—who in all the excitement had totally forgotten her earlier mission—darted into the melee, emerging a few seconds later triumphantly swinging the purple platforms by their long suede ankle ties. "Thanks, Gaym, you're a legend."

"Hmpf" was Damian's only response. He shook his head in disgust at her casual way with vintage clothing, and the three of them started off down the drive.

Jinx trailed a few metres behind her brothers all the way home and got into bed in an absolute daze.

She daydreamed her way through the last few days of the Christmas holiday, constantly replaying the scene with Jamie in her head—and imagining a fair few more besides. She finally stepped off cloud nine and started throwing things haphazardly into her trunk for the beginning of term about an hour before her dad was due to drive her back to Stagmount. As she tied her curtains back and threw open her windows, however, Jinx caught sight of George pulling his boots on down by the stable block. It took about twenty seconds for her to decide she'd prefer to go for a ride in the forest than think about school anymore. It took another twenty for her to race down the stairs, out the doors and present herself, huffing and puffing with her riding hat in her hand, in front of him.

2   *Home on the Farm*

Jinx stood up in her stirrups as she galloped along a very muddy track in one of the forest enclosures not far from home, folded herself forwards toward Pansy's pricked ears, loosened her reins, and gave Damian's game old hunter her head. They were soon going so fast her eyes were streaming and the trees and bushes they whizzed past melded together into one big streak of blurred green.

Jinx sat back in the saddle and peered over her shoulder to look for her brother George as she felt the horse slow up underneath her. She laughed out loud as she spotted him about half a mile behind her.

"Hey, retard!" she yelled, "I thought you said there was no way in HELL I'd beat you?"

George's stirrups were so short his knees were practically touching his ears, and he was bouncing up and down like a huge and demented jockey. He grimaced at Jinx but didn't reply. He urged Dillon on towards his sister, who had pulled Pansy back into a gentle canter before slowing to a jerky, high-step-ping trot and then an ambling walk.

Jinx drew in great lungfuls of the fresh forest air and stretched her arms high above her head. Flexing her neck from side to side she realized she hadn't felt this physically or men-tally sharp since the day she'd arrived home from Stagmount at the end of last term. She'd managed to hold it together until the end of school, but winced as she acknowledged the fact that she'd spent most of the Christmas holidays in a haze of tears, stubbornly refusing to return any of her friends' numerous phone calls and generally stomping about the place, complain-ing bitterly about every family activity she'd not been able to get out of.

Since Tarquin's party Jinx had divided her lying-on-her-bed-and-thinking time pretty evenly between the new object of her affections and her best friend. The only thing, she thought now, to make her Jamie story perfect was if Liberty were able to hear it too.

Jinx laughed at her still-too-breathless-to-speak brother as he pulled up alongside her.

"I can't remember the last time I beat you in a race," she said. She sat up and wiped her grimy sweat- and hair-covered hand thoughtlessly on her clean jeans and smiled with some-thing approaching genuine happiness for the first time since Liberty had been flown away from Stagmount in the Harrods helicopter by her furious father near the end of last term. Jinx hadn't heard a single word from her and had worried about her whereabouts and welfare constantly since.

"I was going easy on you," said George with a sideways smirk at his sister, delighted to see her looking and acting more like her usual easygoing self. "I thought letting you win would cheer you up. I wouldn't have bloody done it if I'd known you'd be this smug, though."

"Shut up, G." Jinx was laughing so hard she had to clutch the front of her saddle for support. "I won that fair and square and you KNOW it. But if you're still not sure," Jinx said as she gathered up her reins, narrowed her eyes and made as if to belt off across the huge green they were approaching, "why don't we go again?"

George grabbed her left arm and shook his head.

"I thought so," Jinx said, raising an eyebrow and smiling archly.

"So," George said casually after they'd meandered along in companionable silence the entire way across the open green and were now approaching the home straight, "still no word from Lib then? Christmas just wasn't the same without you two goons shrieking, shoving, and laughing all over the place, and Mum and Dad are really worried about you. You mooching about the place so miserably all the time isn't fair on them."

Jinx's eyes filled with tears. She stared determinedly at Pansy's pricked ears in front of her. She was torn between shouting at George to mind his own business before storming off in the most almighty huff or admitting that he was right and that she *had* been treating her family badly.

"You're right, G.," she sniffed, having decided to do the right thing after a quick mental tussle. "I'm absolutely gutted about Lib. And I know I've been awful to you guys. Even at New Year's."

George said nothing, but nodded encouragingly at her.

"It's that thing, you know." Jinx squirmed in her seat, for she had a real aversion to "deep and meaningfuls." "Where you KNOW you're being a bitch even as you're doing it. You don't want to be behaving like that and you wish you could snap out of it but your bad mood has been going on for so long it's become almost, like, a default setting. Do you know what I mean?"

"I'm a guy, Jinx, remember?" George said this with a small, self-satisfied shrug of his shoulders. If he could have patted himself on the back at the same time he would have done so. "We don't do that kind of shit."

"Shut UP, G.," Jinx shouted, spinning round in her seat and giving him the finger. "That's the biggest bunch of bollocks I've ever heard. Do you want me to continue baring my soul or what?"

"Of course I do." George looked at his watch, then winked slyly at his sister. "I'm just pleased that it's only taken you—ooo—about three minutes of chat with your second-biggest brother to revert to the self-obsessed narcissist we all know and love."

He ducked as Jinx swung her riding crop at his head. The sudden movement surprised Dillon, who'd been moseying along in very relaxed fashion with his nose practically touching the ground in front of his face, and the horse jumped about four feet in the air without any warning whatsoever. Jinx winced and shut her eyes. When she opened them a second later a very disgruntled-looking George was sitting in a muddy puddle, completely soaked through with muddy streaks all over his face and neck. Dillon, meanwhile, had obviously decided he needed to get home as quick as was equinely possible. Since he was fast becoming a small ginger blur in the distance, he'd also evidently discovered a reserve turn of speed that he'd been hiding earlier.

"Shit, George." Jinx, trying desperately to hold back what she was sure would be an uncontrollable case of the giggles if she let them out, jumped off Pansy's back and held a hand out to help George up. "I am so sorry. I seriously didn't mean for that to happen."

George shook his head and grabbed hold of Jinx's hand as if he was going to let himself be helped out of his puddle.

"Argh, you bastard!" Jinx screamed when George yanked her hand towards him and she lost her footing. She toppled forward, then skidded on her knees in the deep mud until she was lying on her front adjacent to her brother. "I can't fucking believe," Jinx said, lifting her head and mumbling through a mouthful of dirt, "I fell for that!"

"Yeah, literally!" George sprang to his feet and grabbed hold of Pansy, who was standing like a mule and staring half-heartedly after Dillon, before collapsing with laughter. "Well, Sis, it looks like one of us will be walking back. And since it was you who started this little incident," George said as he swung himself athletically onto Pansy's back, gathered the reins together, and flicked his sister the V, "it's sure as hell not going to be me. Bye!"

Jinx sat in her puddle and glared angrily after her brother, whose maniacal bursts of laughter were carried back to her on the wind as he galloped towards home. Torn between crying and laughing, she chewed her lip and used her sleeve to try and wipe the worst of the mud off her face as she decided which emotion was going to win.

With a sigh she stood up and ran her hands through her hair, wincing as her fingers became stuck in a particularly filthy clump. She peeled off her sodden jumper, tied it round her waist and began the long trudge home, the occasional giggle escaping her mouth every time she thought of George's extreme surprise at his impromptu fall to Earth.

Jinx decided that when Liberty found a way to contact her she would, and that in the meantime she had to get a grip on herself and stop agonizing about it. She also realized she'd hardly given a thought to going back to Stagmount for the new term yet, but now that it was imminent she was looking forward to seeing the gang again.

Jinx was washing the mud off the bottom of her filthy jeans and ancient trainers using the hose pipe just outside the tack room and feeling pretty pleased with her new mature outlook on life when Caroline Slater flew round the corner wearing her tan Ugg slippers.

"Jinx," her mum yelled breathlessly, skidding to a halt

in front of her surprised daughter. Caroline *never* wore her Uggs outside, and regularly threatened pain of death to anyone—namely Jinx—who might borrow them and think of doing the same. "I thought I heard the gate slam, thank God you're back!"

"What's wrong, Mum?" Jinx asked, quickly turning off the tap and shaking the water off her jeans. "Is everything ok? You've got your Uggs on! If Dad's cross that I went out riding, then—"

Caroline looked down at her feet in dazed surprise. She'd left the kitchen at such a stretch she hadn't noticed what shoes she was wearing until Jinx pointed them out.

"Never mind that," she said, grabbing Jinx's hand excitedly. "I've been pacing about for the last hour, just dying for you to get back. When George eventually appeared and told me you were walking home I nearly combusted!"

"Why Mum?" Jinx was none the wiser and her feet were beginning to freeze. "What is it?"

"Liberty phoned," Jinx's mum yelled, gripping both of Jinx's hands. "She's in Washington, D.C.!"

"What?" An expression of sheer, unadulterated delight spread slowly across Jinx's shocked face. "When did she phone? How *is* she? And what the hell is she doing there?! Did she leave a number? Oh God." Jinx hugged her mum and started jumping up and down, taking her protesting mother with her. "I'm so PLEASED!"

"Oh, Jinx." Caroline drew back and put her hands on her daughter's shoulders. Her eyes had filled with tears to match her daughter's. "I can't tell you how pleased I am, too. We've all been so worried about you—and her! For the first time ever I've not known what to say to make you feel better about things.

"Come on, darling." Caroline linked arms with a by-now very tearful Jinx as they headed towards the kitchen. "Let's go inside and have a cup of tea and I'll tell you everything I know."

They settled into the comfy sofa to the side of the back door, and Caroline told her the story. Jinx crossed her legs underneath her, gripped her oversized blue ceramic mug with both hands, blew on the scalding hot tea it contained, and stared at her mother in amazement.

"So," Jinx eventually said, "you're telling me that Amir is so furious with Liberty he has *disowned* her and sent her to the States to live with her mum? In Washington? I almost can't believe it."

Stella Fox, that vengeful bitch of the first order, had, after falling out with Jinx and the others, e-mailed photos of her and Liberty on a night out in London to Liberty's rather conflicted Muslim father. Amir Latiffe had promptly chartered the Harrods helicopter to fly him to Stagmount near the end of last term and arrived in such a towering rage over his daughter's perceived indiscretions that—amidst many screamed and shouted declarations of how Liberty had blackened the good name of Latiffe forever—he had flown her back to Saudi Arabia, resolutely insisting that she would never set foot on British soil, and Stagmount's soil in particular, again.

Jinx had been in bits about it ever since. Even though Stella definitely had very serious personality issues and had been asked to leave the school by Mrs. Bennett, Stagmount's headmistress, Jinx couldn't shake the nagging feeling that she herself was partly to blame for what had happened to Lib.

She couldn't help but think if she'd gone a bit easier on Stella, nothing might have happened to her best friend. And although she knew that as soon as Liberty found a way to contact Jinx she would do so, the seemingly endless silence had really been getting to her.

"Yes," sighed Caroline happily. "I think it's the best thing that could have happened to Liberty. That man is far too unpredictable. He made life incredibly stressful for Liberty, never knowing what kind of mood he'd be in, or what threats he might make next. I think she lived on a knife's edge with him."

"Yeah, but..." Jinx could hardly get a word in edgewise before she was interrupted again.

"Come on, Jinx!" Caroline sat up and fixed her daughter with a narrow-eyed stare. "I hope you're not going to start defending him, because I shan't be able to listen to it. Your dad and I were absolutely appalled by what he did. I know you and Martin sometimes have rows, but really! That was something else and I don't think I'll ever forget it."

"I know, Mum." Jinx found a window of opportunity as Caroline drew an indignant breath and decided to take it. "Christ, I was there, remember? Of course I wasn't going to speak up for him. What I *was* going to say was that although Lib will be delighted to have been sent to live with her mother, I bet you she still feels sad about her dad. Even though he was often a complete and utter bastard to her, I think she did love him. Maybe that's changed, I don't know. God, I can't *wait* to speak to her."

"Well," Caroline said, standing up and brushing the dog hairs off the back of her skirt, "her mum whisked her off on some kind of holiday retreat in California for a week or so over New Year's, and they've just gone home to Washington. Liberty will have left for the airport now, but she said as soon as she lands at Heathrow she'll call you."

"Heathrow?" Jinx asked, grabbing Caroline's hand.

"Yes!" replied Caroline. "She'll be back at Stagmount tomorrow."

"Mum," Jinx said, suddenly leaning forward and hugging Caroline around the waist, "I love you so much. I'm sorry I've been so terrible to live with all over the holiday. I'll make it up to you, I promise. What time is Dad back? I'd better jump in the shower."

"Luckily for *you*," Caroline laughed, "Dad phoned just after Lib. Granny's back is playing up again so he's had to wait with her to see the osteopath and won't be home for another couple of hours. Let's go and get you all packed up and ready to go."

3 *Back to Stagmount*

"Jesus Christ," said Martin Slater, swerving to avoid an inconveniently placed road sign and just managing to keep both his cool and his racing green E-class Mercedes on the road as he rounded the sharp corner of Stagmount's long drive that led to Tanner House, where all the lower sixth lived. "Who the hell are *they*?"

"God, Dad, not you too," Jinx said, giggling as she looked up from the text message she'd just received from Chastity, who was also en route back to school, and spotted what had caused their near miss. "Men are so bloody predictable."

Sashaying along Stagmount's drive, a few metres in front of the car, were three visions of identical blonde loveliness. She could hardly blame him for staring—indeed, she had passed many happy hours in assembly and chapel doing exactly that herself. The girls were so stunning, and such complete carbon copies of each other, it would have been nigh on impossible for man, woman, or beast to ignore them.

"Those, Dad," said Jinx with a knowing smirk, "are Stagmount's very own and very infamous Russian triplets: Olga, Masha, and Irina. You must have seen them before—they're in the year above me and Liberty and everyone, and they've been here as long as I have. Don't you remember George falling practically flat on his face when he saw them at speech day last year?"

"No I don't," Martin said as he parked the car. "All I remember from speech day last year was the interminable length of it all. I must have dozed through most of it—or tried to anyway. So who are they? I must say they certainly look a lot," Martin faltered before continuing, "*older* than you and your friends."

Jinx flipped the rearview mirror over to her side in order to spy on the sisters without having to turn around.

It was impossible to tell them apart unless they were standing in front of you and you had been watching them covertly for three and a half years, as Jinx and her friends had, monitoring every difference. Despite their unceasing surveillance, Jinx still had no idea which was which from this distance—or any, come to think of it—but they were all so beautiful and perfect she supposed it didn't actually matter.

What Jinx and the others didn't know was that each could be easily, instantly recognized by the differently coloured large stones set in the center of the gold rings that each wore on the third finger of her right hand. Given to them by their oligarch father before they left Moscow for Stagmount four years earlier, Olga's was a blue diamond, Masha's a green one, and Irina's pink. Despite sharing literally everything else, the triplets never swapped these over.

Five feet, nine inches, and perfect size sixes, all three had expertly highlighted honey-blonde hair that fell to just above their elbows in graceful waves. All of them were wearing pale-blue skinny ksubi jeans tucked into tie-up black Ugg boots. The one in the middle was wearing a black silk Prada bomber jacket; the triplet on the left was wearing a Stella McCartney beige trench coat over a charcoal grey polo neck; and the girl on the right was swathed in an oversized Nicole Farhi cashmere throw in berry-red.

Jinx considered their undulating progress of perfection in silence for a few seconds before turning back to a decidedly dazed Martin. If Jinx didn't know better she'd have sworn she heard a groan escape her dad's lips as the girls drew alongside the car and, with exact synchronicity, waved cheerily at Jinx before walking through Tanner House's front door.

"Curiouser and curiouser," muttered Jinx, who was also watching them go in. "They *were* in the upper sixth last term so I've got no idea what they're doing in Tanner. Either they've been moved down—which wouldn't surprise me given what I know about their so-called work ethic—or they're dropping something off. And I can't see it being the latter. They're lovely girls, but I don't know them that well and I've never once seen any of them run a single errand. We always say that people are too afraid to ask them to do normal things because they're so beautiful."

"Well," said Martin, flinging the driver's door open and dashing round to the boot with what looked to Jinx like unseemly haste to get in the door before the girls disappeared, "since we're finally here, let's get you in and sorted."

"Jinx Slater!" Brian Morris, Jinx's housemaster and a very good egg, stood alone in the small reception area. There was no sign of the Russians anywhere. Mr. M. clutched a clipboard to his chest as he threw an arm around Jinx's shoulders before clasping Martin's hand in a firm handshake. "Has anyone ever told you you're like a bad penny? Always turning up! How are you both? Good hols I trust?"

"Lovely, sir," said Jinx, conveniently forgetting that she'd spent most of her time at home mooching about in the most almighty sulk, delighted to see her favourite teacher back in such high spirits after all the traumas at the end of last term. "And isn't it fanTASTIC news about Liberty! Do you know when she's coming?"

"Yes it is and yes I do," smiled Mr. Morris, winking at his favourite pupil. Jinx had saved him from being fired—and probably worse—when the dreaded Stella Fox had falsely accused him of sexual harassment at the end of last term, thus earning herself a special place in his heart forever. "We've been told to expect her first thing in the morning, definitely in time for assembly. She's flying straight to Heathrow from Washington and coming directly here from the airport. I imagine she's in the air right now, so don't worry—you won't have too long to wait."

"Wow," sighed Jinx, "I can't wait to see her. We haven't not spoken for this long since we first met, and I've really missed the bitch!"

Jinx extracted another twenty pounds from her dad's pocket without him noticing when he'd hugged her good-bye, and now she was sitting happily on her bed and contemplating her room. She leapt up with a huge grin and wrenched open her cupboard door. She peeled one of the myriad photos that adorned the inside of it from its blue-tacked fixing and lay back down on her bed holding it in front of her.

A black-and-white Polaroid, taken by Jinx's mum Caroline, who obsessively documented every single thing that ever happened to any member of the Slater family—including snapping dead pets in their shallow graves whilst the rest of the family sobbed at a respectful distance. The picture showed her and Liberty on the first day they'd met. It was three and a half years ago, but seemed like twenty. They both looked so small and afraid, tiny first years on the first day at school. Jinx loved that picture, and she loved Liberty even more. God, she was relieved they'd gotten away pretty much unscathed by last term's upset.

"Chas," Jinx screamed, dropping the photo onto her bedside table and jumping up as Chastity Max-Ward pushed open the door and stood in the frame, looking impossibly glamorous in a Prada coat with skintight navy blue ksubi jeans tucked into the ubiquitous Ugg boots, clutching a bottle of red wine and sporting a gorgeous skiing tan. "How the hell are you? I've missed you!"

Jinx flung herself towards her second-best friend without waiting for an answer, and they squealed with delight as they jumped up and down on the spot, deliriously happy to see each other after a month apart.

Punctuated by the occasional ear-splitting squeal, they talked at high speed at each other for a good ten minutes without pausing for breath, until they both laughed and collapsed, exhausted, onto Jinx's bed, belatedly realizing that in their excitement they hadn't taken in a word of what the other was saying.

"So," Chastity said breathlessly, yanking off her boots and bundling her long blonde hair into a messy ponytail on the top of her head, "Lib's back tomorrow?"

"Yep," said Jinx, grinning widely and bunching a pillow behind her back against the wall. "I can't tell you how awful it was until she phoned." She paused. "Well, how awful I was, if you want the truth. I couldn't deal with it at all and the poor family got the brunt of it. We're all the best of friends now of course, but I did behave fucking badly. I feel quite shady about it to be honest!"

"Come off it, Jinx," Chastity said, reaching across her for another pillow. "We *all* do it. Christ, I'm sure they've done it themselves. Look what a bitch I was to Mum and Ian all last term. And he's such a nice bloke! He couldn't have been any nicer when we were skiing and I really, really like him now. I wouldn't worry about it any more if I were you."

Chastity was expertly uncorking the bottle of very expensive Pinot Noir the newly lovely Ian had given her as a going-back-to-school present when Jinx slapped her forehead and squealed again.

"Oh my God," she screamed, "in all the excitement I forgot to tell you! I can't believe it!"

"What?" Chastity demanded as Jinx jumped up and down. "*What* haven't you told me? Come on, you can't leave me in suspense like this!"

"Only that the triplets are joining us in the lower sixth this term," Jinx said triumphantly, very pleased to be the imparter of such great gossip. "They're moving back into Tanner and everything."

"Really?" asked Chastity, emitting a long low whistle. "Olga, Irina, and Masha are in *our* year now?"

"Yep," Jinx said, opening her window, leaning out and lighting a cigarette. "Mr. M. tells me they fucked up their pre-final exams, so they're being moved down. Mrs. B.'s obviously in a panic about her league tables."

"Wicked," replied Chastity. "I've always been *fascinated* by them. How cool!"

"Didn't you do ballet or something with one of them in the

second year, Chas?" Jinx asked, carefully stubbing out her cigarette and placing it on the windowsill with an eye to smoking the rest of it later.

"Yes!" Chas slapped her own forehead, wincing as she misjudged it, leaving a red mark right in the middle of her eyebrows. "I did! I can't believe I'd forgotten all about it. Irina was in my tap-dancing class. She was lovely—always smiling and very funny, actually—but I was always too mesmerized by her beauty to ever dare speak to her."

Chastity frowned and took a sip of her wine. "Although," she continued, "we were never sure if it was Irina or one of her sisters. Some weeks she was amazing—so good the teacher would practically wet herself—and then other times she slouched and stomped and no one could understand it. We all thought it was hilarious of course, but the teacher would almost be crying with disappointment. Then the next week she'd be back to brilliant."

"Imagine," said Jinx admiringly, "if you had an identical triplet—even a twin—the mind-blowing stunts you could pull! Wouldn't you be pranking people all the time? I know I *totally* would. I wonder what the others are like—do you know anything about them?"

"What others?" Liv and Charlie, who had been best friends since they'd stolen the gardener's tractor two and a half years previously and tried to do hand-brake turns in it on the grass tennis court, yelled in unison as they pushed and shoved their way into the room and into each other before diving on top of Jinx and Chastity, screaming hellos and happy new years and spilling lots of red wine all over Jinx's clean sheets in the process.

"Fucking hell," said Jinx, righting herself and staring up at Liv, whose shoulder length brown hair had been cropped to within an inch of its life and dyed so black it looked blue. "Your hair looks *amazing*. When did you do that?"

"Well," said Liv, self-consciously running a hand over her new ultra short and ultra fashionable do, "I've had the same-old, same-old hair since I was born, practically, so I thought, you know, new year, new term, new *do*. I did it last week in London. My mum's still not speaking to me, but I love it!"

"Jinx is right," agreed Chastity. "You look freaking fantastic. So much older too...hey! Maybe I should get mine done?"

The others fell silent as they contemplated Chastity. With her long blonde hair and jangling Tiffany bracelets, Chastity's appearance was strictly fluffy, but once riled she was famous for throwing the most almighty hissy fits. As they looked at her, her friends were all wondering how to tell her that having her golden mane chopped off would surely be the worst personal style decision she could ever make.

"But Chas," Jinx exclaimed in a sudden fit of inspiration, remembering that Chastity adored her mother above all else, especially since her media-mogul father had fallen— missing, presumed dead—off the side of his yacht in the south of France when she was very young. "What would your mum say?"

Charlie swiftly jumped in. "Jinx is right, Chas. Don't you always say your mum loves your hair like that?"

"That's true," Chastity said, fondly patting the huge pony-tail she had bunched on top of her head. "She'd be gutted. I guess I'm stuck with it for the time being."

Liv and Jinx shared a secret relieved look. The fact is Chastity's features were simply too strong to cope with a crop like that, although none of them fancied telling her. Far better for a peaceful start to the term to let her think she'd made the decision on her own.

"Right," said Jinx determinedly, standing up and survey-ing the filthy sheets she'd only put on her damn bed twenty minutes previously, "I can't take this anymore. Look what you bastards have done to my bed!"

"Sorry, Jin," Charlie apologized, trying to brush off the worst of the wine but leaving an even worse stain in its place. "Why don't we go sit in the common room? I'll grab a few drinks and meet you in there."

Jinx, grumbling good-naturedly about the mess they'd made of her room, linked arms with Chastity on one side and Liv on the other and forced them to skip down her corridor towards their favourite common room complete with squashy sofas, giant bean bags and—best of all as far as the girls were concerned—a huge plasma-screen TV fully equipped with Sky Plus, DVD, and CD players.

"Ooo," Jinx said with a sly grin when Jamie and New Year's Eve popped unbidden into her mind as they approached the door, "there's something *else* I've got to tell you lot too. Remind me when Liberty gets back."

Completely ignoring her friends' protestations that it

would actually KILL them to wait a second longer for her gossip, Jinx pushed open the common room door.

"Bloody hell," muttered Liv in hushed tones, stopping suddenly and causing a pileup behind her, "what's *he* doing in here?"

The sight that greeted them was unlike any other Jinx and the others had witnessed in that room, and they stood in the doorframe, speechless with shock and admiration.

The Russian triplets were sitting near the window, around a card table none of them had ever seen before. It wasn't the bottles of vodka so casually laid out on the green baize in front of them, or the gold-tipped black cigarettes smoldering so insouciantly in the ashtray, or even the huge piles of ten- and twenty-pound notes in the middle of the poker game they'd obviously been enjoying for some time that shocked the three in the doorway.

No, it was the presence of a very moody-looking, tall, raven-haired man sitting there so cozily with the triplets, as if it was his God-given right to be in the strictly female-only lower-sixth-form common room that threw our girls into a spin. Man! The triplets obviously were as indifferent to school rules as people claimed they were. The dude, who must have been at least thirty-five, looked towards the door, gave Jinx, Liv, and Chastity a very obvious once-over and nonchalantly raised a hand in greeting.

"Who the hell is *that*?" Charlie blurted out after dashing at high speed through the door and skidding to a halt in front of the mystery man the others had been studiously pretending to avoid.

The triplets looked up from their intense study of their card hands at his movement, simultaneously waved, smiled, and chirruped "Hi, girls" at the three in the door, before turning back to the game, identical expressions of fierce concentration etched on each remarkable face.

Fanny Ho, a boyish Chinese girl who had smuggled her girlfriend Maureen Mo from Hong Kong to Stagmount the previous term, keeping her hidden in her bedroom until she'd finally cracked under the pressure of harbouring an illegal immigrant and admitted all to a very sympathetic Jinx, breezed out of the adjoining bathroom and sat herself happily down at the poker table.

Fanny had also been in the year above, but had to stay down in the lower sixth last term due to a nasty bout of glandular fever that had left her totally wiped out in bed for six months. None of them had realized it before, but she was clearly great pals with the triplets. Jinx was surprised. She really liked Fanny, and thought her escapade last term was one of the funniest things she'd ever seen. Jinx was only sorry she'd been sworn to secrecy. But she'd promised never to tell anyone and she fully intended to keep that promise until the day she died.

The triplets and Fanny dissolved into conspiratorial laughter and it was left to the man to stand up and extend a courteous hand to a shocked Charlie.

"My name is Igor," he said self-importantly and in heavily

accented English, "and I am the bodyguard of the Prozorov triplets. I will stay at Stagmount School and watch over the ladies
until they complete their studies."

"Really?" asked Charlie, her face turning pink as he pumped
her hand up and down with what looked like excessive force.
"Well, I'm Charlie. It's, um, lovely to meet you."

"We always see you girls around school," said Irina, drawing their attention back to the card table, "and we think you
look like the most fun from your year. Where is your friend?"
She pointed at Jinx. "The pretty, dark-haired girl? You two are
always laughing and joking together, and we always say you two
are naughty sisters just like us."

Jinx, who was privately thinking that Fanny and Maureen
had nothing on *these* girls when it came to pranking everyone
into thinking they were the same person, was delighted that
the stunning triplets so obviously wanted to make friends with
them all. If nothing else, it looked like the vodka would be
pretty much free-flowing for the rest of the school year.

"That's Liberty," Jinx said with a smile, having quickly
decided it would be just too much effort to explain the rea-
sons for her late arrival back at school. "She's flying in from the
States. She'll be here first thing tomorrow—she'll be so excited
that you three are in our year. She always talks about your
amazing clothes!"

"How kind," said Masha, glowing warmly at Jinx and throwing a delighted smile at her sisters. "We always try to look our
best. We love it when people notice our clothes!"

"Come and have a vodka with us," urged Olga, banging her

glass on the table in invitation. "We are nearly finished with our game anyway."

"Don't mind Igor," added Irina, noticing the concerned looks Jinx and the others were directing at him. "Except for when we need a fourth at cards or something we treat him like he is invisible. He likes it," she continued when the girls looked at each other in shock at such blatant rudeness right in front of his face. "He has to be alert for danger at all times."

The triplets raised their hands in front of their faces at the exact same time and in the exact same way as they emitted the exact same sarcastic "ooo, *scared*" impression.

Jinx looked at Chastity, Liv looked at Charlie and the four of them settled happily into the nearest sofa, no further overtures required.

When Mr. Morris tried to pop his head round the door a couple of hours later to enquire about the high noise levels coming from the common room, he found his path blocked by an intractable Igor. Despite Mr. Morris's anger with the stubborn bodyguard, Igor refused to stand aside and let the housemaster though the door, thus giving the girls a few precious minutes to stow the vodka bottles in the games cupboard, open the windows and spray a load of Irina's uber-expensive, limited edition Solange Agazury-Partridge's Stoned perfume around the room to mask the smell of the black cigarettes. Mr. Morris probably wouldn't have cared anyway. He was renowned for his easygoing attitude towards the girls under his care, whom he regarded as young adults and treated accordingly—letting them smoke in the garage outside reception so long as they cleaned up the butts on a regular basis and keep alcohol in moderation in their rooms. All the girls loved him, but Igor clearly didn't know—or give a shit about—any of that.

Although she was pretty trashed by now, Jinx nudged Chastity, pointed at the inflexible Igor and gave her the thumbs up sign. "S'brilliant," she slurred.

Mr. Morris frowned as he switched off the common room lights and made his way to his small flat at the side of the main house.

5 *First Assembly*

"So," Mrs. Bennett said. She gripped the edge of the eagle-shaped, maple-carved lectern on the dais in front of her, vastly enjoying the sound of her own sonorous voice as it echoed pleasingly around the cavernous, wood-paneled assembly hall, where Stagmount's entire student body and staff had gathered to hear her first day of term speech. "In summation, I am going to announce the head girl of each year."

"Oh God," whispered Jinx, nudging Chastity and pointing at dreaded Daisy Finnegan, who'd positively reveled in her role as chief lower-sixth pen pusher and suck-up throughout last term. "I just *know* she's going to be it again. Look at her—I can't bear it!"

They had woken up with terrible headaches at seven o'clock and lain around giggling raucously at absolutely nothing whilst they waited to give Liberty a heroine's welcome back

to Stagmount. They had killed—or rather, toasted—a few crois-
sants and brewed a carafe of Jamaican ground coffee beans
they'd found in the back of a store cupboard in her honour.
Unfortunately, and as Mr. Morris told them when he and Myrtle
the dog emerged, yawning, at ten to eight, Liberty's plane was
delayed on the ground at Heathrow, so she wouldn't be back at
school until at least morning break time.

"Look," hissed Chastity in Jinx's ear as the two of them
leaned over to the left to peer at Daisy, who was sitting a few
rows in front and to the side of them. "She's pretending to be
all casual about it, but check out how white her knuckles have
gone clenching the front of that pew."

"Puke indeed," giggled Jinx, deliberately mishearing and
flicking a deeply satisfying V sign at Daisy when she turned
round to glare self-importantly in the general direction of the
muffled noise they were making. "I'd like to blow chunks all over
her. And maybe," she continued with a most undignified snort,
"I'll do just that when we get out of here. My tummy feels like it
needs a good old clean-out."

"To be fair," Chastity whispered back, "you could probably
easily do it if you just got a whiff of her death breath. In fact, you
could probably do it right here right now just *thinking* about it."

Jinx wrinkled her nose in disgust but had no chance to
respond, for Mrs. Bennett chose that very second to loudly
announce, "And our penultimate head girl, for the lower sixth
form and for the second term in a row, is Daisy Finnegan."

Daisy stood up and smirked smugly around the room as
her appointment was acknowledged by the sounds of some very

forced and feeble clapping. She looked on the brink of saying a few no-doubt exceedingly well-prepared words, but closed her mouth again as Mrs. Bennett fixed her with an icy stare. Daisy smoothed a lock of greasy ginger hair from where it had escaped the straggly ponytail she usually wore high on her head before sitting back down, the infuriatingly smug expression still plastered across her greasy face.

"Who is *that*?" Irina asked Jinx, leaning over to whisper in her ear from the row behind. "We've never seen her before. Is she in our year?"

"Yep," muttered Jinx. She had no idea which of the sisters had addressed her, and kept a beady eye on the teachers, who were lined up in diagonal rows on either side of Mrs. Bennett and were beginning to crane their necks and shoot pointed glares in their general direction. "Unfortunately she is. We'll fill you in later."

"*Quod Denique.*" Mrs. Bennett permitted herself a small titter at the vast sea of faces staring blankly back at her—she just loved to throw Latin words and phrases into ordinary conversation. "Or, for those of you who haven't been paying quite as much attention to your homework as you should be, and—"

"Get on with it, for fuck's sake!" whispered Liv to Charlie, who tittered nervously as she noticed Miss Strimmer and Miss Golly, Stagmount's much-hated sports staff turning the twin laser beams of their furious eyes towards her.

"—last but not least," continued Mrs. Bennett, sending a silent prayer heavenwards that this was indeed the case, for she had left this appointment to the bursar, "I would like to introduce Mr. Dirk Hanson, Stagmount's first-ever football and cricket teacher. Where are you, Mr. Hanson?"

Mrs. B. didn't need to look around for long. Within seconds, an impressively stacked man of about thirty-five was racing from the back of the hall to the front, a streak of lime green in a heavily branded Adidas tracksuit with white stripes down each leg. The girls were too busy staring in wonder at him to say anything, and Mrs. Bennett stood stock still behind her lectern, staring just as hard.

At the very last moment before he reached the stage, and just when it looked like he was going to crash into the front of it, Mr. Dirk Hanson threw himself into the air and performed a backwards-forwards roll in mid-flight. He jackknifed before landing on his hands next to the very shocked headmistress. He flick-flacked himself into normal standing position and, as he did so, every single person in the room got an eyeful of the exact outline of his package through the thin fabric of his sportswear trousers.

"Fucking hell," guffawed Jinx, whose jaw was nearly on the floor, "did you see that? I think he did it on purpose. He is hilarious!"

"Don't you mean did I see *those*?" replied Chastity, laughing just as hard. "He looks like a total prick but imagine the *fun* we're going to have with him."

"Where do we sign up?" agreed Liv. "I don't think spring term has ever looked like this much fun before."

"Hello girls," drawled Mr. Hanson, smoothing his gelled hair back into place, smug in his belief that he was cutting something of a dash up there onstage in front of all these little ladies, his tracksuit perfectly complementing his St. Tropez-tanned face and torso. "I'd prefer to be called Coach—if, of course, that is agreeable to Mrs. Bennett?" Any doubts that his question was anything other than rhetorical were proved false when he carried on without waiting for an answer, flashing the headmistress his most blinding smile in consolation. "Coach D. Hanson."

Although Mrs. Bennett was seething inside, apart from a small shake of the head she regained her outer poise remarkably quickly. "Well, if that's what you are used to, then that is what the girls must call you. Coach D. Hanson everybody," she said, sounding for all the world as if she was introducing a new act at a cabaret night. "I'm sure you will find lists of his various training sessions on the sports board. That's it. Here's to a great term; school dismissed!"

The entire school filed out of the room in Mrs. Bennett's wake but at a much slower pace than her breezy exit, and with about a trillion decibels more noise as they avidly discussed the newcomer.

"I have never," said Olga to her sisters as they traipsed towards the door, followed by a dark-suited Igor, "seen anything like him in my life."

"I know," said Masha with a giggle, waving as they passed a few girls from the upper sixth before they caught up with the girls from their new class. "It is most odd, but I have suddenly acquired a strong desire to learn to play cricket and football."

"Me too," smirked Charlie. "It's funny, that. Come on dudettes, let's hit the notice boards before they get swamped!"

6 *Mrs. C. Has the Hots*

Stagmount's corridor, which had the dubious claim to fame of being the longest in any building in England, was filled to bursting point with girls of all shapes, sizes, ages, and hairstyles clustered around the sports area of the notice boards. Seeing the glamorous lower sixth make their approach, a gaggle of younger girls instantly melted away from the team lists and training schedules they had been busily rifling through and stood respectfully aside.

The girls giggled as they noticed that some joker had already crossed out the coach's name at the top of the list and written "DIRK DIGGLER" in thick black marker in its place. The three pay phones opposite all had long lines of junior girls who were not permitted to have cellphones, waiting impatiently to speak to their parents and beg them to sign the permission slips needed for any extra lessons in the lower school.

To the casual observer, the mud-stained brown carpet and newly painted pale-lemon walls belied nothing more unusual than a walkway to math. To the girls, though, the corridor was the site on which feuds and promises were hung, drawn, and quartered before being squeezed dry of every last shred of gossip. It was used by all years at all times and was thus an emotional hotbed of various jealousies, hatreds, admiration, and crushes. The latter were always, *always*, directed from younger girls to older ones.

Queenbees of all ages and their cliques reigned supreme and side-by-side, but were always careful not to tread on the toes of anyone older than they. Protocol simply insisted upon it.

A first year, for example, would rather walk on hot coals than have to pass a big group of six formers, who would be far too wrapped up in their friends or whatever it was they were looking at to even notice the junior's passing. The junior, conversely, would think of "the encounter"—as it invariably became in her mind—for weeks.

So Jinx and the rest paid no attention to the younger girls, who had all removed themselves to a respectful distance as the lower sixth made a beeline for the training lists. They had been in awe of the sixth-formers when they'd been in the lower school, and it was simply the natural order of life that the lower years should now be in awe of them. The unquestioning adoration directed at the girls of the sixth was helped by the fact that as soon as they reached the sixth form, school rules exempted the girls from wearing the school's dreary uniform. The more

fashionable amongst the sixth had even earned a slavish following amongst a group of third-years who actually kept notes
on who wore what when. The Russians, Liberty, and Chastity
all featured in this list, but the rest of them wore their skinny
jeans and leopard-print ballet pumps too often to be counted.
Needless to say, and hilarious as they would have found it,
none of them had any idea of its existence.

True to form, the lower sixth hardly even registered the
younger girls' existence as they shrieked and laughed and
clutched each other whilst reminiscing about their new football
teacher's antics that morning in assembly. He'd only been at
the school for about five minutes but was already approaching
mythical status.

"Bloody hell," snorted Liv with sarcastically exaggerated
disbelief as she eyed the A4 pages lining the cork board. "Look
at this. Not one of Coach D. Hanson's junior training sessions
has a single space left in it."

"God," Jinx replied, looking over the same lists with a
knowing smirk. "It's amazing what a quick flash can do for a
Stagmountian's sporting ambitions."

"All the little ones will be growing crushes on that terrible
man as fast as you can say 'prick,'" agreed Chastity, not noticing
the large number of red faces this remark caused amongst the
girls still waiting for them to finish with the board.

"We are signing, aren't we?" asked Irina, confused.

"Of *course* we're signing, um, love," Jinx said, having privately decided last night that she was never going to refer
to the triplets by name again, patting who she thought was

Masha on the shoulder. "None of us is going to miss getting down and dirky for anything. Ooo," she said suddenly to
Chastity, who was writing her name at the top of the sixth-
form list with a flourish. "Make sure you put Lib down, too;
she'll kill us if we forget her!"

All signed up, the girls linked arms and trailed off in the
direction of classroom 4B, where they had to meet their tutor,
eccentric Mrs. Carpenter, to get their timetables for the term,
giggling nonstop about Coach D. Hanson and his acrobatics
show that morning.

"Hey," Liv said as they pushed open the door, "do you
think he'd been practicing all night? We should call him Coach
V. Handsome from now on. He obviously fancies himself
enough."

Roaring with laughter, the girls settled into their usual
seats. Chastity and Jinx sat next to each other in the very
centre of the back row, leaving the seat on Jinx's right-hand
side free for Liberty to claim when she got back. Liv sat next
to Chastity and Charlie sat on the other side of Liberty, closest to the big picture window that looked out over the playing
fields towards the sea. The five of them had shared every back-
row opportunity they could for the last three and a half years
and—apart from when Charlie had been forced into giving up
her seat to the dreaded Stella Fox for most of last term—had
no intention of changing anything just because they were now
in the sixth form.

Mrs. C. wafted into the room in an overpowering cloud
of Bulgari perfume, clutching her mug of strong coffee and

dressed in one of her customary all black and very stylish outfits accessorized with various pieces of chunky silver jewelry. She beamed around the room as she swung herself into her ergo-nomic chair and shuffled a bunch of papers on her desk.

"Well girls," she said, leaning forward conspiratorially and smiling around the room, a sure sign to her class that she remained as gloriously indiscreet as ever, "I'm sure I hardly need to ask what you thought of *that* little display."

"Oh, don't worry, Mrs. C.," Liv piped up, "we're all signed up and ready to learn the offside rule or whatever it's called. We'll keep you posted, for sure."

"Excellent work, Olivia," replied Mrs. C., using the exact same tone of voice she would have employed if Liv had just turned in a perfectly written composition or scored straight A's in a series of tests. She was clearly in one of her extremely good moods. "Please make sure that you do. Now then." She took a great gulp of her coffee and looked round the room again, more purposefully this time. "Am I right in understanding we have three new friends joining us this term?"

Irina, Olga, and Masha waved prettily at Mrs. C. from where they were sitting in a huddle underneath the window. She stood up to welcome them before suddenly spotting Igor, who was being his usual intractable self and sitting silently in the middle of the empty row behind them.

"Oh," she murmured, patting her hair and sitting back down rather suddenly. "Hello."

The barest ghost of a smile seemed to flicker about Igor's mouth before disappearing entirely.

"I don't believe it," hissed Jinx at Chastity. "Look at her! She fancies him! What the bloody hell is going on round here? Is there something in the water, do you reckon?"

"This," replied Chastity, an expression of sheer delight etched across her face, "is going to be a very interesting term indeed. What with one thing and another I reckon we're in for a bit of a rollercoaster ride."

7 *The Discovery*

Jinx, Chastity, Liv, and Charlie sat clustered around
the end of one of the long tables in the lower dining rooms
where the whole school rushed at half past ten every morning
to gorge themselves with hot teas and sugar-coated carbs to
ward off hunger pangs in the notoriously tricky hours between
break and lunch. Heads bent close together and brows fur-
rowed with concentration; they were poring over the timetables
Mrs. Carpenter had handed out in a rush at the end of tutor
group that morning and stuffing themselves with biscuits from
a loaded plate in the middle of their space. Jinx was on her
fifth cup of tea and ninth ginger nut—although none of them
were counting—when Liv screamed, jumped onto her chair and
started doing a war dance.

"Fucking hell, Liv," grumbled Chastity, who had sloshed
a load of tea over the front of her Smythson diary, covered in

the softest leather in the palest pink. "I *wish* you wouldn't make these sudden movements."

"I don't believe it!" Liv yelled, completely ignoring Chastity and waving her timetable above her head and making such a spectacle of herself that the attention of every single person in the crowded dining room was absolutely riveted on her. "I don't fucking believe it!"

"What?" said Jinx, giggling both at Chastity's extremely cross expression and Liv's mad dancing. "What don't you believe?"

"Have none of you retards," said Liv, clambering down and giving one of the assistant junior housemistresses—who had been foolish enough to glare and shake her head at Liv whilst she'd been dancing on her chair—the finger, "spotted the glimmering sign of freedom we've ALL been given this term?"

"O.M. fucking G.," screamed Charlie, excitedly banging one fist on the table as she enunciated each syllable and offering up her other hand to Liv for the obligatory high five they always shared when they had good news. "I've just spotted it. I can't believe it either!"

"Shit," said Jinx, jabbing her finger at the timetable in front of her after avidly looking around at all the others. "We've all got Tuesday afternoons totally free!"

"Lib too?" Charlie asked anxiously from the opposite side of the table, craning her neck as she tried to read the two sheets spread out in front of Jinx upside down and smirking happily when she saw it was true. "Shit, we are actually going to have the best term ever."

"Yep," Jinx crowed, "we've *all* got it. From twelve o'clock every single week until the end of term. First one's tomorrow. What are we going to do—"

Jinx couldn't finish her question since someone had come up silently behind her and covered her eyes with their hands in the silent "guess who" gesture the girls used whenever they managed to sneak up on each other unawares.

Jinx inhaled. Breathing in the familiar smell of Aqua di Palma perfume mingled with top notes of tobacco, Juicy Fruit, leather, and denim, she felt like crying with happiness as she turned round and enveloped a gorgeously olive-tanned Liberty in the most almighty bear hug.

"You little witch," Jinx said, smiling widely as she released her best friend before quickly appraising her with a one-second once-over, "are those Miu Miu shoes?"

"Yep," replied Liberty, a definite smug twinkle in her eye as she pointed the toe of one stunning raw silk shoe in beautiful burnt orange with a golden wedge heel in front of her and waved her foot about in front of their faces. "They're well nice, innit! And what are we going to do about what?"

She collapsed onto the empty seat next to where Jinx had been sitting, grabbed Jinx's hand and squeezed it really hard.

"I can't tell you how happy I am to be here," Liberty said, not-so-surreptitiously wiping a tear from the corner of her eye with her free hand. "I've missed you guys so much and I couldn't stand not knowing whether I'd be back this term or not."

"Tell me about it," Jinx agreed. She shook her head in relief at the sight of Liberty sitting next to her like this and pulled her close in another massive hug and spoke softly into her ear. "I couldn't believe it when Mum told me I'd missed you on the phone."

"I know," said Liberty. "Your mum said you'd been really upset. I was worried about you, Jin. Did you have good hols?"

"No," Jinx replied with a shake of her head, "I was a total wreck for most of it. The last week wasn't too bad, but I want to hear about you—I've been *dying* to know. What happened when you left here? What's going on with your dad? How is it living with your mum and what the hell were you doing spending New Year's Eve in a hippy commune?"

"Bloody hell," whistled Chastity, "that's a lot of questions."

"Christ, Jinx," said Liv, laughing, "we've only got ten minutes before the end of break! Why don't we talk about all of that later and fill Lib in on what she's missed so far this term?"

"Okay, okay," Jinx agreed before waving Liberty's timetable dramatically in front of her face. "First things first. Check this out, Lib."

Liberty studied the sheet, a slow smile of realization spreading over her face.

"Have you seen it!" yelled Chastity, bouncing up and down in her seat, so excited she couldn't contain herself a single second longer. "We've all got them! All of us have got the same free periods every Tuesday from twelve o'clock onwards!"

At this outburst all five girls jumped onto their chairs, linked hands across the table and danced up and down, screaming the whole time with exuberant and very loud overexcitement.

Mrs. Frick, an assistant housemistress at Steinem House

who was sitting at the head of a table of lower-school girls, shook her head in disgust at this childish display but decided against going over to remonstrate with them. She didn't fancy being ridiculed in front of her young charges, most of whom were staring admiringly at the lower sixth, clearly highly impressed by such frankly devilish behaviour.

"Miss, miss," said Katie Green, an unattractively chubby new girl in the second year with big vacant eyes and a permanently wistful expression on her rather stupid-looking face, as she tugged on Mrs. Frick's sleeve. "Did you look after any of those girls in Steinem?"

"No, Katie," snapped Mrs. Frick. "Thankfully I did not. And I am not 'Miss.' My name is 'Mrs. Frick.'"

"Sorry, Miss," replied Katie, gazing longingly after the lower sixth as they danced and skipped their way through the wide swing doors of the lower school dining room to get to their favourite double art lesson. "I didn't know. At my old school we called all the teachers 'Miss.'"

"Well," said Mrs. Frick snidely, "at Stagmount we don't."

Katie didn't hear any of this last statement. She stared at the doors Chastity had kicked open with unnecessary force, which were still swinging on their hinges, and exhaled a shaky breath. She felt weakened by the five arrows Cupid had shot into her heart at once, and certainly had no time for any of Mrs. Frick's inanities. She resolved there and then to find out all she could about her new heroines and to somehow, someday, make herself known to them.

Everything the Way It Should Be

"Come on then, Lib," Jinx said. The two of them lay snuggled together under the duvet of her single bed at ten o'clock that evening after they'd chilled out in the common room with the others since supper, talking about nothing much and watching MTV. "You've got to tell me. What the hell happened with your dad when you left here?"

"Honestly Jinx," said Liberty, "I don't know what I would have done with myself if Dad had stuck to his original plan. I seriously don't think I could have stood to live in Riyadh for the rest of my life. It's a fucking hellhole and I hated every second of it."

"Dammit, Watson!" exclaimed Jinx, determined to get the full story before they went to sleep. "I want details!"

"Watson?" said Liberty, scratching her head, obviously confused as hell by this unexpected reference. "What do you mean?"

"You know," sighed Jinx, exasperated, "Sherlock Holmes's sidekick. Anyway, don't stop. I've waited *months*—well okay it was only one, but it certainly seems like more than that—to hear this story!"

"Okay, okay, give me a bloody chance," Liberty said, stretching her arms above her head as if she were about to engage in a serious sporting activity.

"Sorry, darling, you're right," said Jinx instantly, snuggling down further under the duvet in preparation for a big bout of listening. "Hit me with it and I promise not to interrupt again."

"Okay, so when we flew out of here in that fucking helicopter," Liberty said carrying on in the small voice she always used when she was sad, "he turned to me and said that we were going to Heathrow and flying straight home to Riyadh and that he would never be speaking to me again."

"What about your passport?" Jinx asked, forgetting her earlier promise to keep quiet in her bid to get the whole gory story in one swoop. "How could you have gotten there without it?"

"He can do anything he wants," Liberty sniffed disdainfully. "He probably asked one of his fucking mates in the government to sort it out for him. Anyway, the point is he flew me straight back there and didn't say one word to me throughout the entire flight, the car journey at the other end, and for the first two weeks of the holidays."

"Oh my *God*," said Jinx, shocked even though she knew of old the type of emotional blackmail and bullying Amir Latiffe was capable of. "I can't believe it, you poor angel."

"My bitch of a stepmother totally ignored me too," Liberty

continued, "not that I gave two shits about her. Although to be fair, having me around again was probably her worst freaking nightmare as well. The only person I had any human contact with was Maia, one of the cleaners. She gave me lots of hugs and snuck me in the odd packet of fags when she could. She even managed to get me a couple of Western magazines from God knows where. If Dad had found out she'd have lost her job for sure, so I'll be eternally grateful to her. In fact, the night before I left for Mum's I gave her two hundred pounds—it was all I had on me but she seemed well pleased with it."

"Shit," Jinx said, gripping Liberty even tighter, "I can't even begin to imagine how terrified you must have been stuck on your own out there with no one to talk to and no idea what was going to happen next."

"Yeah, it wasn't pleasant," replied Liberty in the world's biggest understatement. "Not at all. Anyway, I'd kind of resigned myself to the fact that I'd be trapped in Riyadh for the foreseeable future, but what I couldn't resign myself to was the fact that I had no way of contacting you—or anyone, even Mum. He took my mobile as soon as we got to the airport, disconnected my computer and all the phones near my room. He's also got one of those machines that record every call ever made, so he'd have known if I'd used one of his. I was *desperate* to talk to you, but I didn't want to piss him off any more than he was already. So I decided the best thing to do was sit tight and wait his mood out."

"I can't even begin to imagine it, sweetheart," Jinx said, wiping a furious tear from the path it was wending down her cheek. "I mean, I obviously knew how cross he was and I had a fair idea he'd be making your life a misery as punishment, but I had no clue just how bad it was for you."

"It was completely horrendous," agreed Liberty, privately thinking that right now there was no place on Earth she would rather be than lying in this small single bed with her best friend in the world at her beloved boarding school.

"Jeepers," whistled Jinx. "So what happened to make your dad change his mind?"

"You know," mused Liberty thoughtfully, "I've thought about this so much and I still don't really have a clue. The only thought I've had that makes any sense at all is maybe my step-mother was so pissed off at having me mooching around the place all depressed that she insisted he send me away. I don't know. All I *do* know for sure is that one evening Dad bursts into my room and very tersely tells me to pack my stuff up as I'm going to live with Mom. Tomorrow. And in freaking Washington, D.C. of all places."

"Bloody hell," said Jinx, properly shocked by all of this. "I'm surprised you're so normal still, Lib—I'd have gone stark raving mad by this point!"

"Yes, well," Liberty replied, "since I wanted to get the hell out of there as fast as possible in case he changed his mind or something, going mad wasn't really an option."

"I suppose not," murmured Jinx, thinking that Liberty had kind of changed. Not in any really obvious ways, but she seemed a hell of a lot more mature and sure of herself than she had last term.

"So the next thing I know I'm on a plane out of there," she continued, "and I still hadn't spoken to anyone about anything, so I didn't know for sure what to expect, but Mom was waiting at the airport to meet me."

"Phew," whistled Jinx. "I bet you were glad as hell to see her."

"I was," Liberty agreed. "The whole thing was pretty emotional, as you can imagine. She had no idea what had been going on; she'd just had a phone call that morning telling her what flight I'd be on and to make sure she was there to pick me up. She's got no idea what's going on with Dad either. So she drove me back to her place in Georgetown, where she's living with her new husband, Chris. He's a politician and quite quiet, but he's a really nice guy and obviously madly in love with Mom."

"What's it like out there?" asked Jinx, thinking that this was one of the maddest stories she'd ever heard. "Have they got a nice place?"

"Yeah, it's beautiful," Liberty said, smiling in the dark as she thought about it. "A gorgeous colonial town house near the university. I'll dig out some photographs for you tomorrow—you'll totally love it."

"So then you went off to California for New Year?" asked Jinx. "What was that all about? Mum said the two of you had gone to some sort of hippy commune."

"Well," Liberty said, laughing, "it was more like a spa, but there were loads of weird beards there. Cell phones were banned—not that I had mine anyway since Dad never gave it back, and there was no Internet. They had poetry readings and jazz nights and it's supposed to be the most 'relaxed' place in the world. It was cool, you know, hanging out with Mom, catching up on everything and generally sorting my head out, but I'm so pleased to finally be back here. For most of the hols I honestly thought I'd never see you again."

"So are you going to live with your mom permanently now?" Jinx asked, still reeling somewhat from all this crazy information and trying to take everything in. "I can't even *tell* you how happy I am it's all worked out like this. Honestly Lib, I don't know what I would have done with myself or how I would have coped if you'd been made to stay in Saudi."

"Tell me about it," said Liberty, "I've been having the exact same thoughts—but in reverse, obviously. Anyway, that's pretty much the long and short of it. Did you ever hear anything about what happened to Stella?"

"No," Jinx said shortly, "and I don't care either. I never want to see that bitch again in my life. She nearly ruined yours, and I'll never forgive her for it. The less we talk about her the better as far as I'm concerned."

"You're right," Liberty agreed solemnly. "I can't believe I fell for all that shit and I can't *believe* what she did to me. You'll be pleased to know I've made a solemn vow to myself that I'll never be sucked in like that again."

"I know you won't," said Jinx, yawning widely and switching off the lamp on her bedside table. "And don't worry, neither will I. It was like torture not being able to pick up the phone and speak to you whenever I wanted, and I never want that to happen again."

"You're exhausted," said Liberty, "and so am I. Let's hit the hay and talk more in the morning."

"You're right," Jinx agreed, "I am tired. Those triplets had us hitting it hard last night. You must be knackered too, what with all your traveling of late. Goodnight darling, sleep tight."

"You too," whispered Liberty, "you too."

Settled and happy, Jinx and Liberty both fell asleep thinking that everything was finally back as it should be.

9 Cutting Loose

"Paul!" Chastity screamed, leaning precariously out of the taxi window that she, Jinx, and Liberty had taken from Stagmount to Brighton's seafront, and waving manically at her boyfriend. "Over here!"

"Fucking hell," Liberty muttered in an undertone to Jinx as Chastity threw open the cab's back door and propelled herself into a stream of heavy, fast-moving traffic with no thought for either her personal safety or the taxi driver's mental stability, and launched herself onto Paul, who was standing at the entrance to the pier, holding a bunch of roses. "Did you see that? Nice to see she's still bloody crazy."

The three of them had dashed out of their English lesson on the subject of the Romantic Poets with Doctor Brown, the last of the day for them every Tuesday now, and quickly decided to make the absolute most of their first free weekday afternoon ever.

"Shit!" Jinx exclaimed suddenly as two guys wearing thick black wetsuits and carrying surf boards under their arms ran past them down the steps to the beach before launching themselves into the darkly raging sea and paddling furiously. "What with all the excitement since we got back to school I *still* haven't told you bitches about my New Year's Eve!"

"I knew there was something I was supposed to remind you about," said Chastity, pulling Paul back down onto the stones next to her and a ready-rolled spliff out of her pocket. "Spill!"

By the time Jinx had finished telling her friends every detail about Jamie and her unscheduled flying leap down Tarquin's grand staircase into his arms, all three of them were staring at her, mouths agape. Even Paul had been hanging onto her every word.

"So this Jamie then," Paul said, looking—if this was possible—even more pleased by Jinx's revelations than the girls did, "he surfs, does he?"

"Yep," said Jinx proudly with a toss of her head, delighted at the unprecedented opportunities for showing off this story was giving her. "He's practically a pro."

"And he's in a band now as well?" Liberty asked wistfully. "A proper band?"

"Yes," Jinx said, not *quite* so sure of herself this time, but still feeling smug as hell. Anyway, she was *sure* George had said something about the two of them being in a band at university. "He plays guitar."

"Wow," said Chastity, grinning delightedly at all of them.

"Well, we all thought he was great when we met him last term and we can't wait to get to know him properly!"

"Totally," Paul agreed. "Much as I love hanging out with you girls it would be nice to have at least one other guy here, too. He sounds great. When can we all get together?"

"He is great," Jinx agreed, feeling slightly panicked at the realization that her friends seemed to think the two of them was a done deal when it was clearly anything but. "And I really, *really* fancy him, but he's my brother's friend. I can't just go round inviting him to things…can I?"

"Of course you can," said Chastity, making a massive snorting noise. "If you don't ever see him how the hell are you supposed to get him to ask you out?"

"She's right," Liberty instantly agreed, "you've got to get him to come out with all of us one night."

"I can't!" squealed Jinx. "I'm too embarrassed. What the hell would I *say*?"

"Oh for fuck's sake, Jinx," Chastity said crossly, "stop being such a wimp. How do you think I would ever have got it together with Paul if I hadn't sent him that note?"

"Wasn't it an anonymous letter, Chas?" giggled Liberty, digging Jinx in the ribs at the same time. "Correct me if I'm *wrong*, but I seem to recall it was Paul who asked YOU out and you confessed to the letter a month or so later."

"Whatever," snapped Chastity, glaring at Paul to let him know that should he even be thinking of saying a word to prove her wrong he would regret it. "My point is that if she doesn't say anything then he'll totally forget her and probably start going out with someone else. Jamie *is* gorgeous after all."

"Thanks a bunch," Jinx muttered, throwing a pebble towards the sea with great force and taking a deep toke on the last of their spliff. "I feel really, you know, *confident* about the whole thing now. Some friends you lot are."

"Come on, Jinx," Liberty wheedled, "we're only trying to help. You are the best, prettiest, cleverest, most charming and funny friend I've ever had, and if he doesn't jump at the chance to hang out with you then the guy's obviously a total retard and not worth any of your bother, okay?"

"Thanks, angel," said Jinx, putting an arm around Liberty's shoulders and squeezing her tight. "You're right—I know you are. I just feel really, like, totally *squeamish* about calling him up out the blue. But you guys are right. I'm going to do it."

The girls and Paul were sitting at a table in the window of Lal Quilla, their favourite Indian restaurant at the back of East Street. Liv and Charlie never turned up, claiming "unfinished business." The table in front of them groaned under a plethora of silver dishes containing creamy curries and various side dishes.

"Paul!" shrieked Chastity just as a blob of bright red vindaloo sauce landed on her cream Burberry trench coat. "Look what you've done!"

"Sorry babe," Paul said, leaning over to wipe up the mess using his napkin.

"Oh for fuck's sake," said Chastity crossly, batting his hand away, "you'll just make it worse. I'll do it my bloody self. After six months together you'd think you'd have learned to be more careful."

Liberty and Jinx exchanged a quick, shocked glance. They'd almost never seen Chastity and Paul bicker like this, but these days it seemed to be very much their normal mode of interaction. They finished their meal mostly in silence.

"Great day, guys," said Jinx as they finished signing their credit card receipts and started looking round for their coats. "The best. And special thanks to Chas and Paul for providing the entertainment."

"I know," Liberty said slyly, "dinner *and* a show—who'd have thought we'd be this lucky!"

"Shut up, you stoner cretins," squealed Chastity, shoving Jinx in the back and propelling her at great speed through the front door of the restaurant and out onto the street. "It's high time you two got boyfriends of your own and stopped laughing at mine."

"Stoner cretin?" said a deep and sexy voice in Jinx's ear as her inevitable flight across the pavement and into the railing that separated the sidewalk from the busy seafront road was broken and stopped by a pair of strong arms that encircled her waist from behind. "Surely that girl can't be talking about you like that, Jinx Slater?"

Jinx could not believe her ears. She couldn't, simply couldn't, countenance the fact that the best thing that had happened to her in her life to date was happening—and without any warning whatsoever, just like the last time in fact—again.

"Jamie?" she whispered, feeling like swooning all over the place but managing to hold it together as she turned round, making a conscious effort to do so as deliberately and sexily as she could manage. "You are the absolute last person I expected to see! What the hell are you doing here?"

Jinx focused her attention on Jamie and was delighted to see he was looking as hot as ever in faded, low-slung Evisu jeans, a navy blue T-shirt emblazoned with a dragon picked out in silver and gold threads and the same Onitsuka Tiger trainers he'd been wearing on New Year's Eve.

Jinx pulled herself together and, feeling doubly pleased that she'd made an effort with her makeup and worn her nicest grey skinny jeans with her leopard-print slip-on shoes and favourite black polo neck, shot him a wide smile. Studying his gorgeous face, she realized he was amused about something or other. Oh God! He must think she was an absolute crazy. Why oh why couldn't she just bump into him in a nightclub or a bar or when she was doing something normal? Using the tiniest corner of her eye to check him out, Jinx realized he was desperately trying not to laugh and decided she needed to urgently pull herself together. She gave him what she considered her most mature questioning glance—not that she wanted to rush their encounter in the slightest or anything, but she felt it was important to keep up at least the pretence of conversational momentum, even though she herself would have been happy to stand and stare at him all day.

"I live here, remember?" he said in response to her quizzical look, his grin so cheeky and inviting it almost stopped Jinx's heart right there in its tracks on the pavement, gesturing along the street in the direction of Stagmount. "That's my block. You've been to a couple of my house parties, right?"

"Right," she murmured, "right. Of course I have. That one last term was great by the way."

"Hey mate," Paul jumped in, offering his hand to Jamie. "I'm Paul, Chastity's boyfriend and general friend to this lot of reprobates. I picked Chas up from your place last term—it looked like it was kicking off in there."

"Hi Paul," Jamie said, clasping Paul's hand in his own before turning his grin towards a beaming Chastity. "Of course I remember you—and I've met you a few times, haven't I, Chastity?"

"You sure have," Chastity replied, slightly too skittishly for Jinx's liking—she had one bloody boyfriend already for Christ's sake! "And it's lovely to see you again. You should come out with us next time, shouldn't he Paul?"

Ignoring the furious looks Jinx was shooting at Chastity and a frantically nodding Paul, Liberty couldn't stop herself from jumping in feetfirst either.

"Jamie," she said, giving him a bigger hug than Jinx thought appropriate given the circumstances, "it's *great* to see you! Chastity's totally right, we should definitely arrange a big night out."

"That," said Jamie, turning to Jinx and wrapping a warm arm casually around her shoulders, "sounds like a great idea. I'll organize it with this stoner cretin I've got here, shall I?"

"Perfect," snapped Liberty, beaming at him and winking at Jinx. "Make sure that you do."

"Liberty!" Jinx hissed in her ear, "cool it, will you?"

"So," continued Liberty breezily, completely ignoring Jinx, "were you off home when Jinx threw herself at you?"

"*Liberty!*" Jinx hissed again, but to no avail.

"I was out checking on my car actually," Jamie replied, hooking his thumbs into the belt hooks at the front of his jeans and rocking slightly as he stood there in what was—according to Jinx anyway—an almost *maddeningly* sexy fashion. "My house-mate Daz borrowed it yesterday and it hasn't been seen since. I thought I should check that it still had four wheels, an engine, windows—you know, the usual stuff."

"Tell me about it," agreed Paul, shooting an amused glance at Chastity, who was learning to drive and kept forcing him to take her out and about so she could practice. "I've been worried about mine lately."

"Hey," Jamie said, jangling the bunch of keys in his pocket, "were you guys on your way back to Stagmount?"

"Yep," said Jinx, staring up at him through her lowered lashes, "we were just about to hail a cab."

"Well in that case," Jamie said, ostensibly speaking to the group, though all his attention was focused on Jinx, who was holding her breath and had suddenly gone very still. "Why don't I drive you? I should take it for a quick spin anyway and check that Daz hasn't done any lasting damage."

"Thanks," Jinx said delightedly. "We'd love it, wouldn't we girls?"

"That's really kind of you mate," said Paul, who always made a point of delivering Chastity and her friends directly to their door before heading home himself. "And it means I can get straight off from here."

Whilst Paul and Chastity snogged each other's faces practi-cally *off* on the pavement, not giving a damn for the sensibilities of anyone who might walk past and see them and made totally unnecessary—in Jinx and Liberty's opinion anyway—baby noises as they said their goodbyes, Jamie strode off down the road to pick up his motor.

Liberty let out a low whistle as she and Jinx clutched each other and stared appraisingly after his exceedingly pleasant rear view as he disappeared into the distance.

"Bloody hell, Jinx," she said, digging her blushing best friend in the ribs and cackling madly. "That boy is HOT! No wonder your face is currently changing colour even faster than Chastity's was earlier."

"He is hot, isn't he?" Jinx replied dreamily. "And don't you think he's just so, like, goddamned *nice* as well?"

"Of course," Liberty assured her. "I always think it's super sexy when boys make a real effort to be nice to a girl's pals, too."

Jinx blushed as she thought about it. She thought Liberty was totally right—the way Jamie had taken such an interest in her friends was beyond sexy. The fact that he'd made such an effort to make a good impression on *them* made her feel like he was really interested in *her*.

"And he was great with Paul," Liberty said, nudging Jinx and jolting her out of her reverie. "I really like him."

"Jinx the minx!" yelled Chastity, running over to join the two of them after Paul had jumped on his bus and blown her a kiss from the open door. "I am seriously impressed. He's gorgeous and obviously mad about you."

"Do you really think?" asked Jinx, blushing again and beginning to wonder if her cheeks would ever return to their normal pale peachy colour. "Isn't he just being friendly 'cos of George and stuff?"

"Shut up, Slater," Liberty and Chastity yelled in unison. "Your problem," Chastity continued, pointing at Jinx with a very fierce expression on her face, "is that you don't take yourself seriously enough. If you want him you can get him—of course you can—but you've got to make a bloody effort. Put—ha!— your back into it girl."

Whatever Jinx might have had to say about this was lost to the increasingly fierce wind blowing off the sea as Jamie pulled up alongside them in a mud-splattered old black BMW estate, George Michael's "Faith" blaring out the speakers.

"I fucking love this song," said Liberty, yanking open the passenger-side front door and shoving Jinx onto the tan leather seat before slamming it shut and jumping in the back, pulling Chastity after her. "Nice car, dude!"

The four of them sang along at top volume all the way along the seafront. Jamie's car smelt pleasantly of dogs and salt, from all the time he spent hanging ten no doubt; the boot was stuffed to the brim with wetsuits, and a huge breast-shaped pot of surf wax lay by Jinx's feet. She picked it up and giggled as she read the top of the tin. It was called Mrs. Palmer's Mighty Mound and claimed to have smaller, harder nipples to guarantee satisfaction. Jinx shivered deliciously but imperceptibly as she read this. Jamie had swept a great pile of CDs, yellowing newspapers, and magazines onto the floor to give the girls space to sit down. The song ended just as Stagmount came into view, looming above the cliffs. Even though myriad lights were twinkling through the gloomy sky it had a very austere look about it.

In summer, visitors professed astonishment at the huge Gothic building's warm beauty; in winter they invariably likened it to a prison. Today was so wet and miserable it was very much the latter. The stone seemed to absorb the sun; golden and welcoming from May to September, it quickly turned grey and foreboding in winter.

"I've always wanted to come up here," Jamie said with a sideways smile at Jinx while using his rearview mirror to wink at the girls in the back, "but I never quite got round to it. I thought I'd get lynched for sure if I got caught. Infiltrating Stagmount is in most of my pals' top-ten fantasy events."

"You're not alone," said Chastity with a giggle, leaning forward and resting her arms on the back of Jinx's headrest. "Paul's friends all say the same thing. And Mrs. Bennett told me once that during the World War II they had to hand the place over to the army and there was a sign up in all the dorms that said, 'If you need a mistress in the night, ring this bell.' According to her that bell had never seen so much action in its life."

"Did she say that?" asked Jamie, surprised. "That's not quite the language I imagined the headmistress of England's most exclusive school for girls to use. I guess she's keen to move with the times, huh?"

"Well," said Chastity, "she probably didn't use those *exact* words, but you know what I mean."

"Chas just loves to paraphrase," said Jinx, emitting a most unladylike snort and immediately wishing she hadn't, given the present company she was currently trying to impress. "She never lets the truth ruin a good story."

"So," Jamie said, turning to Jinx and resting a hand lightly on her thigh as they waited to turn off up the hill at the traffic lights by the marina, "if I find myself in need of a mistress in the night, what bell do I press?"

Jinx squirmed in her seat as he locked eyes with her. She was totally surprised by the intensity of the shockwaves of pure, unadulterated lust that immediately began coursing through her entire body and, once again, found herself frozen to the back of her seat and bereft of speech. This whole losing the ability to talk thing was getting pretty freaking tiresome pretty freaking rapidly. She made a quick mental note to get a bloody handle on herself ASAP.

"You ring Jinx, of course." Liberty, realizing Jinx wasn't about to say anything of any note anytime soon, jumped in to help her out. "She loves nothing more than a good old chat in the middle of the night."

Jinx, Chastity, and Liberty all laughed. Jinx loved her sleep and was notoriously rude and fierce with anyone who dared to phone at what she considered an unreasonable hour. She always intended to put her phone on silent before she went to bed, but rarely managed to get round to it as she usually fell asleep as soon as her head hit the pillow. But at that moment she firmly decided it would never be switched to silent again. She also knew that in the unlikely event she was ever woken up by Jamie she'd be the exact opposite of cross about it. Rude maybe, she thought with a delicious shudder, but certainly not cross.

What did make her cross was when the lights went green and Jamie had to take his hand off her leg to change gear. She sank back in her seat and surreptitiously studied his profile as he drove. God, he was a good driver—fast, but totally in control. There was something incredibly sexy about being tightly buckled in next to a great-looking guy who took his corners fast but never made you feel unsafe. And his tunes were pretty fantastic, too. Out of ten, Jinx decided, a small smirk spreading across her face, she would give him eleven.

"Tune," she said appreciatively, as Maximo Park's "Our Velocity" came blaring out of the speakers.

Jamie didn't say anything, but turned to smile at her before turning the volume up loud.

When Jamie pulled an expert handbrake turn and swerved into the space next to Mr. Morris's outside Tanner House, Liberty barely had time to say goodbye to him before Chastity grabbed her by the hand and pulled her out of the car.

Yelling something decidedly shady and improbable over her shoulder about homework, Chastity dragged Liberty through the front door and straight into Jinx's bedroom where the two of them would sit on the bed giggling whilst they waited for Jinx's return and the most almighty run-through of every aspect of the evening.

"So," said Jinx brightly, picking up her handbag and turning to Jamie, "thanks so much for the lift. I really appreciate it and so do those ungrateful bitches."

He laughed and turned off the engine. "Allow me," he said, jumping out of the car and strolling round to her side before opening the door with a flourish.

"Thanks," said Jinx, yet another—Christ, she thought, this

was becoming bloody relentless—massive blush staining her cheeks. She was convinced it was an unsightly purple colour, but it was, in fact, a very pleasant pale strawberry. "You *are* kind!"

He didn't step aside to let her pass, so she stood rather awkwardly in front of him and wondered if he was going to kiss her. She was too focused on the highly distracting combination of praying the answer to her silent question was yes, the gorgeous stubble that graced his strong, tanned jaw with flecks of gold and his generous, widely smiling mouth to notice that her fingers were crossed so tightly they were beginning to hurt.

Jamie threw an arm around her shoulders and drew her in close to him in a hug that was anything but friendly as far as Jinx was concerned. She leant her head briefly against his chest and breathed in that wondrous smell. It bought back such intense memories of New Year's Eve and all her subsequent daydreams about him that she felt her knees might actually give way at any second. Jinx clenched them together—she was determined to hold it together and not start gibbering like an idiot at him again. No way. From now on Jinx Slater was going to be in control.

"Hey," he said, his voice decidedly lower than it had been in the car, "I'm really glad you ran into me, Slater. And your friends are great. We'll definitely arrange that night out."

He let go of her, leant forward and dropped the tiniest, lightest and most sexy kiss Jinx had ever had right on her lips.

The lust that Jinx had felt in the car was instantly bested by the most animal feeling she had ever had. It was so unlike anything she'd experienced before that when she was telling

Liberty about it later on, she swore she'd seen actual stars. She had no time to say anything before Jamie bent forward and did it again. Jinx couldn't believe that such feather-light kisses on the lips—so light she couldn't have sworn they'd even *happened* were it not for the white-hot laser beams of lust that shot through her body as they were administered—could physically affect her in the same way as if she'd been punched hard in the stomach. When he tugged gently on the curly strands of hair sticking out of her short ponytail, she felt actually winded. It threw her into such a spin that she had no time to react before Jamie flung open his door, settled himself back behind the wheel, started the engine and backed out of the space.

Jinx stood on the curved stone path outside Tanner House's front door and watched Jamie razz it off down the drive towards Brighton and his flat—throbbing, unidentifiable music once again pumping out of the half-open windows. Her stomach was churning in the most disturbing ways and—if she'd been able to use her brain at all—she would have understood the true meaning of "dazed" for the first time in her life. Fuck, he was *amazing*.

And *fuck*! What with all the excitement she realized she'd forgotten to give him her phone number. Well, stuff it, she decided, unaccountably finding it impossibly hard to think straight; if he wanted to speak to her it would be pretty freaking easy for him to get hold of her. The ball was most definitely in his court and, Jinx mused happily, that was no bad thing.

10 *In a Daze*

Chastity and Liberty did not stop talking to Jinx, and anyone else within earshot, about how amazing Jamie was. And Liv and Charlie—who had mysteriously sprained her wrist the other day, only minutes after she recovered from a badly twisted ankle, but seemed strangely reluctant to give the others any more details about it other than that she'd tripped over again—were also pestering her daily that they be allowed to meet him, too. Jinx was playing it cool, but inside she was both delighted and smug as hell that the guy she was obsessing about had been such a huge hit with her friends. And although Jinx hadn't quite descended from cloud nine yet, she *was* beginning to wonder if Jamie would ever call to arrange the night out they'd all talked about.

"Jinx is not with it at all," Liberty complained to Chastity one night as the two of them trudged back to Tanner House from the Old Reference Library, heads lowered against a driving wind that seemed determined to blow them off their feet. "But I can totally see why."

"Me too," sighed Chastity in agreement, "that guy is hot. Like total! I just wish he'd crack on with it and bloody well ask her out. Then she might return to the land of the living."

Jinx was blissfully unaware of any of these conversations taking place as she lay on her bed for hours at a time, staring unseeingly at the ceiling. Her eyes were usually open but she saw nothing in front of her as thoughts of Jamie played in a constant loop in her mind and Smiths records played nonstop on her iPod.

She'd never experienced an all-consuming crush like this one before, and it hit her hard. Her eyes practically rolled round in the back of her head as she replayed the car-park scene over and over in her mind, occasionally adding in a few new scenes of her own just for the fun of it. In fact, she so often found those tiny kisses and that lightest tug on her hair accosting her mind at any unexpected moment they felt like it, that the whole business was beginning to get just a bit impractical. How the hell was she supposed to conjugate French verbs or talk intelligently about the importance of the growth of a poet's mind with special reference to Wordsworth's *Prelude* when all the time she never knew when to expect that kick to the stomach that heralded the instantaneous return of the most physical memory she'd ever experienced and the inevitable blanking of whatever it was she happened to be doing at the time?

A week after their night out, Jinx was sitting in the library, supposedly poring over the English essay she was writing on the subject of "Is *The Winter's Tale* a tragic comedy or a comic tragedy"—funnily enough Jinx couldn't quite manage to work herself into a sweat about it—and which was due in like yesterday, and distractedly chewing her pen when the ear-splittingly loud peals of the fire alarm sounded, jump-starting all the girls into instant action.

Joyous at the thought of anything remotely exciting happening—even a fire, hey: *especially* a fire!—to take their minds off the terrible weather and the mountains of homework they'd all been given, the whole school rushed outside as one, squealing and elbowing their way out through the double-height double doors, which were made of the strongest oak, had come from a castle in France and were reputedly at least three hundred years old. Once outside, they quickly started milling about in the courtyard in front of the main entrance, shrieking at the tops of their voices in the mistaken belief they could compete with the din the alarms were making, pushing and shoving each other into very ramshackle lines and generally behaving absolutely contrary to the strict health and safety rules and codes of conduct the school had in place for such an event.

"Olivia Taylor." Daisy Finnegan was closing in on Jinx's little group, a determinedly self-important look etched onto her ugly face. "No one would ever guess you were in the lower sixth, carrying on like that and making a spectacle of yourself."

"What the—" Liv looked round in shock from where she had Charlie in a headlock and was attempting to throw her over her shoulder into the well-stocked flower bed in front of Mrs. Bennett's big office window. "Oh. It's you."

Liv turned back round when she saw who was addressing her. She completely ignored Daisy who was standing behind her still bleating inanely about something or other, and carried on her fight with Charlie. What had started out as a definite play fight was rapidly becoming a real-life brawl, each trying to prove she was stronger than the other.

"Oi!" Jinx yelled when she realized what Daisy was talking about, grabbing Liv's arm and yanking her away from Charlie. "What the fuck's going on? Cut it out!"

"Yeah," agreed Liberty, who had wrapped her extra long Missoni scarf so many times around her neck it looked like she didn't have one, pulling on her black leather Chanel gloves as she gave the pair of them a disbelieving look. "It's, like, totally not a cool look to be rolling around in the fucking shrubbery in front of the whole school."

"Thank you, Liberty," sniffed Daisy in the mistaken belief that Liberty had intervened to help her out. "It's nice to see that at least some of us at Stagmount have manners."

"Fuck off, Daisy," Liberty replied immediately, "why don't you go and pick on some of the lower school, *we're* not interested."

Katie Green had been loitering nearby throughout the entire skirmish, thrilled to witness her favourite senior-school girls in such exciting action at such close quarters like this. She was less than impressed when Daisy—completely ignored by her own year, she was trying to save what little face she had left—turned on her and in no uncertain terms told her to hurry up and join her house and form for the mandatory roll call of every girl in the school that always took place immediately following a fire alarm. Katie was even less happy when she heard the others giggling at Daisy's no-nonsense tone. She was too dim-witted and self-obsessed to realize that the girls she was so enamored of were not laughing at *her* but at Daisy, and she felt a deep hatred for the head girl of the lower sixth, who had dared embarrass her like this in front of her heroines. True to form, not one of the lower sixth noticed the black expression plastered across her face as she stood in her line, scowling mutinously at Daisy and the Tanner House line to her left.

Finally, and certainly not quickly enough for Mrs. Bennett's liking, the entire school was split into the six houses the girls lived in. Despite having always studied together, the sixth form had been divided into four alphabetical groups amongst the four main-school houses for their first three years at Stagmount, and this was only the second term they'd all spent sleeping under the same roof in Tanner House.

Mrs. B. looked around for the dratted bursar. He never seemed to be there when she needed him. She was making a superhuman effort to drown out the clanging bells she was sure were going to leave her with a bad case of tinnitus, but dimly registered that of late this absence had been very much the case where the damned bursar was concerned. As she stood at the top of the steps that led towards the drive and the front door, Mrs. Bennett pulled the jacket of her Jaeger skirt suit tighter around her, impatiently tapped her foot and made a mental note to have it out with the bloody man at the earliest opportunity.

"Girls!" she yelled, waving her arms above her head, trying hard but failing dismally to divert her school's attention away from the ear-splitting cacophony and towards her. "GIRLS!"

Whatever Mrs. Bennett might have said next was lost to the wind as most girls rushed forward out of their lines, the momentum of the stampede irresistibly dragging these three along with them. They found themselves propelled to the front of the quad just in front of an apoplectic Mrs. Bennett, where they joined the crowd in craning their necks to gawp at a very bedraggled figure rushing piteously along the drive towards the quad from the direction of the sports hall.

"Look! It's Dirk!" yelled Liv across the crowd to Jinx, jumping up and down and waving her arms above her head to attract the attention of her friend, whose curly blonde hair she'd spotted bobbing about in the midst of a particularly excitable group a few scrums along. "Watch him go! Run, Dirk, RUN!"

What with all the excitement, none of the girls immediately noticed that the noise of the fire alarm had come to a sudden stop, leaving a series of eerie, echoing silences in its wake. The one hanging in the air above the girls' heads was filled with expectation; conversely, the one above Mrs. Bennett's was loaded with an almost palpable fury.

Dirk seemed oblivious to all the tension as he ran, ever slowly, the final stretch to the stone steps, where Mrs. Bennett was standing. He shuddered to a stop and collapsed right in front of her feet. It was only then, his face hidden in the arms he had used to fling himself pathetically onto the lowest step, his upper torso twisted backwards to the crowd, that the girls saw the wet, dark stain that covered his hair–and which, they noted with a grim fascination, was rapidly flooding the expanse of his white aertex-covered back with a livid spread of red.

Mrs. Bennett's grim-set white face turned a chalky grey colour as she leant forward and surveyed the crumpled figure in front of her. The girls had been stunned into a shocked silence. The only noise for a couple of awe-filled seconds was that of the rain that had begun beating down against the wax proofing of the rain jackets worn by only a suck-up few. Two things then happened simultaneously. Dirk raised his head and moaned piteously. As he did this, what appeared to be a celery stick fell from his collar to the floor, where it bounced halfheartedly before coming to rest on the drive near his outstretched, trainer-clad foot. As a few surprised guffaws escaped the crowd, the bursar dashed through the door and skidded to a halt beside Mrs. Bennett, whose jaw was so low by this point that the crowd could see all the way to her tonsils at the back of her throat.

The bursar, puce in the face and sweating profusely even standing in the cold rain, stared wildly around as if in a daze before dashing down the steps and dragging Dirk to a seated position, using the collar of his shirt for leverage. Everyone was too busy staring at the strange triptych occupying the front steps to notice intractable Igor slip through a side door that led to the basements below Steinem House, look around covertly, smooth his hair down and stroll nonchalantly to the back of what had been the Tanner House line but now resembled the crush in front of the main stage at Glastonbury.

Everyone, that is, except Katie Green, whose solid bulk had allowed her to easily resist being swept forward alongside her classmates in the stampede.

Katie watched with interest as Igor checked his mobile phone and smiled slightly before assuming his typical body-guard stance of slightly parted straight legs finished off with a direct stare and sharply folded arms. She *knew* it was of note, but she just didn't know why. Never mind, she thought to her-self smugly, it would come in useful one day. The mental dossier she was building up on the likes, dislikes, movements, allianc-es, clothing, general ambience, and overheard conversations of the lower sixth was becoming so huge there was barely room for a single other thought inside that tiny brain of hers. One thing was certain anyway—somehow she was going to make the lower sixth be friends with her. As far as she was concerned it was only a matter of time. Katie was as sure of this as she was utterly convinced—rightly, as it happens—that Mrs. Frick hated her more than she hated all the other girls in her year.

Katie's vaguely moronic musings were interrupted when the school matron in chief, Sister Minton, fondly nicknamed Mister Sinton by the girls since time immemorial in honour of the bristly moustache that grew unchecked between her promi-nent nose and surprisingly full lips, bustled onto the scene. Her starched blue uniform with its prim white edges creaked stiffly as she walked, and the school fell silent as one.

"Good God, man," she said, her words landing crisply into

the stark silence as she inspected Dirk, reached out a finger to his shirt, licked it and shook her head, a derisory smile playing about her lips. "Do pull yourself together. It's tomato juice." She paused and ran her tongue around the inside of her mouth. "Albeit mixed with a lot of vodka, I'd say!"

"But I..." Dirk stammered as he came to, looked round with a dazed expression on his silly tanned face, and realized the intensely, excruciatingly, unbelievably embarrassing fact of where he was and what he was doing. "I thought...."

"Yes," cut in Mrs. Bennett in icy tones, "I would very much like to know what you thought. And," she finished on a high note, "exactly what the bloody hell is going on here!"

"I was in the gym, having a shower," Dirk mumbled, "when I heard voices coming through the air vent that links to the gym. I thought," he continued, louder and more confident as he progressed, "it was nothing more than people working out. Then I smelt smoke so I decided to investigate." He looked around in disbelief, as if he could hardly trust the words that were about to come out of his own mouth. "I mean, smoking? In the *gym*?"

"And?" Mrs. Bennett only needed to slightly raise her right eyebrow as she said this in her coldest voice to rapidly drag Dirk's attention back to the much more pressing matter at hand. The school had never been as quiet as they all were now. Muffling coughs, stopping sneezes, leaving the gum in their mouths unchewed, the girls knew instinctively that as soon as Mrs. Bennett remembered their presence right here on the front line they'd be sent back to their various houses without so much as a by-your-leave and never know what had caused Dirk to be doused in Bloody Marys yet obviously believe it to be his own blood. And since that, obviously, would be total misery, they were all very much united in their telepathically arranged silence.

"Well," the coach bristled self-righteously, "I don't know about *you*, Mrs. Bennett, but I for one will not tolerate the use of tobacco, and certainly not in the sports hall! Anyway," he carried on swiftly, with an audible gulp when he registered the blackest look he'd ever seen pass across his boss's terrifying face, "I threw on my clothes and jogged over to the basketball court so I could catch the law-breakers in the act—whoever was up there was *definitely* smoking. Unfortunately," he said with a sad downwards glance at the feet that so rarely let him down, "I skidded on the new flooring surface as I was running over and my trainer squeaked really loudly."

Jinx had to suppress a snort of laughter at this point, and Liberty clutched her hand in sympathy. Dirk really did cut the stupidest, most pathetic figure they'd ever seen, lying practically supine on the floor before the head's feet like this—especially with that stupid celery stick lying next to him like a discarded relay baton in the special vegetable race.

"Yes," he continued, blissfully unaware of the very quiet hilarity this was causing amongst the watching girls, "that was definitely what gave me away."

"Mr. Hanson!" Mrs. Bennett's words cracked as if she'd fired them out of machine gun and once again woke Dirk to the reality of whom exactly he was dealing with here.

"Yes, anyway," he mumbled rather petulantly in response,

"so the next thing I know there's a sound like the crack of a shotgun and I'm covered in blood. Well," he said, "tomato juice or whatever it was. So, thinking I'm under siege and my life is in danger, I run out of there as fast as possible, trying to reach the cover of the main entrance, only to find all of you lot out here waiting for me like a welcoming party at the end of a marathon. What's *that* all about?"

"Girls," Mrs. Bennett said, belatedly realizing that the girls had heard every word of this bizarre exchange on the front steps, "you've been outside in the wet and the cold for quite long enough. Before you go, I want to see every single member of the school in the theatre tomorrow morning before break-fast. Seven-thirty A.M., and not a second later. What happened here today was an absolute disgrace, and had there been a real fire…" Mrs. Bennett shuddered in an uncharacteristically theatrical fashion. "Well, I don't like to think what the consequences might have been. But I am going to get to the bottom of all of this, mark my words."

Not particularly cowed at all by these dire, veiled threats of retribution and punishment, the girls shuffled off much more slowly than they'd arrived and with only about a third of the volume. As soon as the lower sixth had passed the corner of Friedan House that made up the last end and side of the very scuffed-up and far-less-verdant-after-its-trampling quad, and turned the corner to Tanner and thus away from Mrs. Bennett's all-seeing eyes, if not her ears, the volume rocketed right back up to what was standard when they were all together. That is to say, very loud indeed. Hot topic number one, obviously, was who the hell had seen fit to throw a fully loaded Bloody Mary cocktail at Dirk's head from the mezzanine balcony of the gym that looked over the indoor tennis courts!

From where she was dawdling near the end of her house line, patiently waiting for all the older girls to scramble through the double doors first, Katie Green's ears pricked up like a loyal dog's when she heard the unmistakable sounds of the lower sixth's shouts of raucous laughter. She noticed Mrs. Bennett roll her eyes in exasperation at the exact same time. She also saw Mrs. Bennett dismiss Dirk with a wave of her hand and turn to harangue the bursar about his tardiness to the scene, his tardiness *generally*, his downright infuriating unavailability and above all the lack of support she felt she was receiving from him this term.

Finally, Katie witnessed Daisy Finnegan rush to Mrs. Bennett's side from where she had been loitering in the middle of the quad, a disgustingly sycophantic look plastered across her spotty face as she offered her assistance in this, as she put it, "terrible time of crisis."

Katie smirked as she spied Daisy being dismissed as summarily as Stagmount's football coach had been a few seconds earlier, then made her way through the doors and turned left in the direction of her own house, chewing the inside of her lip in a thoughtful manner as she walked.

11 *Triple Double*

Desperate to get dry and warm, Jinx, Liberty, and Chastity crashed through the front door of Tanner House into the foyer thinking only of hot showers and their tropically heated common room. They were startled to see Olga, Irina, and Masha lounging on the overstuffed bright pink sofa wearing their matching 2Bfree very cool roll-top tracksuits and flicking through three copies of the same issue of *Marie Claire*. Their long blonde hair was drawn into three very neat identical ponytails and their matching "barely there" makeup was pristine. There was no way on Earth these three had been at the mandatory post-alarm roll call in the freezing cold quad like the fairly ratty-looking others had.

"Hi girls," said Irina, sitting in the middle with an alarming-looking double-page, black-and-white fashion shoot from the magazine that lay open across her loosely bent thighs. "Did we miss anything?"

The triplets dissolved prettily into laughter at this and the others were so impressed by their complete mastery of such an extreme level of nonchalance that they had to join in.

"No," Chastity said through a decidedly porcine snort, "you didn't miss a thing."

"What are you talking about?!" yelled Liberty, furiously unwinding her stunning green, pink, gold, and purple striped Missoni scarf and throwing it dramatically to the floor. "What about the fire alarm and Dirk and the Bloody Mary! They missed LOADS of things!"

"I know," replied Chastity, who had fallen prey to a fresh fit of hysterics at Liberty's outraged reaction and was gripping the side of the coffee table in front of her for support, her long blonde hair covering half of her profile like a lopsided, coquettish curtain. "I was being sarcastic, for Christ's sake."

"Hey," said Jinx, looking around in surprise. "Where's Igor? I'm sure I haven't seen you three without him once yet this term."

"Oh," Olga responded swiftly, tugging the smooth end of the ponytail that was hanging over her left shoulder. "We told him he could go for a walk and we'd be fine in here for an hour or so. So tell us, what happened?"

"God," said Jinx after a giggle that drowned out the last question, to Olga's evident annoyance, given the small frown that passed across her ravishingly high-cheek-boned, heart-shaped face. "He really *is* under the thumb, isn't he? Do you think it pisses him off?"

"Does what piss him off?" Olga looked innocently up at Jinx

through lowered lashes. The tortoiseshell-rimmed rectangular reading glasses she was wearing lent her the air of a very sexy secretary. Jinx hesitated.

"You know." Jinx squirmed. "Having to do what—well—what you lot say all the time. When he's, um, you know, like…a grown man and everything."

"No!" the triplets yelled simultaneously, clutching each other as if this was the funniest thing they'd ever heard. "We're in charge and he knows it!"

At that moment an icy wind blew through the warm lounge area. Someone had flung open the front door with great force and stood there for a second before slamming it shut. This caused such a fierce gust to whistle through the room that the roaring fire in the grate flickered, hissed and seemed on the brink of going out.

"Bloody hell," said Chastity crossly, complete with a correspondingly angry shiver. "This is like being in a bad horror film. For Christ's sake whoever's out there, either come in or go out but whatever you do—and I certainly don't give a shit either way—JUST SHUT THAT FUCKING DOOR!"

"Ladies," Igor said with a pained glance at Chastity before shooting a sinister glare around the room that seemed to linger especially malignantly on the triplets, "good evening."

"Good evening," the girls chorused, barely hiding their laughter at Chastity's bad timing—and the previous conversation between Jinx and Olga that they were sure he must have overheard.

"So," Irina said, her super glossy pale-pink smile full of

mischief, "we were just explaining to these girls how we let you go out for a walk, Igor."

"Did you enjoy it?" Masha enquired, fake solicitously in the face of Igor's unreadable blank glare. "Was it nice to be out in the fresh air...all alone?"

"I never shirk my duty," Igor replied after a long pause. He appeared to teeter on the brink of saying more, but remained silent at the back of the room, arms folded and unreadable eyes narrowed.

The triplets shared a quick, conspiratorial, concerned look and stood up as one, laying the magazines on the coffee table in a line in front of them with perfect, unthinking symmetry, before waving goodnight to the rest and ushering Igor in the direction of their corridor on the third floor.

"Well," said Jinx, collapsing with a very satisfied-sounding sigh onto the end of the recently vacated sofa and picking up one of the discarded magazines. "That was weird, to say the least."

"Yeah," Chastity agreed, unzipping the sides of her long boots, kicking them off and settling in to the opposite end. "I've never seen Igor express any emotion whatsoever, but tonight he seemed really out of sorts."

"The triplets are so bloody rude to him though," Liberty said. "I'm not surprised he seemed pissed off—I bloody would be if someone I worked for spoke to me like that!"

"I can't believe they just couldn't be bothered to go to roll call," sniffed Daisy Finnegan, her grease-covered and currently bright red nose pointed as high as she could physically manage.

She had come in just behind the others and witnessed the whole exchange. "They really don't seem to care about Stagmount at all."

"Shut up, Daisy," mumbled Jinx, flinging her head back against the cushions and closing her eyes. The three memorably unsanitary years she'd spent cooped up at close quarters with Daisy Finnegan, suck-up artist extraordinaire, in Wollstonecraft House had given her not only the strong feeling that she'd be utterly delighted if she never had to see or speak to her again, but also a very healthy disregard for anything—however true—that might pop out of her mouth.

"Newsflash to Fingers," Jinx said, rolling her eyes heavenwards and letting out a long, bored sigh, "nothing's changed and no one gives a shit about anything you say. Still."

Daisy's eyes bulged with fury, but she didn't say anything as she stamped her foot, flicked her greasy French pleat in disgust and stomped off in the direction of the corridor she shared—unfortunately for them—with Jinx and Liberty.

Chastity, who had been texting Paul on her mobile phone, so engrossed in whatever message her flying fingers were tapping out that she'd completely missed Jinx and Daisy's exchange, suddenly screamed in rage and threw her phone against the opposite wall. Jinx and Liberty didn't say anything as the handset crashed to the floor, reduced to a mangled mess, tiny spare parts flying everywhere, but turned to stare at Chastity open-mouthed.

"Fucking Paul!" she yelled, throwing the magazine she'd picked up earlier in quick succession after her phone. "Sometimes I fucking *hate* him."

Jinx and Liberty remained silent, their eyes wide with shock. They had never once heard Chastity say anything bad about Paul. Quite the reverse in fact! They often joked about how totally vomit-inducing they found her usual sickly sweet conversations. And if they happened to unfortunately find themselves in the same room as the loved-up pair when they hadn't seen each other for, ooo, about ten minutes, they always made as fast an exit as possible to avoid the gross-out slurping sounds and despicable baby talk.

"What's he done then?" asked Jinx. "Is everything okay?"

"No it's fucking NOT!" Chastity banged her fist on the table for emphasis. "That's it. I've fucking had enough."

"Whoa there, Chas," said Liberty, grabbing Chastity's hand. "Stop freaking out and just tell us what's going on."

"He's totally changed recently," Chastity said, hanging her head sadly. "I don't know what's got into him. We've hardly had any rows at all in the whole seven months we've been going out, and now all he does is make stupid sexist remarks that really piss me off. He only stops patronizing me when he wants a shag."

"So what did he say just now then?" asked Jinx. She only just managed to inject the necessary tone of concern into her voice. This was freaking interesting—she'd *never* seen Chastity lose it like this, and as far as she could see Paul was a really decent guy.

"He said ages ago that he was looking after his parents' house for a couple of weeks starting on Saturday," sniffed Chastity, "and he hasn't mentioned it for a while so I thought I'd text him and see what was going on."

"And?" Liberty asked, a consoling hand placed just so on Chastity's knee in order that the flawless French-manicure she'd spent an hour and a half doing that morning could be examined.

"He said he still was, so I suggested we have a huge house party there next weekend. I thought we could all go—you could invite Jamie, Jinx, and maybe your brothers—and a few of Paul's friends from college." Chastity stopped speaking and another look of fury passed across her animated face.

"Sounds great," Jinx said, smiling at the mention of Jamie as she instantly forgot about Chastity's woes.

"Well, it's not going to fucking happen so you can take that smile off your face for a start," raged Chastity.

"Shit," muttered an instantly deflated Jinx. "I'm *sorry*. Do carry on."

"He replied, 'Great idea—let's have you, me and one other girl.'" Chastity's condemnatory voice rose to a shrieking pitch as she finished her sentence.

"Bloody hell," said Jinx, stifling a snort of amused laughter, "you need to relax, Chas. George says things like that all the time. I'm sure Paul's only joking. And anyway—" here a definite snort did manage to slip out—"if he isn't—I'll do it!"

"Yes," agreed Liberty, a huge smirk plastered across her stunning face. "You're a total babe, Chas. I'd do it too! In fact, where exactly is this party taking place? I must stick it in my diary!"

"Shut up!" snapped Chastity. "I haven't finished yet. That's not even the worst of it."

"Come on then, Chas," Jinx said, already bored with what she saw as Chastity's total inability to laugh at herself. "What *else* has he done?"

A stony-faced Chastity stood up, grabbed her bag and made to leave without saying a word.

"Come on, Chas," chorused Jinx and Liberty, "we were only joking!"

Chastity said nothing in response as she picked up her boots and shoved the *Marie Claire* under her arm, but as she stalked off down the corridor the pair on the sofa distinctly heard a very dismissive "what a pair of total *bitches*" float through the half-ajar door towards them. They looked at each other as if to say something about this, but before either one of them could comment on Chastity's evident all-consuming wrath they clutched each other and burst into the most furious fit of hysterical giggles they'd suffered all term.

12 *Screw This for a Laugh*

After being rudely awoken a whole hour and a half before their usual time and then forced to struggle down the drive to attend Mrs. Bennett's punishment roll call, where the entire school had sulkily endured a mega telling-off, none of the lower sixth were in good moods by the time they made it to breakfast. Most unusually, there had been no giggling whatsoever on the trudge back to Tanner, and the collective bad mood of the lower sixth showed no sign of changing for the better any time soon. The triplets were the only ones who looked as sprightly as ever. They'd disappeared upstairs as soon as they got back—no doubt to apply the truckload of makeup their studiedly "natural" look required—and hadn't been seen since.

"What about bloody Dirk?" Liv asked, spraying toast crumbs all over the table, still sounding completely amazed at the weird antics of the football coach none of them had properly met yet. "What the hell was *that* all about?"

"Well, I think it had something to do with those Russians." Daisy Finnegan's smugly self-satisfied voice cut over the top of them, rudely interrupting the conversation she had been shamelessly eavesdropping on from the next table across. "Why weren't they at the fire alarm? And who," she continued, then paused, as if what she was about to say was very profound indeed and should therefore be listened to most carefully, "drinks straight vodka apart from them? I think it was them who threw the drink over Coach Hanson and then set off the fire alarm to give themselves time to escape the scene. My dad told me that their dad makes Bill Gates look like a pauper."

"Daisy." Jinx fixed her old nemesis with the worst death stare she could summon up. "I can't help but wonder just how many times this week you're planning to force me to get rid of you. You certainly seem to be enjoying the sensation anyway. Now, for the last and final time, will you just FUCK OFF!"

"Go on, Daisy," Liberty added. "Leave us alone."

"There's a good girl," said Liv, with a sly wink at Mimi and Chloe, as Daisy picked up her bag, shot Jinx a very black look, and stalked out of the kitchen, slamming the door behind her. "Easy does it."

"She drives me fucking crazy." Jinx pushed her plate away and glared round at the others as if daring them to say she'd gone too far. To be honest, she had a sneaking suspicion that she *had*. It wasn't like Daisy had been rude to her or anything, or even said anything particularly annoying, but the bad mood currently sweeping the lower sixth was catching, and snapping at Daisy had become something of a natural reflex for Jinx.

"Yes," Liv replied thoughtfully, clearly not listening to a word Jinx was saying. "And I hate to say it—sorry Jinx—but I think she's probably *right* that it was the triplets who drenched Dirk in vodka-based cocktails."

"Me too," Charlie agreed. "They *weren't* at roll call with the rest of us; we all saw them when we came in so we know they were back here way before we were; and you've got to admit it's exactly the kind of thing they wouldn't give a toss about."

"It's pretty funny, whichever way you look at it," Liberty interjected, surprisingly sensibly. "I mean, who cares if it was them or not? It's no skin off any of our noses."

"I know," Jinx moaned, putting her head in her hands. "Look at us, all fighting and snapping and bitching and having basically no fun at all. I'm bloody bored of nonstop homework and all the teachers talking about exams all the time like it's the end of the world. This fucking weather is driving me crazy, too."

She didn't mention it, but Jinx was also beginning to think that she would never hear from Jamie again either. It was, she thought, bloody unfair that just when she decided to admit to all her friends—and herself—that she really liked him, he should disappear off the scene without so much as a tiny text to say goodbye. Embarrassing too, she reflected unhappily.

"We need a massive night out," Chloe said, her big green eyes shining under the fringe of her sleek brown bob for the first time since she'd joined them at the table. "We'll all go bloody stir-crazy otherwise."

"I've got it!" Liberty banged her mug on the table. "What about Paul's house party? That's supposed to be next week, right Jinx?"

"Chastity's Paul?" Liv asked, interested. "Sounds ace."

"Hold on," said Jinx, shaking her head at Liberty. "Were you even *there* last night? They had a massive fight, remember? About his bloody house party—and from the sounds of it I wouldn't get your hopes up too high, kids."

At that moment Chastity flounced into the room. Although she looked gorgeous in her skinny grey Top Shop Baxter jeans teamed with a black cashmere polo neck, lots of chunky silver jewelry, and dark brown Ugg boots folded down half way to her ankles, the thing that really made her look stunning was the beaming smile plastered across her face.

"Hiya," she trilled, greeting them in her happiest singsong voice, perching herself precariously on the opposite end of the table closest to Mimi and Chloe and leaning over to grab a piece of toast from the rack in the center. "How is everyone?"

"Well," Jinx said with a disbelieving snort at Chastity's new-found sunny disposition, "at least one of us is in a better mood this morning. I take it you've made up with Paul?"

"Yes." Chastity sighed dreamily and smiled around the table. "We're back on."

Jinx was pleased to see her pal back on the up, but she couldn't help thinking that it was bloody unfair that Chastity could behave so badly, screaming and yelling blue murder, and still have Paul running after her, when she, Jinx, behaved like the coolest girl on the planet, all sweetness and light, jokes and gags, and yet remained resolutely ignored by her major crush. The way she was looking at it now, she had to admit it was possible Jamie had not even registered her existence at all. She chewed unhappily at her thumbnail as the horrid realization that he probably thought of her as nothing more than George's annoying little sister began to take hold in her brain.

"Don't bite." Liberty interrupted Jinx's unhappy reverie as she slapped her friend's hand away from her mouth. "Come on, you know how cross you'll be later on when you have to file them *all* down to match!"

"Okay." Jinx moodily sat on her hands. "I won't. And don't slap me again—I can't stand it."

Liv, sensing another storm brewing at their usually happy breakfast table, stood up and clapped her hands together.

"Right," she said in the brisk sergeant-major voice she always used to rally her troops. "Since Chas and Paul have made up we need to start Operation House Party."

"You're on," Mimi responded immediately. "We need something to look forward to or we'll all go stark raving mad."

"Actually," Chastity cut in, looking slightly flustered again, "Paul's parents are coming back early, so we definitely can't do it there."

"Doesn't matter," Liv said, ever practical and keen not to let the good mood slip away. "We'll have a night out instead."

"Yep," agreed Jinx, "it doesn't matter *what* we do, so long as we've got something to bloody well look forward to."

"What about that Sugar Club on the seafront?" Charlie asked. "Liv and I went there with my brother last term—the music was awesome and we danced all night. We've all got our fake IDs, right?"

Everyone nodded. Fake IDs had been an essential part of their lives since they were about fourteen. Liv had one of her twenty-year-old sister Liz's old driving licenses; Liz had given Charlie one of her friend's old halls-of-residence entry cards; Jinx had a University of Bristol student card that one of George's many blonde girlfriends had left behind after a dirty weekend in the New Forest; Liberty had the brunette version—stolen to order by George after she'd banged on about how unfair it was that Jinx had one and she didn't; and Chastity's mother's fiancé had created an amazingly good fake copy of his British Library card on his Mac and slipped it to her on Christmas day. He'd even laminated it—he was *so* back in the good books.

All rifts and unhappy thoughts forgotten in their delight at the prospect of some actual fun in their immediate futures, the lower sixth pushed their dirty plates to one side, conveniently forgot to hear the bell announcing the start of the daily chapel service, pulled their chairs forward and gathered in close around the table for a serious discussion about the weekend, headed by Liv and Charlie.

13 *It's Amazing What Thoughts of a Party Can Do*

Anyone who had seen them earlier would be shocked at the transformation for the better in the moods of the lower sixth as they marched up the steep, narrow and winding stairs clearly marked DOWN that led to the top floor above the main entrance, the tower of which housed Stagmount's excellent, world-renowned modern languages department.

They'd started huffing up the DOWN and vice versa purposefully to piss off their former French teacher, Mrs. Susan Dickinson—aka The Dick. She, to the great relief of the girls, the other staff, and the parents, none of whom had warmed to her, had resigned suddenly at the end of last term, alongside Mrs. Gunn, Jinx's old housemistress from Wollstonecraft. Only Jinx knew the truth, for it was she who had caught The Dick and Gunn sucking face and probably a lot of other things she didn't much care to think about—thank God it had been pretty dark in there—in the bike sheds at the end of last term. She had, rather cleverly she thought with a tiny smile, pretended to record the sick event on her mobile phone and used the threat of revealing the imaginary footage to blackmail them both into resigning pretty much straight away. She giggled to herself as she imagined the unspeakable couple snuggling up in bed together every night and getting up to unspeakably filthy activities in their vegetable patch, happy as Larry she was sure. Total gross-out!

Racing down to the pitch twenty minutes later, on a total high to be out of that boring class, hair blowing in their faces thanks to the wind coming straight off the sea with no breakers in its way, the lower sixth were amused when they clocked a line of blushing third-years coming towards them up the hill in the direction of the changing rooms they'd just vacated and left in a filthy mess. Constantly looking over their shoulders to where Dirk was sorting the pile of red and blue bibs into two piles—incongruously tanned for the time of year and sporting yet another bright white Adidas tracksuit with matching trainers—giggling and waving, the younger ones were clearly even more smitten with the idiot than ever.

In the summer term this particular pitch doubled as an athletics track, and was surrounded by a high verge complete with lots of benches for parents who didn't wish to sit on rugs during the traditional summer sports day picnic. But, with the darkly churning sea furiously smacking into the cliffs beneath them, it looked bleak as hell today.

The triplets—wearing the pink-and-white football shirts with matching socks that they'd purchased in town especially for this occasion to the great hilarity of the rest of the lower sixth—provided light relief from the dour aspect of the environment as they ran elegantly towards their destination. Their long blonde perfect ponytails streamed out behind them like three sheets of golden silk and their long slim legs had taken on a charming pinkish tint thanks to the cold air. Jinx found herself looking at them and wondering if they *ever* found themselves in embarrassing situations or looking less than their best. The sigh she let out as she inwardly admitted to herself that both of these eventualities were highly unlikely was lost to the wind as the girls came to a stop in front of Dirk. The coach fiddled with the gelled spikes of hair he spent hours every morning training to stand up from his head and grinned like a maniac way more at the triplets than anyone else.

Katie Green stood outside the swimming pool changing rooms that the girls used before and after their football lessons and stared down at the lower sixth. An expression of wistful longing masked the jealous fury that was running rampant through her veins as she considered Daisy Finnegan's proximity to Jinx, Liberty, Chastity, Liv, and Charlie—her heroines, the girls she thought about as she tossed and turned in bed every night. Daisy didn't even *like* them. So how was it fair that she got to spend all day and night with them when Katie couldn't? They don't even know I exist, Katie thought, and resolved to do something to change this. She was convinced that if only the lower sixth knew who she was they would love her. She hadn't thought of anything to make them notice her yet, but as soon as she came up with a suitable plan she resolved to put it into immediate action. Her crush was definitely becoming unmanageable—these members of the lower sixth who had barely registered her existence were literally all she thought about. Katie's current thoughts were interrupted however, when Betsy Johnson, one of the most popular girls in her year, sprinted out the door towards the main school, obviously late for something or other.

"What are you looking at, cock face?" Betsy shot Katie a look of such pitying disdain as she passed her that the other flushed a dull red before turning to trudge through the door towards the shower block.

Down on the pitch the lower sixth, busily warming up for their first football lesson by sprinting round the edge of the vast field, were unaware of any scrutiny.

14 *Curveball*

Jinx was slumped in the old reference library trying to concentrate on the complicated French translation that was due in Mr. Christie's pigeonhole first thing tomorrow morning while examining her nails at the same time.

She picked at a couple of chips in the bright pink Jessica varnish—the bloody stuff was called "flirty," she thought morosely, not that *she'd* been doing much of that lately, except in her head—she'd applied in a very slapdash fashion in front of the telly the night before, until she gave them up as a bad job and rummaged around in the depths of her handbag for the small mirror emblazoned with the legend "don't treat me any differently than you would the queen" on one side and "I'm bored, please send drugs" on the other which she always took about with her. She held it up in front of her face and leant back slightly to study her eyebrows as best she could in the dim

February afternoon light that was struggling to stream through the latticed library windows.

"Oi," hissed Liv, looking up from where she was sitting, directly opposite Jinx on the narrow library study benches. "Have you finished that French prep?"

Jinx shook her head and frowned. The last thing she needed was a bloody *homework monitor* watching her every move from across the way. Especially Liv, for God's sake!

"Well crack on, love," Liv said, running an exasperated hand through her very short hair. "I want to have a look at it when you're done. I'll swap you my English essay."

Jinx sighed, pushed all thoughts of Jamie and why he hadn't yet called her to one side and turned her attention back to the boring translation. Why did nothing interesting ever happen to the deathly dull characters in these ridiculous stories? Who gave a toss about Madame Dupont and her boring bloody son going on yet another silly outing to the fucking market, which seemed to be staffed entirely by tossers, morons, and retards?

The pair of them had been hard at it with their heads firmly down for a good forty-five minutes by the time Jo, Mrs. B.'s secretary, bustled over, shaking her own Titian-coloured head at the sheer injustice of having had practically no time alone to put her feet up and enjoy a good old read about Britney, Paris, and Nicole's latest goings on.

"Jinx Slater." Jo tapped the back of Jinx's chair to get her attention. "I've been all over the school looking for you." She paused and looked confused. "I didn't expect to find you in *here*. Are you working?"

"Yes," Jinx said, looking round indignantly. "I DO occasionally work you know. Especially this bloody term—we don't seem to do anything else these days."

"Too true," muttered Liv, a brief but unmistakable look of disgust passing across her extraordinarily innocent-looking face before she sighed and returned her attention to the large pile of books in front of her.

"Well anyway," said Jo, handing one of her black- and red-lined memorandum notes to Jinx, "someone phoned for you. I would have left it in your pigeonhole as usual, but he said it was extremely urgent that you call him back as soon as possible."

Jinx raised her eyebrows. She had no idea who would call her at school like this; everyone she knew had her mobile number. She never went anywhere without it and very rarely received calls on the school line.

"Funny name," Jo said, directing a knowing smirk at Jinx, "for an uncle."

Jo bustled off self-importantly in the direction of her desk and Oscar-night dress disasters whilst Jinx unfolded the paper. When she saw what it contained she couldn't stop herself from emitting a loud shout of laughter, causing several people in the library to turn round and give her evil looks for daring to breach the peace during important revision time like this.

"FOR: Jinx Slater," it read in Jo's curly, black, and very posh handwriting. "FROM: Your Uncle Jamie Trouser-Snake. RE: He urgently needs to know if you are available to accompany him to special-needs line dancing on Saturday afternoon. Please phone him ASAP."

Jinx smiled delightedly. Her heart pounded at what felt like a hundred beats a minute, her face was transfused with a peachy glow, and she experienced a physical clench of excitement grip her stomach and refuse to let go. She transferred the number scrawled at the bottom of the sheet into her phone. She tapped the digits as happily into the little keyboard as if she were banging out a truly amazing house remix on a set of silver decks at the closing night of the Space bar in Ibiza.

"Bloody hell," giggled Liv after leaning across the desk—flashing the top of her bright pink lacy French knickers at the whole room in the process—and reading the note herself. "Well Slater…I'm impressed! You've done the perve, now it's time to do the swerve!"

"What?" hissed Jinx, jumping up and shoving her books haphazardly into her "I Love Me" white canvas book bag with a big glittery purple heart on the side. She chucked her lip gloss, pencil case, phone, and the half-eaten king-sized Mars bar she'd been thoughtfully nibbling on as she wrote into her handbag without much more ceremony.

"I'll tell you behind the bike sheds," Liv replied with a surprisingly lewd wink given her general countenance of beyond-reproach innocence, grabbing Jinx's hand and dragging her as fast as possible towards the door and freedom. "Come on!"

Liv and Jinx sat on orange plastic stacking crates next to the grounds man's tractor in the semidarkness of the garage behind the tuck shop and drew deep tokes from a strong skunk spliff. Liv, who really was an extraordinarily *handy* kind of person to have around the place, had produced it from her pencil case with a flourish as soon as they'd crawled under the slightly open sliding garage door and settled themselves comfortably a safe enough distance from the front.

"So what's all this perve and swerve business then?" Jinx asked with a small, stoned-sounding giggle, clutching the note tight against her thigh, where it lay in the pocket of her Sass and Bide grey skinny jeans and passing the smoking spliff to Liv.

"First you perve, and then you swerve." Liv looked at Jinx, inhaled and creased up before continuing. "It's standard love talk, Jinx. My sister and her friends say it all the time. Basically, when you, like, really fancy someone and you've got a major crush on them and you're thinking about them all the time, that's called perving—when you *perve* over them. And *then*," continued Liv, "when you decide to do something about it, seal the deal, cross the line, make a move, or whatever you want to call it, that's when you *swerve* someone. And the action of swerve is swerving. Get it?"

"Like total," Jinx said, plucking the spliff from Liv's outstretched fingers and smiling with delight. "I love it. In fact, I can't wait to tell George—he gets off on stuff like this—he'll definitely love it too."

"So, back to the matter at hand," said Liv, exhaling an impressive smoke ring as she did so, "it's bleeding obvious that Jamie is, like, totally digging the Jinx-meister's action. When are you going to call him?"

"I don't know," Jinx squeaked, suddenly terrified at the thought of having to hold an at least reasonably sentient telephone conversation with the object of her heart's desires. "He said 'ASAP' so maybe...um...tonight? And what the hell am I going to *say* to him when I do get him on the phone?"

"You've got to plan it," said Liv firmly. "And you've got to work out what you want to do on Saturday before you speak to him, too—that way you'll be able to make things go your way without any effort at all. Hey, you need to relax!"

"Fuck!" Jinx started as if she'd been shot when the garage door began to creak open. Someone was obviously hauling it open from the other side and she hastily stubbed the rest of the spliff out before shoving it deep into one of her extra tight pockets when she suddenly felt a decidedly warm spot pressing against the outside of her thigh. Dammit! She winced as she thought about the inevitable burn mark in her brand-new, most favourite pair of jeans ever, but there was no time to do anything else about it. The garage door was halfway open before the pair inside breathed two massive sighs of relief and started breathing normally again.

"Bloody hell," hissed a somewhat breathless Jinx as she realized the intruders were none other than Liberty and Chastity. "You two gave us such a freaking fright. I thought I was going to get expelled for sure this time! What the hell are you doing sneaking up on us like that?"

"Don't get your knickers in a twist," said Chastity, marching to where they were seated and leaving Liberty to yank the door back down into its customary almost closed position.

"So, what's new?" Liberty asked, turning round and looking expectantly at Jinx and Liv. "What's with all the running around like crazies-in-the-rain stuff?"

"I have perved. And now," said Jinx with a delighted giggle, "I am going to swerve."

Liv offered her hand to Jinx and the pair of them high-fived before collapsing into hysterical floods of laughter.

"What?" asked Chastity, who was busy fastidiously checking her crate for dirt and dust before she sat down on it, legs crossed demurely at the ankles.

"Yeah, what are you two on?" Liberty asked.

"She's only gone and had a phone message from Sir Jamie himself," Liv burst out, unable to hold this exciting information inside a second longer. "He wants her to call him and said something about going out on Saturday."

"Yeah," said Jinx, "he's taking me to a special-needs line-dancing class."

"I don't get it," Liberty said, looking confused. "Why would he want to take you to that? And you'd better make sure you don't laugh like that when you're speaking to *him*, Jinx, or there's no way in hell you'll be going on a second date. That's for freaking sure!"

"Okay, okay," Jinx mumbled, reflecting that she really must learn to be more ladylike in her enthusiasms. "Point taken. Anyway, it's true. Jamie phoned Jo and said he was my Uncle Trouser-Snake and could I phone him to discuss our plans for Saturday. Well, I take it that was what he meant. It was pretty funny. Look." Jinx paused, rummaged in her pocket for the note, which she was dismayed to see had a big brown burn mark in it from where the joint had caught against it in her pocket, and passed it over. "Check it out."

There was a brief silence as Chastity and Liberty bent their blonde and brown heads together over the note and digested its contents. They looked up at the exact same time a few seconds later, matching expressions of thrilled excitement on their expectant faces, waiting to see Jinx's reaction at their having read it. They were not to be disappointed.

"I think it's fucking ace," said Chastity, grabbing one of Jinx's hands and squeezing it hard, "and if you're worried about missing out on a night with us, well, don't be!"

"Me too, and Chas is right," Liberty agreed before narrowing her eyes at Jinx and staring at her reflexively. "Although what the hell are you going to *wear*?"

"Never mind that now," Liv cut in—she found Liberty's obsession with fashion somewhat draining to say the least although, it must be said, she never looked too badly turned out herself. "We've got to work out what she's going to say on the bloody phone first!"

What with all this perving and swerving, wardrobe issues, and phone-call concerns, Jinx barely knew whether she was coming or going. She sat with her knees pulled tightly up to her chest, linked her arms around them, and leant forward towards her pals, an expression of such rapt attention on her glowing face that any teacher who saw it would assume, rightly, that she was giving nothing less than 110 percent to the task at hand.

They sat there and for two nonstop hours endlessly dissected the note—not that it was particularly nuanced, but whatever!—, what Jinx could possibly wear on Saturday, and what, exactly, she should say on the phone that evening.

Eventually, every possible permutation of everything covered, the girls—who had also run out of weed by this time—rapidly decided it was far too cold to be skulking about like tramps in the dark like this. The four of them linked arms and hot-footed it across the pitches back to Tanner House in search of their three current main interests: central heating, crumpets loaded with butter and jam, and the newest episode of *America's Next Top Model*.

Katie Green sat by the window of her small cubicle room in Steinem House and stared avidly out past the drive in front of her house towards the tuck shop area. She had been sitting like that—in the dark, with her face pressed up against the cold glass of the resolutely not double-glazed window and her hands hugging her chunky knees tight to her flat chest—for at least three hours without moving. Katie had seen Jinx and Liv dash down the steps and let themselves into the garage from the window of the sanatorium, where she had been unsuccessfully begging Mister Sinton for a note to let her off games. At the sight of them, Katie had suddenly—and to the great confusion of Mister S, who'd been waiting patiently for the inevitable waterworks—lost all interest in her losing battle, made her excuses, dashed back to Steinem, and settled down to her vigil, only hoping she wouldn't miss them leaving in the short time it took her to get from the san to her room. She was not disappointed.

Only a few minutes after sighting two of her big five fascinatingly engaged in some extracurricular and no doubt illegal activity, Katie felt she'd practically won the jackpot when she spotted Liberty and Chastity making their own way towards the garage. About an hour after they'd also disappeared behind the sliding door, Katie's excellent vantage point afforded her the interesting montage of Charlie—she could hardly believe her luck at spotting all her heroines in one sitting like this—nearly fall out of a taxi as it stopped abruptly by the main gates, throw some money in the direction of the driver, sway, almost fall, and then begin staggering up the drive as the taxi turned round and sped off towards Brighton's bright lights.

At first, Katie thought the older girl must be drunk. It was only when she noticed Charlie dragging her right leg behind her that she realized the sixth-former was sporting a terrible limp. Katie watched, thoughtfully, as Charlie struggled up the drive, keeping close to the shadows of the small hedge that ran the whole way alongside it. Katie's reverie was destroyed a few seconds later by someone banging on her door as they passed, giggling and then running away. She glowered as she got up to put the light on and thought about how much she really, really hated being at this bloody school.

15 *Phone Banter*

Jinx sat on Liberty's bed, rather incredulously watching her best friend pull item after item of sheer fabulousness from her wardrobe, and then carefully assess its suitability for Jinx's date. Liberty, her wild hair bunched on top of her head in a gorgeously messy bun, scrutinized each garment before throwing it either towards the "possible" pile to her left or the "definitely no" pile to her right. Even when Jinx occasionally dared to take her life in her hands and voice the opinion that things were going in the wrong direction, Liberty totally ignored her, so that the right-side pile was quickly growing considerably larger than the left.

Jinx was messing around with a large pot of Mac gold glitter, blending it into the back of her hand, when Liberty spun round. "I've got it!" she squealed. "I knew there was something I'd forgotten."

"What?" Jinx asked, barely bothering to conceal her yawn of absolute, total boredom. She loved clothes, but really, this was ridiculous. How long had they been shut up in here? Christ, she needed to make the bloody phone call yet. And she still had to copy Liv's English essay and make appropriate adjustments before first lesson tomorrow morning. This evening was fast becoming a bloody farce. But since Liberty would be well upset if Jinx said anything, she resolved to try her best to stick it out and at least pretend to be interested.

"Look at THIS," said Liberty, ripping a photograph off the wall by her bed and pressing it into Jinx's hand. "I LOVE you in this dress!"

Jinx studied the photo, taken last summer half-term by Caroline before the whole family went off to a television awards ceremony in London, where Martin had picked up a gold gong for his work as creative director of a top London advertising agency. She smiled as she realized that yes, even if she did say so herself, she looked pretty damn hot in her multicoloured silk Simultane shift. Her face fell as she realized she'd also drunkenly shoved it to the back of her crowded wardrobe when they got home late that night and had promptly forgotten its existence. Until now, anyway.

"But it's not here, Lib," Jinx wailed. She was now absolutely set on wearing this or nothing—and she didn't think *nothing* would make her first date with the divine Jamie East go down quite the way she hoped. "It's at home!"

"Don't worry about it," replied Liberty. "Why don't we go back to yours on Friday and pick it up? Your mum phoned a couple of days ago and asked if she was ever going to see us again—we could kill two birds with one stone. I'd love to see them all anyway."

"Okay," Jinx said, sitting up and looking enthused for the first time since Liberty had announced her position as head stylist for Saturday's event and decided to act on it immediately. "That sounds great. Let's do it! We'll get on a train straight after Art and be home by dinner. Mum will be thrilled, I can pick up my dress, and George can drive us back here on Saturday afternoon just in time for bright lights, date city!"

"Excellent!" Liberty shoved all the clothes littering the bed onto the floor and flung herself onto the bed next to Jinx. "We can take all our washing back, too."

"Yeah," agreed Jinx, "and have a massive dinner and see the dogs. In fact, the more I think about it the more I can't wait—I feel like I haven't been home in a freaking *age*."

Sitting cross-legged and alone on her bed a few minutes later, having been propelled at high speed out of the next door room by its owner occupant, one Liberty Latiffe, Jinx opened a can of Diet Coke and took a few reflexive sips as she gazed at her mobile phone lying on top of the pile of largely unopened text books on her bedside table. This was fucking ridiculous. Wasn't she supposed to be, like, a way cool dudette? Well, she sure as hell wasn't behaving like one. No, she was acting like the biggest wuss in the whole freaking world. Jinx mentally punched herself in the face and reached for her phone. She was making this bloody call, and she was making it *now*.

"Hello?" Jamie's voice answered after the third ring and Jinx felt her heart leap with excitement at the sound of it.

"Hi Jamie," she said, thinking that—thank God—she sounded remarkably cool, calm and collected even in spite of what was currently happening to the inside of her stomach. "It's Jinx."

"Ah, naughty Jinx Slater finally gets off her butt and calls me back," Jamie said in a very low and sexy voice that seemed positively brimming with innuendo to a totally love-struck Jinx. "Hel-*lo*. I hoped it would be you. Don't move!"

Jinx sat unsurely on her bed. After an uncomfortably long pause during which a reddening and slightly sweaty Jinx mostly wished she'd taken her jumper off earlier, she heard heavy, rushing footsteps thudding across the line until a heavy-breathing Jamie picked it up with a clatter and said, "So, where were we, Slater?"

"Um," Jinx replied uncertainly, just a touch unnerved by the whole business, "you were…"

"Yes, that's it. I was about to ask you out," Jamie said firmly, immediately bringing Jinx's spinning mind right back to the matter at hand.

"So?" he asked, a huge smile lending his voice a very warm, teasing tone, "can I tempt you? Saturday?"

"*Gosh*—a date!" Jinx snapped right back, all unease totally brushed under the nasty navy blue carpet of her single room. "I'd love to, thanks very much."

"Sweetheart, that's great. I hoped you'd say yes." Jamie paused enough to allow a throaty chuckle to drift down the airwaves and hit a beaming Jinx's delighted ear before continuing.

"So here's the deal. I'm having a party at my place on Saturday."

Jinx nodded as she thought that this wasn't quite the *tête-à-tête* she had envisioned, but smiled at the realization that it sounded like a hell of a lot of fun and much less scary than having to deal with him *à deux*. Shit though, what about the solemn promise the lower sixth had made to each other to go out and have a total blast on Saturday night?

"Um, the thing *is*," Jinx said after a quick-fire think, ripping tiny slivers of paper off the sides of the note Jo had given to her in the library earlier, "I've kind of got—"

"Don't worry about it." Jamie's voice cut Jinx's off in the middle of her sentence. "You can bring whoever you like. In fact, I'd say the more the merrier."

"Okay," said Jinx, not really noticing the presumption in his tone. "I'll tell Liberty and Chastity and everyone. They'll definitely be up for it."

"Great, come round at about seven and bring a few bottles. And Jinx..." The lingering pause seemed positively pregnant with promise to Jinx, until Jamie added decisively, "I'm really looking forward to seeing you."

"Me too," she replied, blushing a deep red and distractedly screwing the note into a tiny ball with her free hand.

She was going to crack a gag about trying to keep hold of her shoes this time and hadn't even managed to ask if George would be there on Saturday night when she realized that the silence from the other end of the line meant he'd put the phone down.

Well, she thought to herself, exhaling deeply and banging

on the wall that she shared with Liberty, that went better than expected.

Jinx might have known there'd be no need for her to attract Liberty's attention. She'd barely banged once before her door was flung open and Liberty and Chastity burst in and leapt on top of her on her bed. They'd obviously been sitting in the corridor outside, ears firmly attached to the door, just waiting for the conversation going on inside to end so they could go over every aspect of it in endless detail.

The three of them were so overexcited they didn't notice Liv running down the corridor towards a very bedraggled Charlie, an expression of extreme concern on her face. The pair went into a huddle in the alcove by the common room. Not long after this, Liv started laughing uncontrollably at whatever it was Charlie was telling her. Their tortuous ascent up the adjacent stairs to the first floor bedrooms a few minutes later—the pain in her leg obviously intense, Charlie was leaning heavily on Liv's arm—also went completely unnoticed by their friends. Jinx et al. were now making so much noise in her room they'd already woken up Brian Morris from where he was trying to have a snooze in his office two corridors along and three floors up.

16 *Relax, Don't Do It*

Jinx and Liberty spent two solid hours giggling and shrieking at everyone's horoscopes in all the trash magazines they'd bought at Brighton station for the train home to Hampshire. And now Jinx sat happily on her bed at home and sorted through the pile of mail Caroline had left on her bed.

She hardly had to strain her ears over and above The La's "There She Goes" that was playing on her digital radio to hear Liberty having an extremely animated conversation with her parents downstairs. God, she thought as she breathed in great lungfuls of crisp countryside air breezing in through the open window at the head of her bed and looked around at her pink-and white-striped bedroom, which had remained resolutely unchanged since she was twelve, it was good to be home. It was also great—she grinned massively at the thought of this— to have Liberty back where she belonged, clutched close to the collective bosom of the adoring Slater family. Caroline and Martin, both sporting suspiciously bright eyes, had leapt on her as if she were their own daughter when the taxi the girls had hailed at the station dropped them off at the front door.

Lying back against her perfectly squashy pillows, Jinx fondled her dog Flash's ears with contentment and a very real sense that all was right with the world. Although Caroline often waxed long and lyrical about how unhygienic—never mind the bloody hairs!—it was to allow the dogs onto their beds, the rest of the Slaters paid her scant attention and Jinx was especially enjoying the long and emotional homecoming love that she and Flash were sharing right now.

As early as *she'd* thought polite—which wasn't very, though no one really noticed, Jinx had left her parents and Liberty in the kitchen and sloped off upstairs mumbling something under her breath about needing to sort her washing out. Instead, she'd hotfooted it straight into George's empty room and immediately located three gorgeous pictures of Jamie plastered to the whiteboard above his sink. Jinx had painstakingly unstuck them from their blue tack fixings, moved a few other pictures around to conceal the obvious white spaces left behind by their removal and strolled happily along the corridor to her own bedroom at the back of the house.

She held her ill-gotten gains in front of her, looking at first one and then another as if she were about to play her best hand during a game of poker at a super casino. She grimaced fiercely when she heard Caroline yelling at her about dinner, carefully placed the purloined photos between two empty November pages in the big leather-bound desk diary she kept on top of her chest of drawers and followed Flash and the smell of her favourite garlic- and rosemary-roasted potatoes down the wide main staircase, along the painting-filled hallway, past the dresser that held a riotous bunch of flowers in a blue glass vase, through the red dining room and into the kitchen where the Slaters always ate when there were only a few of them in residence.

Caroline was pulling a huge and wonderful-smelling leg of roast lamb from the Aga when Jinx slipped into her seat and reached for the open bottle of Pinot Noir in front of her. She gave Liberty—who was listening to Martin tell a story about his latest video campaign and laughing in all the right places—a discreet thumbs up to indicate she'd located the dress, then turned her attention to her mother as Caroline started heaping leeks and carrots swimming in her glorious homemade cheese sauce onto Jinx's plate.

During their visits to the Slaters, Liberty had taken to sleeping in the guest room adjacent to Jinx's, both of them having agreed that a night alone in a deliciously comfortable double bed was a small price to pay when they chatted late into the night at school all the time. Whoever woke up first always went and got into bed with the other one. Liberty, sporting a pair of George's old boxer shorts incongruously but sexily matched with a pale peach-coloured silk camisole edged with white lace, peered round the slightly open door.

She said, "Hey, I heard you rustling around and thought we should plan our day. Are we going to get changed here? There's no point in us going back to school and then out or we'll have to come up with some lie about what we're doing and where we're going."

Jinx stretched, yawned, pushed up her "princess sleeping" pink satin eye mask and rolled over to look at her radio alarm clock. It was only half past nine. She snuggled deeper down into the warmth of her goose-down duvet as the radio played her current favourite Amy Winehouse song.

Jinx nodded eventually. "Yeah. You're right. We'll hang out here all day until George gets back and it's time to sort ourselves out and get ready to leave. Then we'll get changed and head straight off to Jamie's."

The girls flung on dressing gowns thoughtfully stolen from the Sanctuary day spa in London by Jinx at the end of her and Caroline's last mother/daughter bonding day, and sauntered off to Gaymian's room. The small flat roof, easily accessed via the big picture window behind his desk, was not only an absolute suntrap but also hidden from the rest of the house unless someone peered right out of Caroline and Martin's bathroom window. These two factors had transpired to make it easily the Slater kids' number one favourite place to get baked in the morning.

"You know, Lib," Jinx said as she leaned against the red brick wall, pulled her dressing gown tighter around her body and turned her face to the dazzlingly bright winter morning sun, "it's really funny to think that the last time I sat here I was completely miserable, wondering if you were okay and if I was ever going to see you again. And now—well, everything's fucking great!"

"I know," Liberty replied, resting her head momentarily against Jinx's arm, "everything *is* fucking great. And I'm so excited for you tonight with Jamie. I'd love it if you two got together. He's so cool and such a dude. Great clothes too!"

"And he's got loads of nice friends," retorted an extremely overexcited Jinx, punching Liberty on the arm so hard she squealed. "We can go on double dates!"

Later, it seemed like the most civilized thing in the world for the two of them to take to Jinx's bedroom after loudly and loftily proclaiming to anyone who would listen that they would be working on their English homework and therefore must not be disturbed for at least the next two hours, and lock the door tight behind them.

"I feel like I'm in a boutique hotel," Liberty said, sighing deliriously as she rolled around in ecstasy on the ridiculously comfortable rug. "I can't tell you how much I've missed *this*. I love coming here."

"I know," Jinx replied, her current satisfaction levels also at an all-time high. "I love school, but I can't imagine how people must have coped in, like, the seventies, when boarders were only allowed home at half-term."

"Speaking of the seventies," Liberty added, directing an obvious smirk over to the uncovered legs on show in the space between the top of Jinx's socks and the hem of her tracksuit bottoms, "are you planning to shave your legs or is this a considered look? Do you think Jamie digs the whole boho thing? Because, just so you know, it's not quite the same this time round..."

"Fuck you, Latiffe!" Jinx screamed, throwing the biscuit

she'd been nibbling at Liberty but missing and hitting the wall instead. "How very dare you! Of *course* I'm going to shave my fucking legs. I'm waiting for *you* to finally finish hogging that bloody spliff and then I'm going to run myself a long hot tub and wallow in it...oh, for an hour at least. And before you start with the beseeching looks, I'*m* in Mum and Dad's bathroom today, so you can piss off to the green one!"

"Touché." Liberty waved her hand in the flame of the rose-scented candle in an attempt to intensify its delicious smell. "I like the green one best anyway. Hey, Jinx—" Liberty paused and rolled over onto her front, eyeing her pal before continuing. "Have you thought about what you're going to tell George about Jamie? Are you even going to bother saying anything, or what?"

"Hmmm," murmured Jinx, who had actually been thinking about this intensively during the last couple of days but had yet to mention anything about it to her friends. "George knows I like him, obviously. But I haven't decided whether I should tell him how *much* I like Jamie. I've been trying to think about what's best, but to be honest we've been so freaking busy lately I haven't come up with anything. What do you think I should do?"

"I don't know." Liberty drew her words out in a manner that indicated she was currently engaging in very deep thoughts indeed. "Maybe...*nothing*. Yes," she continued, sitting up as she warmed to her theme. "What's the point of saying anything when you don't quite know what you're saying yet—if you see what I'*m* saying of course."

Jinx, who saw exactly what Liberty meant and liked the thought of saying nothing a great deal more than she liked to think about George's reaction to the news that she was in love with his best friend, nodded happily.

Lying in water so hot the mirrors wouldn't de-steam for hours after she'd pulled the plug, her face and body bright red from the heat, Jinx reached over to replace the pot of intensive Frizz Ease conditioning mask on the shelf at the side of the roll-top bath and ran the hot tap. She dumped half a bottle of Kiehl's Original Musk into the running water and smiled as the glorious musky scent punched all others out of its way as soon as it hit and mingled with the damp bathroom air.

Discovered by Kiehl's in a mysterious vat labeled "Love Oil" in their apothecary in the fifties, it had been rediscovered by Jinx in the Brighton branch of Space NK on one of her many shopping trips there last year. Truly though, gimmick or not, its heavy scent was redolent of romance. It smelt like the most brilliantly passionate love affair but also, somehow, of the bittersweet nostalgia that follows its end. Not that Jinx had ever experienced much of either, but whatever, here's hoping!

She took a deep breath and pushed her head back and under the water. She held her breath as long as she could before rising, Thalassa-like, from the water and using both hands to smooth her slick, wet hair away from her face against the back of her head and neck. She examined her rather stubbly calves, reached for Martin's new razor—God, he went properly psychopathically *mad* when he eventually cottoned on to the fact his wife and daughter did this far too often—and propped a foot between the taps ready to make her legs shiny and beautiful even in the dead of winter.

17 *George Is a Moron*

Jinx and Liberty both jumped as if shot when their moisturizing session in Jinx's bedroom was rudely interrupted by a sudden fierce banging against the locked door. George had only been home for five minutes but the noise levels were already verging towards antisocial territory.

"You'll have the fucking neighbours round in a minute if you carry that on," Jinx yelled. "We're busy—we'll be down in a second. Fuck off and raid the fridge or something!"

"All right, all right," George said, his booming voice not at all muffled by the heavy oak door. "Keep your hair on, Sis—we don't *have* any bloody neighbours. See you two downstairs."

"I definitely," said Liberty with a worried glance at the door, "think you should keep all the Jamie stuff to yourself. I don't think George would be pissed off about it in the slightest, but can you imagine the bloody *jokes*?"

"I know," replied Jinx firmly, pulling on her old favourite black velvet Miss 60 tracksuit bottoms over her now glistening legs. "You're right, it would be awful. I'd constantly be looking over my shoulder worried about what he was saying and to whom. He's never quite worked out what's appropriate and what's not." There was a thoughtful pause as she slipped on the hot pink Kenzo T-shirt she'd filched from Caroline's dressing room on her way back from the bathroom. "Or maybe he *has* and just doesn't care who he winds up. Either way, I'm not saying a freaking word."

Tripping down the stairs half an hour later in a cloud of L'Artisan Parfumeur's Fou D'Absinthe—Jinx thought her current favourite perfume the scent equivalent of wearing full body armour, and Bulgari's *au the vert*—Liberty's far more subtle choice, shaved, body oiled, moisturized, nails painted and fake-tanned up to the max, the girls felt very pleased with their pre-party preparations indeed.

They pulled up short when, through the banisters and the half-open door beyond, they spied a small blonde girl lounging on the overstuffed white sofa in the huge drawing room the Slaters hardly ever used. Decorated predominantly in varying shade of white and cream, it contained Caroline's beloved baby grand piano, hundreds of family photographs in all kinds of frames, and shelves groaning under the weight of myriad poetry books. It was very much Caroline's room and the family normally only hung out in there to drink champagne and open their presents on Christmas Day.

"Oh fuck," moaned Jinx to Liberty as the girl stood up. "I'm sure that's fucking Lydia. She was such a bitch to me on New Year's Eve—God, I hope she's not coming to Jamie's party too."

"I bet you she *is*," Liberty replied, equally morosely, for she'd heard all about Not So Lovely Lydia's New Year's Eve antics from a still-irate Jinx at the beginning of term. "Otherwise he wouldn't have brought her back here, would he?"

"Finally!" George, clutching a bottle of Laurent Perrier Rose and four champagne flutes, which looked too cozy by half as far as Jinx was concerned, pushed through the swing door from the kitchen and stood looking up at them from the hall with a very cheeky grin. "I thought you might have died up there. Come and have a drink."

Jinx, thinking what an absolute bona fide fool he was, grimaced at him as Lydia stood up—very elegantly considering the ridiculously high heels on her pointy black shoes and the fearsomely tight black pencil skirt she was sporting underneath a ruffled cream silk shirt—and moved over to the marble fireplace, affording her an excellent view of the two halfway down the stairs. Jinx knew she and Liberty were being appraised as Lydia reclined against the marble shelf with her back to the grate, slowly lit a cigarette, and as she exhaled, pushed her chest out and sucked in her tummy—such as it was, it was pretty flat anyway.

"Jinx," she said eventually, in an incredibly fake nice voice, as if the New Year's Eve incident had never happened. "How lovely to see you. And this must be the famous Liberty."

"Hmm," Jinx grunted rudely, barely looking at Lydia—who she still couldn't quite *believe* was in her house like this—before she turned straight back to a grinning George, who was clearly oblivious to any tension whatsoever. "We need to ask you something—can we have a word upstairs please?"

"Sure thing," said George expansively. "Let me dump the champers down here and I'll be straight up."

Jinx didn't bother to reply but pulled a disgusted face, grabbed Liberty's hand and stomped back upstairs, where the two of them hovered round the corner from the bathroom long enough to hear Lydia's tinkling laugh ring out loud, proud, and evidently very pleased with itself indeed from the drawing room.

"Christ!" hissed Jinx, "that's high-pitched enough to break the fucking glass on every frame in that room. Mum would go *mad* if she knew he was letting that slut smoke in there too. What's he thinking of, inviting her to Jamie's tonight? Last time he saw her he couldn't get away fast enough. What a fucking idiot."

"What's up, Sis?" George asked, running up the stairs two at a time before sweeping Jinx off her feet and spinning her round in a huge bear-hug. "Excited about tonight?"

"Put me down!" squealed a not-at-all-amused Jinx, thumping him on the back in protest at the same time. "And what the hell are you doing bringing HER? I thought you hated that bitch!"

"Ah," George said suavely, before turning round to administer the same greeting to a grinning Liberty and thereby buying himself a few seconds to think of an explanation that would satisfy his irate sister. "Yes. Well. Things have—shall we say—*changed* on that front. Ready for the party?"

18 *Big Pimping It*

George pulled their car up opposite the imposing white building where Jamie's penthouse apartment occupied the whole top floor. Jinx reflected that it was a very good thing George had been given such an amazing new car stereo for Christmas. She and Liberty had spent the whole two-hour journey sitting in the back and singing along to the *Dance Anthems* album they'd lifted from Gaymian's room, whilst furiously texting their friends and each other about what a total loser George's girlfriend was.

Unable to hear anything Lydia might have said to them, they ignored her pointedly anyway, reasoning, as they so often did when presented with any situation out of the ordinary, that it was worth it for the practice, if nothing else.

Jinx checked her face for the last and final time in her hand mirror. She was delighted to see her mascara had for once stayed put on her eyelashes and her nose still looked as pleasantly shine-free as it had in the bathroom mirror just before they'd left home.

Liberty nudged Jinx hard in the ribs, winked and pointed up to Jamie's windows and surrounding decked balcony, just visible from the road as George backed expertly into a space right in front of the building. All was in darkness save for a few multicoloured pulsing disco lights that illuminated, off and on, a couple kissing on the balcony. When George cut the engine they could all hear the dull yet wildly exciting throb of some seriously hardcore house music pumping through the night air.

Liberty snatched Jinx's mirror out of her hand and, using the glow from the streetlights outside, pouted at herself for a few seconds from various angles. A pleased smile showed she was extremely happy with the stunning reflection pouting right back at her. She slipped on the crushed silk Miu Miu heels in burnt orange she'd kicked into the foot as soon as they'd set off, opened the back door, stood up, and smoothed down the front of her black Stella McCartney black bubble dress. She'd straightened her long hair so that her choppy fringe swept seductively over one eye and she looked gorgeous. Good enough, as George had rather inappropriately said after doing a double take when he saw her walk down the stairs at home earlier, to eat.

Jinx, in the silk Simultane shift dress, worn over skinny black jeans teamed with her favourite shoes ever—glittery gold Top Shop platforms with a chunky golden heel—and a short black and white houndstooth French Connection swing jacket over the top, looked pretty damn hot-to-trot as well.

The two of them stood on the street and looked each other over approvingly before doing a noisy high five and squealing with excitement, much to Lydia's disapproval. Jinx caught sight of Lydia's I'm-too-cool-for-school disdainful look and flicked a quick two fingers up behind her back. This caused Liberty to snort with laughter and Lydia to spin round again and fix them with a blacker look than one would have thought such a small, silly-looking girl capable of producing on a dark night like this.

And if that look was bad, thought Jinx and Liberty at the same time but unbeknownst to each other, the look she fixed upon the objects of an impromptu wolf whistle from George a few seconds later was something else entirely. This one was positively malevolent, evil enough to send a real-life shiver down both their spines and make them immediately crane their necks in that direction too.

"Fucking hell, Jinx," hissed Liberty, nudging her friend really quite hard in the ribs in her joy at being the first to realize what had caused the commotion, "I can't believe it—look at *that!*"

Sashaying down the opposite pavement, looking as if their names were in fact Sheba, Salome, and Scherazade instead of the rather drab Chekhovian originals, were Stagmount's very own identical Russian triplets. George's was by no means the only jaw that came to rest nearly on the floor as they approached. *Everyone*, including the drivers and passengers of three cars stuck behind a red traffic light, a motley bunch of students drinking cans of cider and wearing ostentatiously holey attire, a glamorous old lady in a mink coat with big hair and a slash of scarlet lipstick who was walking her black pug, a cyclist, and, of course, Jinx, Liberty, and Lydia ranged alongside George on the other, were all equally in thrall to the spectacle of the sisters marching along.

The girls had linked their arms and were striding along in unison, flashes of bright white teeth occasionally glinting in the dark against their glossed lips and lightly tanned faces. Their hair flew out behind them and they looked as if they were playing the three heroines in a Hollywood blockbuster. At first Jinx and Liberty were too stunned by the whole scene, the passersby and everything, to realize that the triplets were crossing the road at high speed specifically to talk to *them*.

"Liberty! Jinx!" said Olga loudly, although neither of the addressees knew which one she was. She beamed at them in the friendliest way and took each of their left hands warmly in both of hers. "How funny to see you here. We are going out for dinner—would you like to come with us?"

"That's *so* kind of you girls," Liberty replied. She loved the fact that the traffic light had gone green, but the three cars had remained in their stationary position and none of the other onlookers showed much sign of moving anywhere fast either. "But we're already kind of late for a party in this building."

"Maybe," said Jinx, raising her eyebrows meaningfully at George, trying to get his attention, "you guys should come and join us after you've had dinner?"

George completely ignored the absolute daggers Lydia's eyes were now shooting into Jinx and Liberty's shapely backs.

He just managed to get a grip on himself and asserted immediately that the triplets were of course more than welcome to attend the party, that they *must* do so. "In fact," he added in an incredibly cheesy tone of voice, "I will be personally very disappointed if you do not."

Lydia pretended she hadn't noticed Jinx and Liberty's fake gagging. The triplets said their goodbyes and sauntered off down the road—nearly causing a ten-car pileup. Lydia also ignored George's conciliatory tone as he offered to take her arm. She turned on her heel and started marching determinedly in the direction of Jamie's front door without a backwards glance.

Jinx and Liberty stood by the door of the bedroom where they were supposed to leave their coats, unable to get in due to the current occupants having very loud sex in there. They banged impatiently on the door while giggling to each other about how furious Lydia had been when the triplets came on the scene. Jinx began to do a very mean impression of Lydia stomping off when she turned round and came face to face with her. Liberty snorted with sudden laughter. She just couldn't help herself. The whole Lydia thing was becoming way too much like hard work. She and Jinx *were* here to have fun after all, and the expression on Jinx's face *was* a perfect comic mix of horrified guilt at finding the subject of her little one-man show suddenly standing in front of her like this, and quick rage at being caught in the act by the same.

"I bet you think this is really funny, don't you Jinx?" Lydia's lip trembled, but she folded her arms and raised her chin so that she seemed built entirely of a series of angry, angular points. "Well, you don't understand it now but you will. You wait until you see someone *you* like slobbering after someone else. Or THREE someone elses, you see how you like it. I bet you go mad!"

"I wouldn't actually," said Jinx firmly, eyeing Lydia with more disapproval than ever. Didn't the fucking girl have any self-control, for God's sake! "And, for the record, Lyds, you're only TWENTY-TWO. I can't fucking stand being patronized by people who are, like, four and a half years older than me and seem to think they've had all these life experiences and whatever and are therefore licensed to preach wisdom to those younger than them. The whole thing's so freaking stupid."

Jinx made a disgusted face, grabbed Liberty's arm and dragged her off to the double doors leading to the decked roof terrace, complete with hot tub, huge Indian-style cushions strewn around the floor, and a white canopy sheltering revelers from too much wind or rain.

"*This* is more like it," Jinx said, looking round once more before deciding her best bet for finding Jamie was if they moved around. "Fuck her. D.B.M. That means: don't bore me. No, not YOU, Lib. Lydia of course!" Jinx rolled her eyes quickly so Liberty wouldn't spot her. "Let's go and get some urgent drinks—I'm dying of thirst over here."

They threw their coats behind a mammoth navy sofa and wended their way through the very well-dressed throng to the makeshift bar that two black uniformed cocktail waiters had set up in the corner of the outside deck and were now fully staffing. George still hadn't reappeared from wherever he'd scarpered off to as soon as they'd come in, but what with the amazing canapés knocking around and a set of wicked beats coming from the silver decks in front of the glass wall of the living room just inside, this party most definitely had the makings of an outstanding night.

"Where are Liv and Charlie?" Jinx leaned over and yelled in Chastity's ear as the two of them swayed next to each other in Jamie's palatial front room, trying to make herself heard above the amazing tunes a female DJ—wearing a short, tight purple boob tube dress over bare shoulders and legs liberally dusted with sparkly body powder, strappy silver sandals and a pair of huge angel wings made of white feathers and silver sequins—was spinning on the decks. As soon as the dirty blonde, slightly louche-looking self-styled angel started playing Prince's "Kiss," pretty much everyone at the party rammed themselves into the living room at once. Big as the room was, since there was not enough space for anyone to throw any shapes to speak of, they were currently all jumping up and down in time to the beat. Bouncing off each other and everyone around them, splashes from raised drinks occasionally landing on their hot skin and momentarily cooling it down, the girls were having the most incredible time.

Jinx had seen Jamie a few times out of the corner of her eye, but hadn't yet managed to say hello to him. He was wearing now faded, once dark blue Wrangler jeans, a white T-shirt with a picture of KFC's Colonel Sanders on the front in neon pink, kind of like an Andy Warhol print, and Spring Court shoes. The overall effect was way cool and pretty amazing to a completely smitten

Jinx. Although the meeting and greeting of all his friends, as far as it appeared to her anyway, was obviously a bloody time consuming old business and Jinx was beginning to wonder whether she would *ever* get him alone.

George had resurfaced and was studiously avoiding catching Lydia's eye whilst chatting up lots of the more arty girls who were mostly wearing variations on tight black outfits accented with flashes of bright neon colour—shoes, handbags, hair bands, or chunky statement pieces of fluorescent jewelry. Lydia, conversely, was in the thick of what looked like an off-duty doting rugby scrum. Lots of well-built boys wearing pink, blue, or white open-necked shirts ubiquitously and unimaginatively paired with pale blue jeans and brown loafers were clamouring to fetch her more drinks or invite her to dance. She looked a hell of a lot happier than when they'd arrived, that was for sure.

Although Chastity and Paul arrived at 8:30, about half an hour after Jinx's crew, there was still no sign of Liv and Charlie and neither of them—most unusually—were answering their mobile phones. Whatever, it was now half past nine, the party was in full swing, and they were all so busy having a total blast they didn't give the missing two more than the occasional, cursory thought and a quick, mental head shake at their amazing negligence.

Jinx and Liberty both noticed Chastity kept edging towards them and away from her boyfriend during a few more energetic songs. Eventually, decidedly rosy-faced, the foursome stumbled outside to cool down in the chill night air. Sweating quite a lot after all that vigorous aerobic exercise on the dance floor, they were also flushed with the combination of great music, stunning raspberry mojitos, caipirinhas, and dirty martinis that the bar guys were dishing out inside at a rate of knots. They found a spare few silk-striped floor cushions scattered around a low table holding tea lights in glass jars, some dirty champagne flutes, and a massive bong. The girls flung themselves down and kicked off their shoes whilst Paul went to the bar on a cocktail mission.

"Fucking hell," sighed Liberty, taking a huge breath as she leant on her elbows and flexed her neck back and from side to side before exhaling slowly. "This party is *fantastic*. Where are Liv and Charlie?"

"Don't forget the triplets!" Jinx said, giggling as she kicked off her golden heels and curled her legs underneath her.

"What about the triplets?" Chastity asked, reaching into the black quilted Chanel handbag on a gold chain her mum had given her for Christmas, pulling out a lump of sticky hash and chucking it at Jinx. "Are they coming tonight, too? When did you speak to them?"

"We bumped into them on the street when we got here," Liberty said. She was not so subtly eyeing a beautiful dark-haired boy who had just sat down at the next table and was smiling right back at her. "They practically created a public disturbance when they stopped to talk to us, as per."

"You're damn right," added Jinx, "and a private one too, judging by Lydia's freak-out when George couldn't take his eyes off them. I never liked her anyway. *And* she had the cheek to tell Lib and I we'd understand 'one day.' The fucking bitch is only bloody twenty-two. Anyway, I think he's well rid of her."

"Yes," Chastity said, in much quieter tones than her normal voice. She looked over her shoulder. Paul was coming towards them holding a circular silver tray laden with fruit-filled cocktails carefully in front of him. "I guess he is."

An Everybody's Free remix came on and Chastity cocked her head to one side, frowning thoughtfully at the lyrics before she turned back round to face the table. Next to her, Jinx, who thought Chastity was definitely not quite as enthusiastic about the evening as she could have been, was offering her a toke on the bong. She held her hair back, leant towards the bong, inhaled deeply and exhaled a potent cloud of smoke alongside an appreciative naughty giggle just as Paul reached them with the tray.

"For fuck's sake, Chastity," he said, looking really cross and not bothering to lower his voice in front of the others, "you know I can't stand it when you get stoned."

"Stop being such a fucking knob, Paul," Chastity hissed, her blue eyes flashing cobalt daggers at him. "You're really bugging me. I can do whatever the fuck I like."

Even though they were pretty baked, Liberty and Jinx looked at each other in horror—they had *never* heard Chastity and Paul speak so dismissively to each other like this.

"Mojito, Jinx?" Paul said, avoiding Chastity's eyes and pointedly turning his back on her to face the others. "Liberty?"

"Um…thanks Paul," said Jinx quietly, not quite sure where to look. "That's great."

Liberty accepted her drink equally meekly. They immediately started downing their cocktails in great long gulps—not least for something to do in the uncomfortable face of such icy *froideur* coming in waves off their formerly loved-up pals.

Chastity stood up without a word, surprisingly steady on her feet given the huge amount of high-grade hash she'd just ingested. She turned on the thin steel heel of her black pointy Prada boots and stalked off in the direction of the relative privacy of the hallway inside. It was obvious to all of them that her intention was for Paul to follow right after her. Without a word and with an extremely pissy look on his face, he did so, leaving behind Jinx and Liberty, who were more than a little drunk, stoned as hell, and just as shocked by the angry scene they'd just witnessed.

"Trouble in paradise," said Jinx, giggling nervously at Liberty. "Who'd have thought it?"

"I would," Liberty replied mischievously, giggling right back at her. "They've been bitching and moaning at each other all term. I'm not surprised in the slightest. Oh look, here come the triplets!"

"And Jamie," Jinx moaned. She spotted him striding along purposefully behind the triplets. What she really felt like doing right now was putting her head in her hands at this unfortunate conjunction, but she knocked that impulse on its head and smiled widely and—she hoped—alluringly in the direction from which all four were descending on them. "Please God let me not make a fool of myself again," she whispered, sending a not-so-silent prayer fleetingly heavenwards.

"Don't worry, Jinx," Liberty said quickly, after catching all but the first word of this plaintive statement on the strengthening breeze coming off the sea. She gave the triplets an admiring once-over, squeezed Jinx's leg in what was supposed to be a gesture of reassurance but mostly succeeded only in wrinkling the silk shift dress even further, and smiled encouragingly at her. "You look stunning. Anyway," she continued, ruining somewhat the previous good effect of her words, "pretty as they are, you're so much more fun than them. And Jamie likes you, we *know* he does."

Jinx's attention was fully diverted from the triplets—and indeed every single other person in the entire world—when Jamie dropped down right next to her, threw an arm round her shoulders, pulled her in close, and dropped a tiny kiss on the top of her head in greeting.

It took Jinx a couple of seconds to come round from the inevitable swoon this action put her into. When she did so she found Jamie's face level with her own. He was staring deeply into her eyes, his lips mere millimeters from her own, and the hand he'd snaked round to the nape of her neck was tugging suggestively on some curly blonde tendrils of hair. He was so close she could see each individual freckle on his nose, the different gradations of colour in his green irises and the creased vertical lines along the bottom of his lower lip. He was going to kiss her, she knew he was, and at that moment she both closed her eyes and did actually stop breathing. She felt the hand tighten against her neck, pulling her forwards slightly and then Jinx felt Jamie's mouth press hard against her own. She parted her lips involuntarily and gasped and pretty much as soon as she felt his tongue enter her mouth he pulled away, squeezed her shoulder, and dropped into the seat next to her.

"So, Jinx," said Jamie, breaking away, hugging her close to

his chest, and tracing the line of her jaw with his forefinger. Even though this position was actually quite uncomfortable and her neck was beginning to ache from being twisted unnaturally to the side, this action sent Jinx into practically the biggest spin she'd ever been in her whole life after the earlier kiss. "What's up?"

"Mmm," she murmured, closing her eyes for a second, savouring the sensation and surreptitiously trying to stretch her neck by rolling her head round without appearing insane. "What a freaking great party. Thanks so much for...ooomfh!"

Jinx sat up in surprise after finding herself suddenly launched from Jamie's supportive arm into an undignified sprawl on her side of the cushion with no warning whatsoever. How did that happen? Where did he *go* in such a hurry? She looked round in confusion before frowning as the reason for Jamie's sudden abdication swam into focus in front of her. Her gaze fell on her brother and stuck there. She might have known George would bloody well have something to do with it. There he was, the grinning idiot, shoving Liberty practically off her seat as he squeezed himself onto the corner of it, smarming over the triplets at the same time as patting Jamie vigorously on the back whilst congratulating his best friend for holding yet another brilliant bash.

"Drinks, girls?" George winked at Jinx. He was obviously beside himself with excitement at his good fortune that the girls he was *really* talking to had actually turned up, and mistakenly assumed his sister would share his enthusiasm.

"Yes, thanks," Jinx snapped straight back, knowing what he was up to and deciding to play him at his own game. "We'd love some, wouldn't we Liberty?"

"Um," George replied, looking around at the triplets' full glasses, their elegantly crossed legs and their charming smiles and mentally cursed his sister in the worst way. *Dammit*. He knew she had him over a barrel. He could hardly not get her what she wanted for fear of looking like a churlish bastard in front of these total honeys, could he? "Sure thing, Sis," he continued in a level voice, smiling winningly at the identical stunners opposite him. "Coming right up."

"Grab me a Corona, mate," Jamie shouted after George's retreat before sitting down again. This time, he was opposite Jinx and Liberty and adjacent to the triplets, who were sitting at the head of the table, most attractively arranged around each other in a coil of slender denim-clad legs, perfectly highlighted sleek ash-blonde hair and a veritable cloud of Opium perfume. Drink order duly noted, Jamie turned his attention back to the incredibly interesting group of young ladies at this table.

"So," he said, leaning forward and smiling inclusively round the table at them, "is it true that you Stagmount girls have got a house*master* looking after you up there?"

The girls were giggling helplessly as George returned with a cocktail in each hand and two bottles of Corona with lime sticking out of the two deep pockets at the front of his jeans.

"I think something's going on outside, mate," he said to Jamie, nodding over to the bar, where the student Jamie had paid to act as chief security man was now in an anxious-looking huddle with the bar men. "They said something about a fight? I'd go and take a look if I were you."

"My apologies, ladies," Jamie said, jumping up and making

a mock bow, "but this delightful chat is most definitely to be continued! Don't move!"

"I spat in it by the way," George murmured in Jinx's ear just as she was finishing her first long swallow of delicious Sea Breeze and he was moving over to shamelessly steal Jamie's prime seat adjacent to the triplets. "Hope you enjoy it!"

"You asshole," Jinx hissed back, swallowing the urgent desire she had to give her brother the worst dead arm he'd ever experienced, along with the remains of her drink. Or, better still, she could give him a dead leg—a really good one of those would have him limping for a couple of hours at *least*. Aside from anything else, she was steaming cross that he'd so effortlessly succeeded in getting rid of Jamie. George had obviously, she thought with a smug smile, mistakenly assumed Jamie fancied the triplets and got him out of the way so the field would be clear for himself. Well, she concluded with another smirk as she pulled the bottoms of her skinny jeans back down over the tops of her shoes, he'd get a surprise and a half when he realized that it *wasn't* the stunning triplets Jamie was interested in but rather his own dear sister.

"Come on, Lib," said Jinx, she grabbed a half full bottle of Smirnoff that no one seemed to be drinking, stood up and beamed at the triplets. God, it wasn't *their* fault her brother was such a freaking moron—and the more she saw of these girls, the more she liked them. "Let's go and find Chastity. We should at least see how she's doing."

"Where do you think Igor is?" Liberty asked as they wandered over to the crowd that was gathering fast by the balcony railings, looking at something happening on the road down below. "They give him the slip all the bloody time now."

"Yeah," agreed Jinx, not really paying too much attention to Igor's whereabouts since she was now much more engrossed in finding out what everyone was gazing at over the side. "He's the worst bodyguard in the world. You'd think their dad would at least get someone who was up to the job, wouldn't you?"

As soon as Jinx had managed to squeeze herself into a small gap between two whooping boys and peer down herself, she turned round with a horrified expression on her face, grabbed Liberty's hand and without a word pulled her along the decking and down the main staircase that led to the street.

The sight that greeted them just outside the front door was so shocking it pulled them both up short for a few seconds. Chastity, her red face transformed by a veritable river of tears running down both cheeks, was screaming obscenities into a very cross-looking Paul's ear.

Just as Jinx was gathering some air into her lungs with which to scream at Chastity to let him go and get the hell off him, a police van, complete with flashing blues and a screaming siren, screeched to a handbrake halt at the side of the pavement.

"Oh fuck," said Jinx to Liberty, grabbing her best friend's arm in horror as three policemen jumped out the back of the van and surrounded Chastity and Paul. "Fuck, fuck, FUCK!"

Chastity, stunned into sudden sanity by the lights, noise, and close proximity to the boys in blue, raised her ghostly, tear-stained face to the policemen and stared at them in bewilderment. Paul, his own face an unbecoming shade of green that was becoming more virulent by the second, looked round at

Chastity. She, very over-dramatically as far as Jinx and Liberty were concerned, fell to her knees by the side of what the voyeurs were pretty safe in their unanimous assumption was her *ex*-boyfriend. She lay curled in a defeated little heap on the pavement, her Chanel bag to the side of her, prostrate at the feet of the police as if she were begging forgiveness.

Without any warning whatsoever, the frozen tableau in front of Jinx and Liberty began to show signs of movement. Paul creakily raised his head once more, turned and proceeded to deliver a direct stream of evil-smelling, orange projectile vomit towards Chastity's stomach area, legs, and—cue involuntary shudder from Liberty—Prada boots. What had appeared to be taking place in slow-motion rewind, a simulacrum more real than the present original, became a hive of frenetic activity.

"What the..." said the eldest policeman in disgust, covering his mouth and nose with his hand in a vain attempt to disguise the smell. "I've seen some sights in my life," he continued, very much in the manner of an actor doing some warm-up exercises before he goes on stage, "let me tell you. But that right there is the most absolutely disgusting one yet. 'Ere, love!" He bent down to address a by-now quietly sobbing Chastity, who was staring at her vomit-covered body in utter disbelief and wondering if she would ever in her life recover from this terrible scene. "Are you all right?"

"I'm the one that's not all right, for fuck's sake!" said Paul bitterly, standing up and steadying himself on the ornate street lamp next to him when it was touch and go whether his legs would support him. "Why are you asking *her*? She..."

Whatever slander Paul was about to commit against Chastity's hitherto good name was lost as another stream of evil sick, more orange—if that was possible—vomit careered out of his mouth onto the pavement next to Chastity. The force of the projection was so great that it seemed to go on forever, and created a fearsome amount of splash-back as it hit. Unfortunately, where Chastity had shuffled on her knees out of the way of the first puddle in order to assess the damage to her person was right next to where the second stream was hitting. Jinx and Liberty found they were too disgusted even to turn away as the splashes landed all over Chastity's face, causing her mascara to drip down from her now stuck-together eyelashes and her hair to stick to the side of her head where the sick landed. It was the most filthy fucking shower any of them had ever seen, and that was for sure.

"Oh dear God," muttered one of the policemen, a nice chap, a born and bred Brightonian who had a lovely daughter at home about Chastity's age, crossing himself and turning to his colleagues. "I've never seen anything like it. This poor lassie—we've got to get her home, lads."

"Oh fuck," said Jinx again, much quieter this time but with even more feeling than the first—she didn't even like to think about Mr. Morris's, or worse, Mrs. Bennett's reaction to them being dropped back to school in the middle of the night with a full police escort.

"Paul," Liberty suddenly said, thinking admirably on her feet around the same dilemma and rushing to his side, "are you okay? Shouldn't you go to *hospital* or something?" She looked pleadingly at the policemen, directing the full benefit of the dual beam of her soft brown eyes into their own, slightly bloodshot versions. "Can't you lot take him? I've never seen anyone being sick like that."

"Yes," Jinx added firmly, understanding exactly what Liberty was getting at and dashing over to help her. "I think she's right. What would happen if he died on the street and you hadn't dropped him off at A&E? I'm sure there'd be a terrible fuss. Well…the *Argus* would make something of it, definitely."

This cunning mention of the local paper finally got through to the policemen. They moved over to the side of the van, where they stood muttering amongst themselves for a couple of minutes before marching purposefully back over to the girls. The only sounds were the omnipresent squawk of the seagulls and the sea rolling the pebbles back and forth on the beach beyond the road. The partygoers leaning over the side of Jamie's penthouse balcony had all been stunned into silence when the vomiting started, and were now avidly awaiting the verdict from the police. Chastity had finally cottoned on to the enormity of the problems they would face if the policemen insisted on taking them "home" as promised, and was now also staring silently at the policemen, willing them to take Paul and leave her alone.

"Right, son," the burliest cop said, looking with extreme distaste at Paul but offering him his arm nonetheless. "Come on. It'd be best if you got yourself checked over."

"I'm fine," Paul said, shaking him off and shooting a seriously filthy look at Chastity. "I'm severely allergic to fish, that's all. I haven't had a reaction like this since I bit into a crispy fish ball thinking it was a chicken nugget three years ago. In fact," he said, his green face quickly turning red with fury at the thought of what he might have been subjected to this time, "I think you should ask this girl here what she had for lunch. Go on!"

"Okay, okay, keep your wig on," said the cop, shaking his head and turning to Chastity.

"What did you have for your lunch then, love? And don't worry, I'm only asking to keep the peace between you two. I'm sure—ha ha—whatever it was won't constitute a criminal offence of any kind."

"I wouldn't be so confident of that if I were you," muttered Jinx in an aside to Liberty, unable to stop herself from cracking the gag despite the severity of the situation.

"I had a tuna mayo sub actually," Chastity said dreamily whilst shooting a contrarily triumphant glance at an apoplectic Paul. "And I really, *really* enjoyed it. I guess I forgot to brush my teeth afterwards, too."

"If you really loved me like you said you did," Paul said dramatically, looking at the lamppost as if it were a tree and he was in fact Heathcliffe, "you would never have eaten fish for lunch knowing you were seeing me later."

"I forgot," Chastity replied nonchalantly before leaning in close to Paul and whispering her punch line so the policemen couldn't hear. "I guess I was too *stoned*."

"Oh dear," Liberty whispered to Jinx after seeing the look of pure, unadulterated fury this revelation caused to pass across Paul's normally cheery face. "I know she's cross, but I don't think she should have said that. I've got a bad feeling about this."

Liberty was proved exactly right for once as, only a second later, all hell did indeed break loose. Paul started screaming at Chastity with such a deranged look in his eye that all the onlookers were convinced he meant grievous bodily harm at *best* and drew in sharp intakes of breath. The burly policeman—who couldn't stop thinking just how like Chastity was his own eldest daughter, the light of his life, his absolute pride and joy—moved in front of Paul and caught him mid-flight. He bundled him off to one side and treated him to a few very stern words about controlling himself, being a man, and accepting when things were over in a reasonable manner. Paul, already incensed by Chastity, became wildly furious at the sound of all this.

"Why don't you phone up STAGMOUNT," he screamed, delivering his parting shot with the true venom of the recently dumped, "and ask them where their lower sixth is right now? I bet the teachers up there would just love to know what their *young ladies* are doing messing around in town at this time of night."

"You bastard," Chastity hissed at him, her fury now easily matching his own, "I can't believe you'd stoop that low. Well, Paul, if you want the honest truth, you can have it—I've been bored as hell by you for weeks now, *months* probably. I only kept seeing you because I couldn't be bothered with the agro of finishing it, and now I wish I'd done it sooner. You're pathetic and I NEVER want to see you again. *Best leave it, yeah!*"

With that, Chastity turned on her heel and strode over to Jinx and Liberty, who tried their best to appear supportive and not to squirm away too much from the bits of sick still clinging all over their second-best friend. All three turned and stared at the policemen, wondering what they'd do with this particular bit of information. Sadly, they didn't have to wait long to find out.

"What *are* you all doing out here?" asked the leanest of the men, removing his hat and scratching his head as if puzzled by the whole affair—which indeed he was. "Have you been at that party up there?"

"No," Jinx said firmly, eyeing Paul and making it very obvious that if he dropped them in it again then Chastity would be the least of his worries. "We've just been mucking about on the seafront."

There was no way in hell Jinx wanted to link the four of them on the pavement with Jamie's party in the penthouse. As if it wasn't bad enough that her brother was inside with the triplets, the whole place was awash with drugs, and she didn't fancy Jamie's chances much as the host if these dudes started wanting to have a look around.

Paul didn't say another word, but looked guiltily down at his feet before stumbling off into the night after a final, despairing glance at his most definitely lost love. Chastity, it must be said, was practically gagging at the time as she flicked unidentifiable lumps of sick from her jeans, so she didn't even notice him leaving.

The policemen began ushering the three girls into the back of the van—having let Paul go they absolutely insisted on dropping the girls safely back to school, as a 'friendly fucking gesture' no less—and slammed the door shut behind them. The three inside the back held onto the security straps for dear life and stared at each other, speechless with horror as they were driven east along the seafront towards Stagmount and beyond. Although at least this time, the unhappy trio thought thankfully, grateful for any small mercies at this losing stage of the game, without any of the lights and sirens that heralded the police's first appearance.

19 *In Deep Shit*

Katie Green looked at her pale pink plastic Swatch watch. It was just past midnight, and she'd been sitting on the inside of her window ledge staring out over the pitches, across the marina, past the lights of the funfair at the end of the pier and towards the town for a little over an hour and a half now. She wasn't expecting to see anything of interest tonight, but she'd developed an attachment to this spot after she'd so fortuitously spotted the lower sixth dashing in and out of the garage that day. Since then, this had become the only place she felt able to try and unravel her muddled thoughts. She quite often now found herself slipping away from the noisy girls in her year to come and sit here quietly on her own.

Katie leaned forward, halfheartedly thinking she really must get to bed if there was to be any hope of her making it to Sunday Service in the morning, and drew in one last deep breath of the bitingly crisp sea air. She drew back when she spotted a shadowy figure making its way along the path from the main schoolhouse towards the old cricket pavilion. Whoever it was clearly didn't want to be discovered—hugging the bushes, it was clear the person was up to no good. Katie drew her blanket around her shoulders and peered more intently out the window. She was just gagging to know who she was looking at.

At that moment, a shaft of moonlight broke through the layers of cloud, illuminating a slender figure with unnaturally white skin and unusually bright orange hair. Fate, for once, had chosen to smile on Katie. She nearly passed out cold with excitement when she realized the furtive figure was none other than Daisy Finnegan, head girl of the lower sixth and completely unwitting recipient of huge amounts of mental vitriol from this particular second-year student.

Daisy had woken in a cold sweat, thinking of next week's chemistry exam, only to realize she'd left her homemade revision table of chemical equations in the cricket pavilion. She muttered crossly to herself under her breath, aggrieved to have forgotten the colour-coded, laminated spreadsheet it had taken her two full days of the Christmas holidays to construct. She liked to have it on hand to glance at whenever she felt panicky about the imminent exams, which was surprisingly often.

It was freezing outside, and even though Daisy was an undeniable suck-up, swot, and a sneak, she was thinking longingly of her bed and wishing she wasn't so conscientious. Jinx and the others were not the only ones feeling the pressure from the teachers. Daisy often wished she could be more effortlessly casual about things, like so many of the others in her year, but the requisite "chill out" gene just seemed to be missing in her.

Whilst Daisy was staggering along the pitches in the freezing cold in search of her lost study notes, the three in the police van had recovered their voices and were subjecting the policemen in the front to a barrage of pleading, sob stories, and desperate last appeals to be released before they reached the main gates. At the same time, they were all so worried about the repercussions from the school they couldn't help but throw barbed remarks at each other in between their plaintive and increasingly vociferous remarks to the coppers.

"Wild horses couldn't have dragged me away from that party," Jinx muttered, glaring at Chastity's puke-covered face opposite her and thinking for the first time that she bloody well deserved everything that happened earlier. "But you and three flying pigs managed it perfectly. Jamie will never speak to me again." Jinx fixed Chastity with a steely glare and began ticking off the rest of her grievances on her fingers. "Liberty never got that guy's phone number, we never got to have any more of those amazing drinks, God knows what's happened to George and, for the grand finale, we're probably all going to get expelled for sure. And Liberty and I were signed out for the whole weekend, so as far as the school's concerned we're not even anywhere *near* Brighton. So yes, Chastity, thanks for a whole bunch of *nothing*."

"You bitch," hissed Chastity. "You absolute fucking bitch. I don't suppose you give a shit that Paul and I have split up and I'm covered in fucking SICK from head to foot, do you?"

"Shut up guys," Liberty said. "We've got approximately two minutes and we've got to *do* something."

Katie Green was also fixated on doing something, and she too had no idea what that something was yet. There was no way she could let Daisy Finnegan get away with creeping about in the middle of the night like this. A unique potential spot of revenge was staring her in the face and she knew she mustn't let this window of opportunity slip shut without making the most of it. There must, she thought, her brain ticking over slowly but determinedly, be something she could do to screw Daisy over. A teacher—that was it! That was the answer to all her problems! She had to somehow alert a member of the staff to Daisy's nocturnal wanderings without drawing attention to herself. But *how* could she do this?

Katie forced herself to think back to the day of the fire alarm, when Daisy had so uncaringly humiliated her in front of her heroines. This exercise was an attempt to drum up an even greater strength of feeling and hopefully find a solution. This didn't take long to work, amazingly enough. After only three minutes of reliving the unfortunate scene—during which time Daisy finally reached the shelter of the Pavilion's porch—and digging it even less in the re-imagining, Katie experienced her first ever Eureka moment. Somehow she had managed to coax a plan out of her addled mind. No, she thought recklessly, clutching her tummy in excitement, it wasn't so much a plan as a bloody *brainwave*. Now all she had to do was put it into action. And this, of course, was the hard bit.

Whilst Katie turned left out of Steinem's inside back door and began creeping silently along the corridor towards the art room, the sanitorium, the old reference library, Pankhurst House, and ultimately Mrs. Bennett's large house beyond, the police van was turning off the coast road and making its way towards Stagmount's main gates and driveway.

Katie paused for breath in front of Mrs. Bennett's front steps and stared at the smart, navy-painted door with its big brass knocker smack bang in the middle. She knew that no one was around, but at this time of night the school seemed eerily quiet and was an undeniably frightening place to be. The darkness didn't help her nerves much either. The most ordinary objects and buildings took on a spooky, paranormal glow under the dim, greenish glare of the streetlights randomly dotted about the place, and Katie took a few deep breaths to steady her nerves before she made her final assault.

The police van that contained a now very subdued Jinx, Liberty, and Chastity, slumped together in a sorry, sickly lump at the back of the van, exhausted and pretty much resigned to whatever sick joke fate intended to throw at them next this evening, slowed to allow the electric gates to roll to the side.

Daisy, meanwhile, traversed the quad in front of the main entrance.

At the same time, the police van swung through the main gates and Katie *banged* fiercely on Mrs. Bennett's door and then flung herself behind a handy Camelia bush in the flowerbed running alongside the outer wall of Pankhurst House.

These three events, some admittedly more unfortunate than

others, converged at exactly the wrong moment. A sleep-deprived Mrs. Bennett, wrapped in a fog of exhaustion and a floral Cath Kidston dressing gown, flung open her door at the same time the police van slowed to a halt in front of one of the speed bumps and Daisy rounded the corner from the main school.

Katie had to shove one of her fat fists into her mouth to muffle her scream of appalled shock when she saw Jinx, Liberty, and Chastity clamber wearily out the sliding back door of the horribly distinctive blue and white van and arrange themselves silently in front of their headmistress.

Mrs. Bennett was so horrified at the sight of them—not least their law enforcement entourage—it was all she could do to push the lingering thought that she must still be dreaming from her mind. When she saw Daisy Finnegan standing uncertainly to the left of the bedraggled but still a zillion times more glamorous three, their headmistress did an actual double take. For once, Mrs. Bennett found it difficult to believe her own eyes!

The headmistress recovered her senses when the burly policeman—who, it must be said, was beginning to wish they'd left the girls, who were technically adults after all, to their own devices down on the seafront—removed his hat and coughed.

"Evening, madam," he said. "Sorry to get you out of bed, but we found these girls of yours down on the seafront and thought you might like them back."

Mrs. Bennett cast an experienced eye over the shady-as-hell girls in front of her, the embarrassed policemen beyond, and wisely decided to get to the bottom of this particular mess using the soft, gentle approach.

"Right then," she said in a tone that brooked no arguments from any of them. "Everyone inside. Chop chop, come on, we can't stand around in the cold like this."

Jinx, Liberty, and Chastity, eyes cast firmly to the ground, began to shuffle up the steps. They were too shocked even to register that—after four years' often intense speculation as to how it would be inside—this was the first time any of them had ever knowingly set foot in Heads House, as Mrs. Bennett's abode was called. After removing their hats, the policemen followed them. Only Daisy hung back. She was reluctant to associate herself with this motley crew and she was quite clear on her intention to calmly and fearlessly tell Mrs. Bennett about her innocent mission and be on her way.

"Don't even think about it, Daisy Finnegan," snapped Mrs. Bennett, crooking an impatient finger and hurrying the malingerer inside. "I am *especially* surprised at you!"

"But…" Daisy's downright foolish attempt to answer Mrs. Bennett back was cut off with what appeared to be a relative of the karate chop, but with not such a straight arm and a hissing sound. Daisy recoiled, and as she did so her trusty sheet of chemical equations caught on the wind and whirled up, up, up in the night air before disappearing on a sudden strong gust round to the back of Mrs. B.'s house.

"Inside, NOW!" the headmistress barked, and a truly terrified Daisy put all thoughts of both telling her side of the story and ever seeing her revision aid again immediately aside and hurried up the steps as quickly as she could.

Behind the Camelia bush Katie was the sudden recipient

of a load of wet leaves and dirty water dumping on her from where it had been pushed along the gutter by the rainwater and directed down the drain right above her head. She blinked furiously as she wiped some thick black grime from her woebegone face and raised her head in time to see the revision timetable fly up into the air and Mrs. Bennett's front door slam behind Daisy. By happy accident, the timetable, which had danced for a while in the wind above the decked terrace at the back of Mrs. Bennett's house, chose that moment to shoot across the side of Pankhurst House and float to the ground, where it landed right next to Katie's bush. Katie reached for it, cast a curious eye over the meaningless symbols on the front before she instantly lost interest and scrunched it without another thought deep into the back pocket of her baggy, brown cords—possibly the most singularly unflattering item of clothing anyone at Stagmount had ever possessed, but anyway, they had big pockets. There was no way in hell she was going back to bed just yet, so she settled into the squelching mud ready to wait this one out for as long as it took.

Jinx, Liberty, Chastity, and Daisy sat very close together on a white- and red-striped silk sofa in Mrs. B.'s dramatic drawing room. Huge earthenware pots containing Triffid-sized green plants were bunched variously around, lending the blood-red walls, massive gold-framed mirrors, and tiny exquisite paintings the air of having been hung in a jungle. A rug very similar to the Bokhara in the study covered most of the dark and highly shined wood floor, its navy blue, red, and dark purple pattern entirely visible through the big chunk of glass that served as the headmistress's coffee table.

The girls barely had a chance to sit down and glance round before the burly policeman took the initiative, apologized for waking Mrs. Bennett, assured her that the girls had been doing nothing wrong, and insisted that he and his fellow officers were merely, *chivalrously* dropping them home at the end of an obviously tiring and emotional night. Mrs. Bennett pursed her lips at this, but thanked the officers for their kind gesture, promised to see that everyone got to bed as soon as possible—she even managed an airy laugh or two, albeit through gritted teeth—before she ushered them out of her house.

Mrs. Bennett swept back into her drawing room and positioned herself on a high-backed, ornately carved wooden chair directly opposite the girls' sofa. She sat there for a few seconds, thoughtfully studying the four overwrought faces in front of her.

Jinx and Liberty looked scared and tired, but basically seemed fine. Daisy, Mrs. Bennett couldn't help noting, was dressed most oddly compared to the others. Maybe, she considered, Daisy Finnegan was not the model pupil they all thought she was, and actually one of those "new geek hardcore ravers" she'd read about in the *Sunday Times* style section last weekend. She simply must be making a statement with her school tracksuit, no bra, and Wellington boots teamed with no makeup to speak of and a flowery blanket over her shoulders. Quite what this statement was, however, the headmistress had no idea. Either way, right now it was obvious to everyone in the room that Daisy really did not want to be there.

Daisy sobbed quietly into her hands. She was shaking like

a leaf and occasionally moaning incoherently through her haze of snot and tears. Daisy was not at all used to being "in trouble." She clearly had no idea it was crucial to maintain an outwardly cool and calm exterior during these difficult encounters if one stood even the slightest chance of getting away with it. Jinx edged away from Daisy, but Mrs. Bennett didn't notice, since she was busy studying Chastity Max-Ward.

Chastity looked, frankly, like she'd been run over and left for dead—and that she now wished they'd finished the job. She also, Mrs. Bennett belatedly realized with a horrified shudder, appeared to be covered in what looked like human vomit. Dear God, but this job was no way near as glamorous as people so often assumed it was.

"Right then, girls," said Mrs. B. "I think it's high time we make for our beds."

Mrs. Bennett made the executive decision to deal with this matter in the morning. Even if they hadn't been delivered to her doorstep in the back of a police riot van she knew just from looking at them that the girls were exhausted and way too upset to deal rationally and sensibly with anything reasonable. And Mrs. Bennett, above all, was a reasonable, rational, and sensible woman. This is why she was so excellent at her job and so popular with the girls, the staff, the parents, and the governors. This is also why she was continually phoned up by newspapers for quotes on everything from education to female adolescence issues and was even beginning to develop quite a following on the Internet. The girls hadn't discovered it yet, but a middle-aged man from Hull had set up a fan site in fulsome praise of the occasional times she appeared on *Newsnight* as an "expert."

"Right then," she said softly, looking at the girls remarkably kindly given the circs, "I think the best thing for all of us is to get to bed as soon as possible. We obviously have a lot to discuss, but I'm sure it will all keep for the morning."

Taking advantage of the head's new, calm mood, Daisy decided to try and explain her non-involvement once again. "Mrs. Ben—"

"Daisy Finnegan," Mrs. Bennett snapped in the iciest voice any of them had ever heard, "if you do not want me to lose my temper I suggest you do not say another single word until I ask you a direct question."

Daisy nodded sadly, sniffing hugely and trying in vain to halt the fresh flood of tears this announcement had brought to her eyes. If nothing else, the others supposed, beginning to feel almost sorry for her for the first time in their lives, at least she had the bloody sense not to respond verbally.

"So, girls," Mrs. Bennett continued, standing up to indicate that this cozy little session was most definitely at an end, "I want you to go straight back to Tanner House and get into bed. You're all absolutely exhausted and there's no point keeping you up a minute longer than necessary. I shall telephone Mr. Morris now and tell him to be expecting you, and we will meet in the morning and get to the bottom of exactly what's gone on here. I'll see all of you in my office first thing after chapel. And girls," she added, "I don't want any of you doing anything silly like sitting up worrying all night."

The girls nodded meekly, stood up and prepared to file

shamefacedly out of Mrs. Bennett's drawing room. Jinx edged past the headmistress and caught the strap of her gold faux snakeskin shoulder bag on one of the high-backed chairs ranged along the dining table. Blithely oblivious for a second, she continued walking before she was jerked back a few steps. The half-bottle of Smirnoff vodka fell out the bag and rolled slowly, portentously along the hall before coming to a stop underneath a magazine stand in the hallway. Mrs. Bennett didn't say a word, but her expression darkened as she darted after it, bent down and picked it up. She looked Jinx in the eye as she passed it from hand to hand.

"Um," Jinx said, aghast at the cruel hand fate had dealt her, "I..."

"Not now, Jinx," said Mrs. Bennett. "Not now."

"But—" Jinx spluttered, desperately trying to think of an explanation.

"No buts," snapped the head, turning on her slipper. "We'll deal with this in the morning as well."

Jinx raced down the steps outside and turned right in the direction of Tanner House, desperate to catch up with the others, who had walked on, oblivious to the vodka-bottle debacle. They walked as fast as they could without running away from Mrs. Bennett's house, maintaining a determined, grimfaced silence until they rounded the corner past the sports hall to Tanner House and gained cover of the line of rhododendron bushes. As soon as they knew they could no longer be observed, they slowed to a trudge and gaped at each other in horror. Jinx was the first to break the silence.

"Bloody hell, Daisy," she said, still not understanding what possible sequence of events had led to her old nemesis from Wollstonecraft House sitting next to her on Mrs. Bennett's amazingly tasteful sofa. "What on Earth have you been up to? I couldn't believe it when I saw you standing next to us out there. Where did you *come* from?"

"I realized I left my chemistry homework in the cricket pavilion," wailed Daisy, still hugely distressed by this extremely unfair case of mistaken identity or whatever it was she was currently embroiled in. "So I got up and went to get it in case I woke up early and felt like memorizing some equations."

"Serves you fucking right then," mumbled Liberty meanly, before instantly regretting it when Daisy cast a truly anguished glance in her direction. "Sorry, Daisy...sorry. I really am."

"And then," Daisy continued, much mollified by the unprecedented apology, "I was walking back to Tanner when out of nowhere a police van came past me up the drive, and when I came round the corner Mrs. Bennett opened her door and then you guys got out and then...well, you know the rest. What am I going to DO? What if I get expelled? My parents would kill me!"

"Come on, Daisy," Jinx said, torn between laughing at the ridiculousness of Daisy's increasingly high-pitched explanation and crying at the thought of her own no-doubt imminent expulsion. "We'll tell her the truth tomorrow and you'll be fine. She'll just probably say you were an idiot for not leaving it until morning and fucking *apologise* to you or something. I really wouldn't sweat it if I were you."

"Do you really think?" Daisy asked, eyes shining hopefully at Jinx.

"Yeah I do. It's us," she said, looking at Liberty and Chastity, "who need to be coming up with the best damn story in the world right about NOW."

"Do you promise you'll tell her I didn't have anything to do with the police and things?" asked Daisy, still not quite able to trust Jinx and the others wouldn't stitch her up as part of some "hilarious" gag. "Really promise?"

Jinx looked over at her and inexplicably felt truly sorry for her for the first time ever. She also felt bad about all the times she'd been mean to Daisy and made up her mind to be as nice as possible to her from now on and hopefully score some karmic points—let's face it, she needed them.

"Of course we will, Daisy," Jinx said firmly. "Don't worry about it. I can't believe what shit luck you've had! But wait till you lot hear what happened to me just now."

"Fuck," said Liberty, clutching Jinx's hand in horror as the latter finished telling the others about the Smirnoff fiasco. "What do you think Mrs. Bennett will *do*?"

"I don't know." Jinx spoke more nonchalantly than she felt. "But there's no point sweating it until tomorrow."

"The only thing I don't understand," said Daisy suddenly, looking at Jinx, "is why Mrs. Bennett opened her door when she did."

The others looked at her blankly. They hadn't thought about this at all.

"What do you mean?" asked Chastity, speaking for the first

time since they'd left the police van. Considering the river of tears she had cried this evening, it was no surprise she sounded like Dracula after a night on the lash.

"Well, think about it logically," said Daisy, sounding—for once comfortingly—exactly like one of the teachers. "She'd obviously dashed out of bed in a rush as if she'd heard something outside, but nothing was making a noise. It's too windy for the police van driving past on the tarmac to make enough noise to wake anyone up, and I was walking silently past the buildings. I was so shocked to see the van drive past me that I didn't think about it at the time, but I suppose I was vaguely aware of some kind of banging sound."

"I don't get it," Chastity said impatiently. "What are you saying?"

"I'm saying," said Daisy, looking over her shoulder to where they had come from and shivering dramatically, "that I think someone knew you lot were going to be driving past at that time and decided to drop you in it by knocking on her door and running away."

"*What?*" asked Liberty, horrified at the very thought. "Who would want to do something like that to us?"

"Someone who's got a grudge," replied Daisy knowingly. "It could be anyone."

"Hold on a second," Chastity cut in exasperatedly. "I don't think it's fair to imply that anyone in the whole of Stagmount might have a grudge against us. We're actually, like, some of the most popular girls at this freaking school."

"Exactly," said Daisy darkly.

It didn't occur to any of them—even Daisy herself—that the person who had brought Mrs. Bennett rushing to her front door might be somebody who had a problem with Daisy. The whole thing was just too leftfield, too goddamn unlikely.

It was now nearly two o'clock in the morning, but Katie Green was far too agitated to feel it. She had watched as the four lower-sixths set off at a smart pace down the drive in the direction of Tanner House. She saw Mrs. Bennett watch after them until they rounded the corner, one hand on her chin, the other on her hip as if she was deeply worried. She noticed none of the girls looked back once, pointedly almost, in the embarrassed manner of people who know they are being watched but can't stand the sensation for whatever reason. She was soaked through, covered in mud, filth, and slime from the drain above, hiding behind a Camelia bush on a cliff top just to the east of Brighton in the middle of the night in the freezing cold and she didn't feel a thing because she was too focused on forcing her barely adequate, cretinous brain to work out what the hell had just happened.

Whatever, one thing was clear: Katie knew she had to get herself back to Steinem House and the safety of her room as soon as possible. The junior crept off, making sure to keep herself in the shadows.

Meanwhile, Liberty, Chastity, and Jinx invited a surprised but pleased Daisy Finnegan into Jinx's room for an emergency crisis discussion meeting at half past eight, right before chapel the next morning. They wouldn't normally bother to attend on a Sunday morning after such a late night, but wisely decided it would do no harm to their cause whatsoever to be observed singing lustily in the aisles. And after getting over the terrible initial shock of it all and Mr. Morris's "disappointed" face when he met them at the door, they each went to bed reasonably confident they'd somehow manage to scam their way out of it in the morning. Thank God for Mrs. B. deciding to postpone things, they unanimously agreed—she really was the most amazingly civilized woman they were ever likely to meet and they were beyond freaking lucky to have her as their headmistress. Contrary to their expectations, within minutes each and every one of them, despite all the upset and histrionics on the grandest scale, was fast asleep as if they didn't have a care in the world.

Katie stood in the dark of her room and shed her seriously messed-up clothes. She stuffed them into a plastic bag and dumped them underneath a pile of clean towels at the back of her wardrobe, figuring she'd wash them later. Using most of her L'Oreal moisturizing face wipes, she cleared the rest of the grime from her face, hands and neck and got into bed. If she was a religious girl she might have prayed for guidance at this point, but Katie was completely lacking in spirituality of any kind. She lay in bed, mindlessly popping Maltesers into her mouth and sucking them until they went soggy whilst wondering what on Earth her heroines had been doing out in town and how come they ended up being brought back to school by the police.

Shocked didn't even come close to how Katie was feeling right now. Shock and awe was more like it—she couldn't help but be deeply, deeply impressed by the radical antics she'd witnessed tonight. What exciting, glamorous lives those girls lived, she thought as she closed her eyes, still sucking at the Maltesers furiously.

Jinx woke up the next morning a few minutes before her alarm clock and stretched happily before tensing rigid as the events of the previous night slowly filtered into her growing awareness of what was going to be a huge headache.

"Fuck," she muttered crossly to herself, reaching for the two-litre bottle of Evian she always kept on her bedside table and banging weakly on the wall, which adjoined Liberty's. "We are in *so* much trouble."

She lay back against her pillow and held her hand horizontally in front of her face to see how much it was trembling. Oh dear, things really did not look good from this frankly depressing side of last night's amazing party.

She reached for her phone and punched out a quick text message to her second-oldest brother, as she always did in times of hangover crisis. No matter what Jinx might have done, she could be assured that George would have gone one better. The comforting thought that at least she hadn't been the *worst* behaved always made her feel a lot better about things. George was also a master at getting himself out of trouble and would surely advise his little sister on the very best damage control methods she needed to put in place right now.

Jinx's door was silently pushed open. In the frame stood a wild-haired Liberty who, judging from the black lines etched deep into the huge bags beneath her eyes, had neglected to take her makeup off before she got into bed last night. Without a word, Liberty lifted the corner of Jinx's duvet, got into bed and snuggled up against her best friend. They lay there not speaking, just staring at each other in appalled horror, until Jinx's phone made its customary trilling sound to indicate she'd received a text.

"'STOP PRESS! Woteva u do, REITERATE that u WEREN'T in the care of the school at the time and there is technically NOTHING they can do to punish u. Peace out bitches,'" she read aloud to Liberty, before adding excitedly, "and he's right of course, Lib. We were signed out for the weekend."

"Yeah," Liberty conceded quietly, "we were. But I still can't see us getting away with anything. Did you *see* Mrs. B.'s face last night? And darling—I hate to bring it up—but you're in a whole world more trouble than us given the bloody vodka bottle."

Jinx said nothing. After a couple of minutes' appalled silence, Chastity walked into the room. And although she was very pale indeed, she was smiling and looked a zillion times happier than she had by the end of last night. Chastity sat down on the end of Jinx's bed and grinned at the pair of them lying in it, who were looking at her rather warily, as if not sure quite what emotion to expect next.

"Don't worry," said Chastity. "I'm fine. I was so *drunk* last night I think I might have overreacted. But," she continued firmly, "Paul and I are definitely over. He's been driving me mad for ages now, but I didn't say anything because I kind of felt embarrassed about it after how much I went on about how I liked him.

It just changed and I don't really know why except I know I want to be single like you guys. I'm so bored of constantly missing out on things with you girls because he and I have got some boring bloody couples thing to do."

"I still can't believe he told the police to phone the school," Liberty said with a disgusted sniff. "What a complete asshole."

"Liberty!" Jinx said sharply.

"What?" asked Liberty. "I can't!"

"Yeah, but it's not really appropriate to start slagging off her boyfriend when the relationship's barely cold in its grave yet," said Jinx, nudging Liberty meaningfully and raising her eyebrows in Chastity's direction. "Is it?"

"Oh God," Chastity said airily, waving a hand dismissively in front of her, "don't worry about it. I'm so over him. What I *do* need to bloody worry about is what the hell I'm going to say to get out of this mess. Have we got any ideas?"

Jinx, with no help whatsoever from Liberty, who took this opportunity to have a small cat nap, explained the situation regarding the intricacies of the signing out system, parental responsibilities versus school control and the fortunate convergence of the facts as far as they pertained to herself and Liberty. As Jinx talked, relief flooded Chastity's face, bringing a little bit of much-needed colour to her cheeks and a pleased sparkle back to her still fairly bloodshot eyes.

"Well, I'm fine too then," she said, exhaling with relief and practically crossing herself in thanks. "As far as the school is concerned I was with Mum and Ian. Since I *was* planning to stay the night with Paul I signed out yesterday before I left, saying I was off to see them. They won't be up yet so I'll text Ian and tell him to say as far as he was concerned I was meeting up with you two in town and we were going to go out for dinner before getting a taxi back to his flat. Your parents say the same thing and we're all fine."

"Brilliant," said Jinx enthusiastically. "Mine will so do that. I'll call them in a minute and give them the briefing. And we'll say that on our way to getting a taxi to go back to school you started being sick—food poisoning or something—and the police stopped to help us."

"We'll say," Liberty added, "we were so worried about you Chas, we thought it was safer to get you back to school in case you couldn't stop being sick and needed urgent medical attention from Mister Sinton. But that you then miraculously recovered in the van on the way back—they can't disprove a thing."

"What about the vodka, Jin?" Liberty asked, worried. "Do you think Mrs. B. will give you a worse punishment than us?"

"Dunno," muttered Jinx, feeling very deflated at the prospect.

Daisy pushed open the door and stood in front of them wearing a ratty pink dressing gown, her infuriating Garfield slippers and massive dark circles under her strangely pale eyes. The three of them laughed delightedly at the sheer simple genius of this plan whilst Daisy stared at them aghast. She could hardly believe her ears—how could they be so flippant and casual about all of this? If it were *her* in this amount of trouble she couldn't be sure that suicidal thoughts wouldn't pass through her mind.

"B-b-but," she stammered, "won't Mrs. B. ask you loads of questions?"

"So what," said Jinx, bored of the whole damn issue. All she wanted was five freaking minutes to herself to think about Jamie and the things he'd said to her before she'd been so rudely taken away from his amazing party. "We stick to our stories like glue and there's nothing they can do. Our parents won't make a fuss—they knew exactly what we were up to and they couldn't be bothered with the trouble if nothing else. And we *are* seventeen, which is practically an adult, even if we *do* live in a boarding school."

"Yeah," agreed Chastity, "and don't worry Daisy—we'll spill the truth for you too. Everything's going to be fine."

"That's really sweet of you," said Daisy with a blush. She wasn't at all used to this level of niceness from these girls and she was kind of wishing she hadn't always set herself so dead against them. Maybe it still wasn't too late to make friends, she thought wistfully, before deciding this was highly unlikely. But it would be equally as nice to put an end to the cold war she and Jinx had sustained for three and a half years.

"I tell you what," Daisy said. "I'll help you investigate who banged on Mrs. Bennett's door and got her to rush out and catch us all like that. If we all put our heads together I'm sure we'll catch the culprit."

"Thanks, Daisy," said Jinx, smiling at her genuinely for maybe the first time ever in her life. "That's really nice of you."

"What about YOU though, Jinx?" Daisy blurted out. "You're going to get in more trouble than the others because the vodka came out of *your* pocket."

"Nah," Jinx said nonchalantly, not even wanting to think about that. "I'll be cool, but thanks, Daisy."

"Yeah," Liberty agreed, following her and Chastity out of Jinx's room, "it is nice of you Daisy. Thanks."

Jinx straightened out her bedding without getting up—one of her special skills was making her bed without actually getting out of it—and lay back against her newly fluffed-up pillows. She was desperate to have a quick think about things in the ten minutes she had left before she simply must get in the shower in order not to be late for chapel. Jumbled thoughts of Jamie jostled for space in her mind with the ghastly end to the party, curiosity about what might have happened with George and the triplets alongside what the hell had caused Daisy Finnegan to suddenly become so nice and what had kept Liv and Charlie away for so long. Sadly, her alarm went off again before she'd made much headway at all. Jinx got out of bed reluctantly, shrugged into her dressing gown and flip-flops, grabbed her Anya Hindmarch wash bag and sauntered off to the showers to think about what she would say to Mrs. Bennett in her office later that morning. She sincerely hoped Mrs. B. wouldn't place the whole blame for the vodka bottle on her.

Liberty, Chastity, Daisy Finnegan, and Jinx stood shoulder to shoulder in the chapel singing "Onward Christian Soldiers" with all the might they could muster. Jinx had no idea just how terribly out of tune she was. A devilish headache was rumbling just of out reach of the three pain killers she'd swallowed with a quick cup of coffee before leaving Tanner House. She prayed it would stay away from her frontal lobes for at least as long as it took her to get back into bed, where she fully intended to spend the rest of the day listening to soothing music and recuperating from their now scarily imminent chat with Mrs. Bennett.

Chastity, meanwhile, was feeling remarkably chipper about things as she sang along perfectly and smiled angelically up at Mrs. Bennett standing in the pulpit above them. The thought that she was now free to do exactly as she pleased like all the others made her very happy indeed. She so wasn't the kind of girl who needed a boyfriend, and since her relationship with Paul had become little more than a major drag she was just relieved to have gotten rid of him and not regretful in the slightest. Chastity Max-Ward was one way-cool customer.

Jinx, Liberty, Chastity, and Daisy paused outside Mrs. Bennett's office door. None of them wanted to be the one to knock. Jinx, Liberty, and Chastity also needed just a couple of seconds to compose themselves and iron out any fits of potential nervous giggles. The handle on the door turned sharply in front of them. Shocked into standing to attention and practically saluting, the door flew open and Mrs. Bennett was in front of them, ushering them into her office amidst gentle enquiries as to why on Earth they hadn't knocked sooner and gesturing for them to sit down and help themselves to coffee and biscuits. All of them—apart from Daisy, who was now shaking with pure nerves alone—were suddenly far too nervous to contemplate holding a cup of hot coffee during this ordeal.

Mrs. B. leant forward delicately on her leather armchair. Legs crossed slightly to the side and at the ankle, she raised her dainty green-and-gold bone-china coffee cup to her lips and took a sip. As she did so, she observed the girls through the black-rimmed Prada spectacles that had slipped slightly down her patrician nose. The four of them were perched on the outer rim of the sofa cushions, keen to appear as eager, alert, sensible, and responsive to their headmistress as possible.

"You are," Mrs. Bennett continued, smiling slightly to soften the blow, "wallys, dingbats, and sillies of the first order."

The girls giggled slightly, not quite able to believe that anyone anywhere in the whole world still used these kinds of insults and storing them up to tell the others later.

"However," the head continued, a steelier tone to her previously warm, reassuring voice, "I was not at all amused to be confronted with the four of you and a police escort at my front door last night. And I intend," she said, looking them in the eye one by one, "to get to the bottom of exactly what it was you were up to."

"Well, Mrs. Bennett," said Jinx, deciding to jump straight in and get this ordeal the hell over with, "we certainly can explain everything to you, and I shall do so right away."

"I hope you can," replied Mrs. B., fixing her with a gimlet eye. "For I can assure you that three members of my lower sixth being picked up in town and dropped off back at school in the back of a police vehicle is most definitely not the kind of image Stagmount either wants or needs."

"Yes," muttered Jinx, momentarily thrown and flicking an aghast glance at Liberty next to her. "Of course, Mrs. Bennett. So...um...where was I? Oh yes," she continued hastily, having recovered her composure, "the thing *is*, we had all arranged to meet for dinner in town, before heading back to Chastity's parents' place in London on one of the late trains and then come back to school—the regular way, ha ha—this evening."

"And?" Mrs. Bennett said as Jinx paused for a much-needed breath.

"And we had a lovely meal at a pizza place, although Chastity had a seafood pizza, which, you know, is never really a good idea what with all the calamari rings on it." Jinx paused again and quickly wondered if calamari was a dangerous enough foodstuff known for poisoning in its own right. She looked at Mrs. Bennett's skeptical face and decided not. "With prawns...and mussels. Yes, mussels, lots of them. Oh, and even some cockles and whelks and...um...those orange seafood sticks you get in supermarkets, sort of shaved over the top of it under all the cheese, I think. It was very stringy anyway."

"And?" Mrs. Bennett snapped, baffled by all this talk of filthy pizza toppings and wondering darkly if Jinx was joking.

"And, well," Jinx said, with a downward glance intended to convey extreme dismay, "with all of that sloshing around inside her and maybe a bad mussel or prawn or something, when we were on our way to the station Chastity suddenly started being sick."

"Yes, Mrs. B.," Chastity said. "It was awful. I just couldn't stop. I vomited and I vomited and I *vomited*, and then I vomited some more."

Mrs. Bennett, remembering with a shudder the sick she'd spotted all over Chastity late last night, was beginning to look slightly alarmed for her Bokhora rug and tasteful soft furnishings.

"It's true, Mrs. Bennett," agreed Liberty with relish. "It was—literally—the sickest thing I've ever seen. It was just pouring out of her as if it would never stop. And it was the most bright orange colour, like paint or something. Man, it was gross as hell."

"Yes, thank you, Liberty," snapped Mrs. Bennett, slightly confused to be addressed as "man," "but that doesn't explain how the Sussex police force came to be involved. If one of you would be so kind, I would like to get this wrapped up sooner rather than later. Contrary to popular expectation, I do NOT delight in spending my Sundays dealing with school matters."

Jinx, Liberty, and Chastity exchanged a quick horrified glance; Daisy's eyes were too swollen to notice, but she exhaled a great shaky breath that suggested she was on the brink of a severe mental meltdown. The fury etched on Mrs. Bennett's normally calm face made the girls wonder if maybe they *wouldn't* get away with it, despite all the fortuitous extenuating circumstances.

"Well," said Jinx, "Chastity was being so ill we had to stop walking and sort of stand with her at the side of the pavement on the busy seafront road. People were slowing down their cars as they drove past—it was that much of a spectacle. Anyway, then the police stopped to see what was going on and offered us a lift back to school. We tried to stop them," Jinx said in her most sincere voice, staring intently into Mrs. Bennett's eyes and holding her gaze without blinking, "but they simply insisted upon it. And anyway, with Chas so ill, we thought getting her back here and into bed must be our priority."

Daisy, who had been staring, mouth agape, was slack-jawed

with wonder at the most virtuoso performance she'd ever witnessed being played out on the stage of this sofa she herself was also sitting on. She literally couldn't believe it, so much so that she'd forgotten her own predicament totally. She only remembered it when she heard her own name in the conversation and snapped back to attention.

"And Daisy," Chastity was now saying earnestly to Mrs. Bennett, "was not involved at all. She just got caught up in the confusion alongside us, but Mrs. Bennett, we absolutely swear on our mothers' lives that she wasn't out in town with us and hasn't done anything wrong. She was only trying to get her study notes back!"

"I'm sure it's not right to swear anything on your mother's life, Chastity," said a somewhat appalled Mrs. Bennett, who'd never heard the charming expression before. "What a horrid, nasty thing to say. Please never let me hear you say that again."

"Sorry," mumbled a very humbled-looking Chastity, suddenly feeling absolutely horrified with herself, staring at the shiny black patent pair of Marc Jacobs Mary Jane shoes she'd rather incongruously matched with her school uniform and thinking about how much she loved her mum.

"So, Daisy, you got up out of bed and walked over there *in the middle of the night* to retrieve some *study notes*?" continued the headmistress, thinking that Daisy Finnegan really must be a little touched in the head and looking correspondingly puzzled as she quizzed her.

"Yes," Daisy nodded, her face looking paler than ever against her ginger hair, her puffy eyes almost popping out of her head in terror by now.

"I am," Mrs. Bennett said, putting her coffee cup down on the low table in front of them and shaking her head, "very, very disappointed in all of you. And I am *especially* disappointed that you, Jinx, have such little regard for your school that you see fit to wander the streets with a bottle of vodka in your pocket."

Jinx shook her own head, albeit hardly noticeably. She *hated* it when adults did that "more in sorrow than in anger" thing. It made her feel bad every time and she folded her arms across her chest, trying to make herself as small as possible.

"You have," the headmistress continued, "not only let me and the school down, but also yourselves. I can only *imagine* what your parents will think about all of this."

She paused to stare out the window as Daisy emitted a series of stomach-clenchingly revolting snorting sounds at the mention of the word "parents." It was all Jinx and Chastity could do to maintain a straight face—they knew their parents would be cool with it. Liberty studied her shoes, a pained expression on her face. She knew Mrs. B. would never say anything to her dad, but this almost made her feel worse. The last person on Earth she wanted to upset was her beloved headmistress, especially when she'd tried so hard to stand up for her in the face of Amir's black rage at the end of last term.

"You're not silly schoolgirls anymore," Mrs. Bennett went on. "You're young adults, and I expect you to behave accordingly. You're halfway through the lower sixth. I'm not only cross with you girls; I'm saddened by the fact that you still seem unable to distinguish between right and wrong."

"We are *so* sorry Mrs. Bennett, we really are," Liberty said. "We promise and swear nothing like this will ever happen again. Truly, if Chastity hadn't been so ill none of this would have happened."

"Well," said Mrs. Bennett, "as far as Daisy's concerned, I'm sure you've learned your lesson and I won't be taking this any further."

"Oh yes," agreed Daisy, tear pricks of relief causing her eyes to shine suspiciously brightly. "I have."

"And as for the rest of you," she continued, fixing the girls with yet another gimlet eye, "I have spoken to or left messages for your parents and—since you were all signed out for the weekend and technically not in the care of the school—I can't punish you as heavily as I would *like* to. Although you, Jinx Slater, can expect further punishment when I have finally managed to get hold of your parents."

The girls winced collectively at the positively icy new edge to their headmistress's voice and shuffled back slightly on their sofa.

"In fact," she went sternly on, recalling how Chastity Max-Ward's stepfather or whoever he was had whistled appreciatively, as if actually impressed by what he obviously saw as her rock-and-roll antics, "I was rather surprised at the levels of nonchalance affected by all of your parents regarding this matter. Apart from your father, Liberty, who I simply did not call."

The girls smirked; they couldn't help it—this was too good. Of course their parents wouldn't make a scene about things; this was an excellent story to be told at the next dinner party, and anyway—where the hell's the point in making a fuss about stuff? At least their kids weren't teenage crack-whores, in gangs, on (many) drugs, and out robbing old ladies. Although if it was possible for Daisy's mouth to fall open any further, they doubted it.

"But what about my parents," she wailed, hot tears spilling rapidly down her cheeks at the thought of how upset and disappointed they'd be with her. "They must have gone mad! What am I going to DO!"

"Calm down, Daisy," snapped Mrs. Bennett, who had a horror of hysteria, particularly, ironically, in schoolgirls. "Your parents were the only ones who didn't answer the phone and since there appeared to be no messaging service I wasn't able to leave one. They are none the wiser about any of this and I certainly won't be phoning up to tell them about your lost revision aid. Although, Daisy," she carried on in more gentle tones, "I think you need to try and relax a little bit. It really wouldn't have killed you to wait until morning to retrieve it, would it? I don't want any of my girls falling ill through overwork. The usual school day provides you with plenty of homework to do, and I really don't think there's a need to go looking for any extra.

"So," said Mrs. B., looking round at the rest, not liking the smirks she'd just witnessed at all, "I've been looking at your timetables, and I see you all have Tuesday afternoons free." She paused slightly before delivering her hammer blow. "And since the three of you have made a sport out of the school rules, making a mockery of them at every recent turn, it would seem, Mr. Morris and I have decided that as the sports hall needs a spring clean before next term, you three will be the perfect ones to help us out in your free time until the end of term, starting this Tuesday coming."

"But—" Chastity attempted a weak defence.

Mrs. Bennett started speaking again, cutting her off entirely as if she hadn't said a word. "I want," the head explained, "the entire place to be turned inside out, all of the equipment labeled and catalogued and put neatly in its rightful place. And," Mrs. Bennett continued, almost purring with satisfaction at her final thrust, "the sports staff will be on hand to make sure everything is done their way. Right."

She stood up and clapped her hands together before throwing open her door and ushering them out. "That's all. I don't want any of you leaving the school boundaries for the rest of the day, and I have told Mr. Morris you are not to receive any visitors, either. I suggest you all take it easy today and think about next week's lessons. I should think you three have had quite enough excitement recently to last a lifetime. I'll let you know when I'll need to see you again, Jinx, but rest assured it will be sooner rather than later."

"Well," said Jinx, linking arms with Liberty and scuffing her shoes on the drive as they walked back home to Tanner House, "that could have been a lot worse."

"Hmm," Chastity said with a sniff, tossing her nose in the air as she so often did when she felt something was beneath her. "I *guess*. We still don't know what she's going to do to *you* for a start. Aren't you worried about what punishment you might get?"

"Of course I am," said Jinx, who really *was* but was trying not to show it. "But it's only Mrs. B. after all—she digs us."

"Come on, Chas," Liberty said, upbeat, "Jinx is right. We got off fucking lightly considering what could have happened last night. So we lose our Tuesdays—big freaking deal. We never had them before and we seemed to survive okay. The worst thing is being confined in a closed-in space with the fucking sports staff for hours on end, but I'm sure we'll cope okay."

"You know what, Lib?" Jinx asked, smiling at her best friend in astonishment as something clicked in her head. "I think you've really changed!"

"What do you mean?" Liberty replied indignantly, snatching her arm away from Jinx in mock fury. "How very dare you!"

"No, no," giggled Jinx, "not in a *bad* way. I just mean you seem a lot more, I don't know, like sensible or something this term. Although not," she added hastily, spying Liberty's disbelieving expression, "in a boring way at all. You're still YOU, you just seem to have your head screwed on a bit tighter, that's all. You're a bit more streetwise, I suppose."

"We still need to work out what happened last night," interrupted Daisy. She'd been chewing her lip thoughtfully as they walked along and didn't really care to analyse whether or not Liberty's personality had, in fact, changed at all. "There's a meeting of all the head girls this afternoon and I'm going to ask the other heads-of-years if they've seen anything or know anything. I'm absolutely determined to get to the bottom of this one. Someone stitched you guys up, and by extension me too, and it's not fair."

"Thanks, Daisy," said Chastity as they started up the path that led to Tanner House's front doorway. "That's really kind of you. If we do find out who did it they're going to get the nastiest shock of their fucking lives. No one makes *me* do chores and gets away with it."

"I'm totally ruined," said Jinx, flopping down onto the sofa as they walked into the reception area. "I need to have a little lie down and a think about things."

"Me too," agreed Chastity, lying down on the same sofa in the opposite direction and coiling her arms around Jinx's bent knees. "Wiped out."

"Broken, destroyed and wrecked," added Liberty with a sigh, lifting up Jinx's legs and squidging herself onto the end of the sofa by Chastity's head.

Daisy looked a tad uncomfortable at this frank exchange. Moving towards the exit and in search of her neat and tidy desk, where all the pens and pencils were lined up in neat rows alongside Post-it notes in every colour, stickers and dictionaries of all kinds. "Right, then," she said. "I'm going to go and make myself another chemistry crib sheet. I'll see you girls later."

"Laters, Dais," the sofa-ridden three chorused, weakly waving her off before collapsing in a heap again.

"So," muttered Liberty, tickling Jinx's feet after a few minutes' comfortable, companionable silence from the three on the sofa. "Are we going to, like, lie here all day long or go and watch music videos or *what*?"

"Music videos," trilled Chastity. "But can you carry us there, Liberty? And can we get our duvets out of our rooms?"

"Yes!" agreed Jinx. "And a packet of custard creams from the kitchen!"

Suitably furnished for an afternoon's extreme relaxation, the three of them got into their Juicy tracksuits, fired up the central heating and settled into the common room. It being Sunday lunchtime with only three weeks left of term, the school was deserted. And since anyone who had stayed in had done so to work, they had the place to themselves.

After three solid hours of *America's Next Top Model* interspersed with VH1 golden oldie music videos during the ads, Jinx, Liberty, and Chastity had roused themselves to chatting about the previous evening. They were more alert than they'd been all day.

"Do you believe that thing about the truth always coming out when you're drunk?" Chastity asked, rolling round on her sofa so she could see the other's faces.

"No, Chas," Jinx replied instantly. "Drunk people don't generally purvey considered opinions do they? I quite often *lie* when I'm drunk—more so than when I'm sober anyway. I normally think it's funny at the time."

"What about during an argument?" queried Chastity, who was thinking about Paul and feeling bad for the first time about some of the things she'd screamed at him in the street.

"Well," said Jinx, knowing exactly what Chastity was getting at, "sometimes—in an argument or whatever—you're so cross you just look for the worst possible, most wounding thing you can say to the other one. And when you're drunk and having an argument you don't have the same sense of boundaries that you have when you're sober. You just want to purposefully upset the other one as much as possible."

"Hmm," nodded Chastity, clearly not yet convinced by this, for although she didn't regret breaking up with Paul in the slightest, she didn't want to make the guy suicidal or anything—what a drag *that* would be.

"And you'll notice," carried on Jinx, wanting to make Chas feel better about things, but also really believing in what she was saying, "it's ALWAYS smug, victim-type people who are the ones to latch onto drunken bad behaviour and emphasize the drunken part of it. I think it's so they can use the excuse of every bit of drinking being bad and negative when we know most of it's hunky dory. It's like one night in fifty that goes bad, and I don't think that's too bad a price to pay for fun and games the rest of the time."

"Fucking killjoys," added Liberty supportively.

"Exactly, Lib," said Jinx with a smile. "They constantly justify why they're always right and everyone else is wrong and it gets freaking tedious if you ask me. It's the ultimate 'I told you so' from boring people who are too afraid of rocking the boat or—God forbid!—losing control of themselves to risk ever having any fun in their lives."

"You're so right," agreed Chastity, feeling a hell of a lot better about things after this pep talk. "I don't trust people who don't drink—what have they got to hide?"

"Who doesn't drink?" giggled Olga, pushing open the door and leading a procession entirely made up of her sisters into the common room, thereby causing the others to forget their conversation entirely. "Are they feeling okay in the head?"

The girls on the sofa laughed delightedly and ushered them over to spill all about the party. Wearing skinny jeans, pumps, and soft cashmere jumpers in blue, green, and pink to match their diamond rings, the trips looked stunning as ever and betrayed not a single shred of evidence of a late night.

"My brother's been unusually silent all day long," said Jinx, winking at the girls. "What ever did you lot get up to last night? We've been dying to find out!"

"Forget about *us*," said **Masha**, running her fingers through her hair so that her green diamond ring sparkled in the harsh light from the long bulb on the ceiling. "We want to know what the hell happened to you girls. People came over to us and said you'd been taken away in a police van. We couldn't believe it, but then George said this morning you had texted him about what to say to Mrs. Bennett. Is it true?"

"This morning?" Jinx almost screamed with shock. "You were still with George this *morning*?"

"Why yes," sighed Irina. "He picked us up from our hotel and took us to Bill's for breakfast. "We really like him and his friends very much."

"That bastard hasn't even texted me back to see what happened with Mrs. Bennett," Jinx snorted, furious at her brother's apparent total lack of concern for her physical and mental well-being. "And now I find out he's been squiring you lot all over town. Well, I'm pleased you had a good time with him but he's going to get a flea in his ear the next time I speak to him."

"So come on then," urged Masha, sitting forward eagerly and clasping her hands together in anticipation, "tell us what happened last night!"

"Yes," agreed Olga, "come on!"

In the face of such pleasing interest in their latest exploits, and from such damned good-looking girls, too, Jinx, Liberty, and Chastity were more than happy to regale the triplets with highly exaggerated scenes from last night's theatrical debacle. Halfway through their tall tales, Igor mooched into the room, threw a dark look at the triplets and settled himself into an old leather armchair by one of the windows. He stared out to sea and didn't appear to take any interest in the girls' conversation. After a few minutes they forgot he was even there and carried on as normal, shrieking and laughing and generally behaving very boisterously indeed. If they *had* paid any attention to him they would have seen him absentmindedly twisting what looked like a replica of the triplets' rings, but in white, on the middle finger of his right hand and staring thoughtfully out the window.

Judging by the glowing reports, George had been at his most charming, funny, and naughty self and had made a massive hit with the triplets. Jinx couldn't help but reflect that at least she'd get amazing presents if one of these birds ended up as her sister-in-law. Not, of course, that George would be likely to be able to keep himself in the good books for very much longer. Trouble had a way of following him around and she didn't suspect this time would be very much different from all of the other relationship disasters he had endured.

At ten o'clock the others had just finished watching television and were beginning to say their good nights and gather all their stuff up, ready for bed, when Liv and Charlie swept into the room in a cloud of what smelt like real ale.

"Where the hell have you two been?" yelled Chastity, jumping up and dropping the duvet she'd just neatly folded onto the floor in her excitement, "we've been trying to ring you both all freaking day!"

"You smell like a bloody brewery," sniffed Jinx admiringly. "What the hell have you been up to?"

"Um," giggled Liv, flopping onto the floor in front of Jinx's sofa and dragging an equally unsteady Charlie after her. "We've been, you know, hanging ten in town."

For some reason this statement caused the pair on the floor to clutch each other and start screaming with laughter. Whatever they'd been up to they were clearly more than a little soused. The others doubted they'd get much sense of any kind out of either of them, but pressed on with their questioning nonetheless.

"Come on," Chastity insisted, "what *exactly* have you been doing? And what the hell kept you last night? Although," she added thoughtfully, "it's actually pretty good for you two that you weren't there earlier or you'd be cleaning out the fucking sports hall alongside the rest of us."

"What?" demanded Charlie, the realization that she and Liv must have missed a whole lot more school chat than they thought slowly filtering into her befuddled mind.

"Yeah," slurred Liv, resting her head on Charlie's lap and peering up at the others through half-lowered eyes. "Spill!"

All thoughts of bed pushed aside, Jinx, Liberty, and Chastity immediately launched into yet more of the luridly embellished tales they'd already spun the triplets. The latter three, even though they'd heard it all before, didn't make any tracks for bed either.

Igor was still sitting in his chair by the window, but since the girls were all so intent on their stories they paid him no attention at all. If any of them had bothered to look at him they would have seen him staring out to sea with an expression of pure longing on his face. He looked the picture of stoicism as he sat there, very occasionally letting out a long sigh. None of them noticed, anyway, since they'd all settled in for a glorious gossip bitch fest and lots of comic speculation as to who might have banged on Mrs. Bennett's door.

None of them took Daisy's theory particularly seriously, and basically assumed the whole thing was down to sheer bad luck. Jinx was much more interested in hearing about George from the triplets anyway. And they in turn quizzed her relentlessly about her feelings for Jamie. Jinx was flattered by their interest, so pleased they clearly adored her brother and so keen to talk about Jamie that she answered their questions for two hours straight without a break. Liv and Charlie were so shocked to hear about Paul and Chastity splitting up they made her retell the whole gory story in exhaustive detail, and what with all the excitement everyone forgot to ask them what *they'd* been up to. They also failed to notice a nasty scratch on Charlie's elbow.

It was past midnight when they got to bed, and every single one of them fell asleep within seconds of their heads hitting their pillows. Whilst every other person who lived in Tanner slumbered, Igor remained sitting in his chair in the dark common room. He got up to open the window and as he did so a tear glinted on his cheek. It was illuminated by the quarter moon which cut almost as stark a figure as Igor tonight, so bleakly did it seem set against the night sky.

20 *A Very Average Day*

Miss Strimmer and Miss Golly eyed a defiant-looking Jinx, Liberty, and Chastity with inappropriate amounts of glee as the three lower-sixths stood in front of them. It was Tuesday, the bell signaling the end of the lunch period had just rung throughout the school and the girls had turned up at the sports hall to begin the first of their afternoon-punishment cleaning sessions.

Lunch had been a particularly filthy effort on the part of the terrible catering company Stagmount used. Slimy chicken with hairs still visible on the undercooked, puckered skin; overcooked cabbage swimming in gross, greasy margarine; and potatoes with black bits in them did not help make the girls feel good in any way about what their afternoon held. Oh no, quite the reverse.

All three were in moods as filthy as their lunch had been

when Dirk flew through the spin doors and came to a halt in between the two female sports staff before slinging a matey arm around each's neck. The girls nearly vomited up their disgusting lunch at this point. The sight of someone *willingly* touching these two total tools was almost too much to bear.

Standing purposefully slouched in front of these three fools, eyes lowered mutinously, awaiting their instructions, Jinx, Liberty, and Chastity could hardly believe what a freaking chore this punishment was obviously going to be. And in more ways than one considering the task masters they had to put up with.

"So," Dirk said to his colleagues, nodding his smarmy head at the sulky girls in front of them. "To what do we owe *this* pleasure?"

"These three," Gosh said with a delighted snarl at Jinx, who was her least favourite out of this very poor bunch, "are going to be spending all their Tuesdays until the end of term cleaning out the sports center, bagging and tagging all the equipment, and basically doing whatever we tell them to."

Strumpet and Gosh had hated Jinx ever since the summer term of the first year, when she'd been instrumental in the freeing of a neighbouring farmer's flock of pygmy goats and the subsequent canceling of a very important tennis match against Millfield. They hated Liberty because she couldn't care less about games of any kind. Also, since she was a favourite of Sister Minton's and thus able to throw medical sign-off notes around like confetti, there was nothing they could do to force her to attend games lessons when she conveniently seemed to get her period three times each month. And although Chastity was an excellent hockey player, captain of the tennis team, and a brilliant swimmer, she was far too wealthy to be liked by this pair, who were extraordinarily jealous of some of the richer girls and made little attempt to hide it.

"Fucking hell," muttered Chastity under her breath to Liberty, "I'm not sure I can stand three weeks of this."

"Shut up Max-Ward," snapped Strumpet. "We haven't finished with you yet, not by a long shot, and if I were you I'd keep quiet until we have."

Chastity fixed Strumpet with a long glare, but was ignored by the teacher, who was giggling like a cretin at something Dirk had whispered in her ear. The way these three carried on was frankly disgusting. Chastity wondered idly whether she should phone her mum and get her to complain. She decided, on balance and after remembering Mrs. Bennett's furious expression on Sunday in her office, against it and resigned herself to whatever was coming next.

"Right then," Strumpet intoned, delighted at having these three exactly where she wanted them for once. "We've come to a decision."

"At last," murmured Jinx to Liberty, earning herself a sharp look from Dirk.

"Yes," continued Gosh. These two often spoke like this, as if they were participating in a conversational relay race, the freaking idiots. "You can all start upstairs in the gym. Normally you'll be separated, but some of the equipment up there is pretty heavy and you'll need to move it to clean it properly."

"And we've got second-year badminton training on the court," said Dirk, flashing an entirely inappropriate lewd wink at the girls, "so don't worry, we'll be able to keep a close eye on you."

"There will be no talking, no laughing, and absolutely NO gum chewing, mobile phones, or smoking this afternoon," snapped Strumpet, who had caught the tail end of the wink and hadn't liked it at all.

"Go on then," said Gosh. "Set to it. We've been told to let you go at half past five."

Jinx, Liberty, and Chastity looked at each other aghast. It was twenty past two now, so that meant over three hours' work in this stinking sweat factory. They trooped miserably up the stairs to the mezzanine level over the courts that housed the gym to the backing track of the sports staff's uproarious laughter at their expense. The girls could hardly believe their bad luck.

Two hours later, covered in dust and absolutely furious at being treated like slaves, Chastity and Liberty were sitting on a pile of yoga mats, talking to Jinx, who was hanging upside down from the monkey bars and very red in the face. They could hear Dirk shouting instructions at the group of second-years who were playing a very noisy game of badminton beneath them, so they also felt no need to lower their voices. In fact, messy and gross and covered in cobwebs as everything up there was, spending the afternoon with your two best friends in the whole world was really not such a bad deal. The girls had got on with the job whilst giggling nonstop about what dicks and pricks such a lot of people in the world were. The sports staff, lots of the other teachers, and more than a few pupils were included in this list, and they'd actually cleaned most of the gym area already. The only things left to sort out were the mats—which Strumpet had infuriatingly insisted must each be cleaned individually and would be checked at the end of the day—so they were taking a much-deserved break before tackling them.

They'd spilt the pile into three and were busily wiping each one clean when Chastity let out a surprised yell. The other two looked up to see her waving a bunch of papers in their direction.

"What is it?" asked Jinx, leaving a grimy trail of black dust on her forehead as she wiped it with the back of one of her mucky hands.

"I don't know," Chastity said, straightening up and unfolding one of the larger squares before studying it intently. "Hey," she said, surprised, "I think it's a plan of the school. How weird!"

"You're right, Chas." Jinx peered over Chastity's shoulder. "Look—this here is the main school building, those are the dining rooms and that's the sports hall. It looks like an architect's impression or something to me."

"But what do all these squiggles mean?" Liberty asked, staring confusedly at the plan in front of them.

"I'm not *sure*," replied Chastity, "but I think it's Russian. Why would there be Russian writing all over architect plans of the school?"

"Maybe," said Jinx, who was more interested in clock-watching their final half hour than she was in the plans, "they're getting a Russian architect to redo the dining rooms or the sports hall or something. In fact, I bet it's this place and that's why they're making us sort it out like this."

"Maybe," Chastity replied a bit doubtfully, "but why would they be left *here*, in the gym, shoved between a pile of yoga mats?"

"God, who even cares?" Jinx said, walking back over to her diminishing pile of dirty mats and pointing at them. "These things won't have been used since last term; maybe there was a meeting in the sports hall and they just got misplaced and then buried under this lot. Whatever, guys, we've only got twenty-five minutes left until we're free to leave this dump, and I for one can't freaking wait."

Chastity put the plans in her book bag and the three of them finished the job in silence without discussing them again. At 5:29 exactly the three of them skipped down the stairs, flashed knowingly irritating grins at the sports staff and prepared to go back to Tanner. As Liberty was zipping up her green, fluffy-hooded Parka jacket, the group of badminton-playing second-years, headed by Betsy Johnson, trooped out through the double swing-doors that led to the reception area of the sports hall, the staff office, and the girls' suite of white-tiled changing rooms.

Katie Green, trailing miserably at the back of the group of second-year girls, didn't look up at first and had no idea the three lower-sixths were standing almost in front of her nose. When she looked up and saw them at such close quarters she flushed a deep, immediate red and started back in shock. The movement caused Liberty to look up from her zip. Liberty, unlike most of the others, did occasionally notice members of the lower school, and when her eyes fell on Katie she thought how unfortunate and unhappy the poor thing looked. And before she turned round to dash through the doors and race after Jinx and Chastity, who had gotten bored of waiting for her and pushed off towards Tanner, Liberty smiled extremely kindly at Katie.

"Hello there," she said warmly, as she pushed through the swing door.

Liberty, racing up the drive in a tangle of scarf, books and bag, immediately forgot this little scene. Indeed, throughout her whole life she would never once think of it again. Katie, conversely, stopped where she stood as if shot through the heart with a golden arrow when Liberty smiled at her. She stared after the older girl in a trance when the latter turned on her Ugg-booted heel and raced off through the doors.

It was only when Betsy Johnson, dashing off to an extra English lesson intended to help her with her mild dyslexia, bumped into Katie as she went past that she managed to pull herself together and slump into the changing room. She could hardly believe it. Liberty Latiffe, one of the ultimate queens of the lower sixth, had smiled at her. Her, Katie Green. She thought about nothing else for the rest of that day and it was the first thing she thought of when she woke up the next morning. She was still analyzing it the following week. In fact, that very night she sat up until four o'clock in the morning writing, screwing up, and rewriting sick little notes to Liberty. Fortunately for

Liberty, she came to her senses eventually and the misspelt declarations of eternal love remained unsent and in the bin.

Jinx and the others arrived home to find Daisy Finnegan sitting on the sofa reading a chunky physics book.

"Hey Dais," they chorused and sat down to tell her about their afternoon in the clink.

Mr. Morris smiled his way past them a few minutes later, followed by the ever-present but much happier-looking Myrtle. Things had definitely changed in Tanner House this term, he thought.

21 *Crushworthy?*

Jinx sat in the library on Monday morning after a way more subdued than normal break time, helping Liberty with a French translation that was due to Mr. Christie that afternoon. When Liberty bent her dark head over her books to attempt at least some of it herself, Jinx looked out the rain-soaked window and involuntarily let out a massive sigh. She couldn't help it; she hadn't heard a thing from Jamie since the party and was beginning to feel seriously down in the dumps. She had considered texting him, but couldn't bear the idea of reaching out to him when he was so clearly not reaching out to *her*.

"What's wrong, Jinx?" asked Liberty, looking up from her books and fixing Jinx with a worried glance. "Have we done it wrong?"

"I'm not worried about our fucking French prep," said Jinx, roughly pulling her curly blonde hair into a short ponytail and shaking her head. "I'm just pissed off generally."

Liberty knew Jinx was dying to hear from Jamie. Only a deaf, dumb, and blind person could have missed Jinx leaping on her phone every time it bleeped with a new text message and her invariably disappointed look when it proved—once again—not to be from him. She studied Jinx without saying anything, but raised an eyebrow at her best friend, silently encouraging her to share her feelings.

"Okay," admitted Jinx with another sigh. She knew that Liberty knew what was wrong with her, but hadn't felt inclined to discuss it at all until now. "I want to know why the hell I haven't heard a word from Jamie. I mean, we had such a great time at the party until…"

"Chastity and Paul fucked it up!" finished Liberty, pushing her chair closer to Jinx's and wrapping her in a huge hug.

"Yeah," muttered Jinx. "But, you know, shit happens and people just have to deal with it. George thought the whole thing was hilarious. Maybe he just doesn't fancy me. Maybe," she added in extremely morose tones, "he thinks I'm a bad kisser or something."

"Liberty Latiffe!" Jo appeared from behind one with the shelves in front of their desk, interrupting their little tête-à-tête, and stood before them with her hands on her hips. "I've been all over the school looking for you. I never imagined I'd find you in *here*."

Jinx shook her head. She was pretty fed up with everyone assuming their lot never did any bloody work. It was as good as slander and she'd had enough.

"Jo," she began, intending to give the secretary a piece of

her mind once and for all, "we *are* in the lower sixth now, you know. We do have A Levels next year and—contrary to popular opinion, obviously—we *do* intend to pass the things."

"Whatever," replied Jo. "Liberty, your father phoned an hour or so ago."

Liberty's face blanched at this information. Jinx immediately forgot Jo, their work, Jamie, and everything else as she registered the look of blank shock on her friend's face at this totally leftfield information. She grabbed Liberty's hand and squeezed it tight as Jo leaned over and placed a telephone memorandum on the desk between them. Jo, wearing a long belted grey cardigan over her black trousers and blue shirt, flapped off in the direction of the main school and her many chores, leaving Jinx and Liberty sitting in stunned silence at their desk.

"Bloody hell," said Jinx quietly. "You haven't heard a thing from him since you left Riyadh, have you?"

"No," Liberty muttered, picking up the piece of paper and studying it intently, "I haven't."

"So…" Jinx said, wanting to ask a hundred questions but also not wanting to freak Liberty out any more than she currently was.

"So," replied Liberty, folding the memo into a series of smaller squares, "it doesn't say anything other than he called and wants me to call him back when I can."

"Are you going to?" Jinx inquired gently, slipping her free arm round Liberty's shoulders and pulling her close. "Do you *want* to?"

"Yes I'm going to and yes I want to, "Liberty said determinedly. "I've actually kind of been expecting him to get in touch. I know we had that massive scene at the end of last term and he didn't speak to me all through the holidays and all but he *is* my dad and I knew he'd want to know what I was up to at some point or other. Also," she continued, smiling at Jinx, "last time I spoke to Mum she told me he's still paying the fees."

"Really?" said Jinx, surprised, for she'd never once thought about who was paying for what. "You never said anything."

"Yep." Liberty nodded. "Mum phoned to speak to Mrs. Bennett about sorting it all out and Mrs. B. told her they'd been paid in full right through to the end of the upper sixth. Apparently he did it at the beginning of this term. And as soon as I heard that I knew he must have gotten over it. I don't know why I didn't tell you—I've been mulling it over in my own mind I guess. The thing *is*," she went on, sweeping her books into her bag, "he's very stubborn."

"And proud," added Jinx, also gathering her things together.

"Yes," Liberty replied. "So I was thinking about writing him a letter or something, but I guess I don't have to now, do I? Let's go back to Tanner. Will you sit with me when I call him?"

"Of *course* I will," answered Jinx. "Come on, let's get out of here."

Jinx and Liberty walked down the drive, heads lowered against the driving rain which had succeeded in soaking them completely in spite of their parka jackets, oversized scarves and matching baker boy hats. The pair of them heard the trilling sound of a text message at the same time that Jinx felt a vibration against her thigh. She rummaged around in her deep coat pocket and grabbed her phone as they turned the corner to Tanner. She pulled her cap down low over her forehead to shield her face from the relentless rain as she opened her new text.

"It's him!" she screamed, punching the top of Liberty's arm, tossing her hat in the air and jumping up and down in delight. "At fucking last!"

"What does it SAY?" Liberty yelled impatiently, stamping her foot and forgetting all about the imminent conversation she was due to have with her father. "Come on, let's have it!"

"It says," read Jinx from the phone's small screen, "'Hey there hot chick, how's tricks?'"

Both of them shrieked at this point, gripped each other and started jumping up and down together with no regard whatsoever for the rapidly deepening puddle they were splashing all over themselves.

Dirk, driving past in the opposite direction in his yellow Suzuki Swift—possibly the most cretinous car in existence and thus very suitable for his purposes, shook his head and thought to himself that, fit as they undoubtedly were, these Stagmount girls were all stark raving mad. He put his foot down, intent on racing away from them as fast as possible.

The girls looked up but barely registered his passing, so intently were they both now staring back at Jinx's phone.

"'If yr free next Saturday,'" Liberty took over the reading, "'bring yr friends and come to Get Down or Get Wrecked at Skate Fest on the seafront. Love Jamie x.'"

"LOVE!" Jinx yelled. "Did you see it said 'LOVE'?"

"Yes," giggled Liberty. "I *did* see that. What the hell is the Skate Fest?"

"I don't know," said Jinx in her normal voice, "but I'm sure I've heard George talk about it. I think it's one of those skateboard things all the surf dudes are into. It's a competition, I think, and there's an after-party for everyone in one of the seafront bars afterwards. In fact," she went on, sounding more convinced as the memories filtered into her brain, "I'm sure George and Jamie went to it last year. Yes, and one of their friends—it was Jamie's housemate Daz, I think—was showing off and tried to do a somersault or something off his board on the ramp and missed it and totally fucked his back up. And another one broke his leg and had to be taken off to the hospital in an ambulance. And everyone got so drunk afterwards none of them remembered anything about it in the morning," she finished with relish.

"Do you think George and Jamie will be in the competition," Liberty asked, wide-eyed at the thought of all these injuries. "It sounds really dangerous."

"I don't think *they* will," Jinx said, retrieving her hat from the bush it had landed in and shaking it violently to get rid of the water that had pooled inside it. "But I'm sure some of their friends will be in it. I guess they'll be watching it with us. Whatever, it's the next to last weekend of term and we've *so* got to go. God, I'm so excited! I thought I'd never hear from him again. I mean, I know about the three-day rule and everything, but it's been nine freaking days since the party."

"I know," Liberty said, beyond delighted that Jamie had

finally seen fit to get in touch with her best friend, thrilled at the prospect of another big night out with no interruptions from Chastity and Paul this time and also secretly hoping the dark-haired boy from the party would be there. "I was a bit worried myself. And what a blast to go to this thing on our last Saturday of term!"

"Totally," confirmed Jinx, smiling widely as she rammed her sopping hat back on top of her head, blithely oblivious to the water—by now dripping down the back of her neck—and gripping Liberty's arm. "Right, Latiffe, let's get you back to Tanner and make this phone call."

They raced the rest of the way back. After shaking themselves like dogs in the reception area, covering the notice board with drops of water and dumping their bags in an untidy heap by the door, they sauntered into the kitchen in search of sustenance.

Sitting back to front on Liberty's desk chair, Jinx blew on her mug of scalding hot tea, nibbled on the corner of a Bourbon Cream biscuit and looked out the window. Listening to her best friend's side of the conversation with her father, she shook her head and wondered for the thousandth time about Amir's sanity.

Until the end of last term, when Amir had chartered the Harrods helicopter, flown to Stagmount, and landed at the school in a towering rage, only to drag his daughter back to Saudi over some perceived transgressions on her part, Jinx had not been able to put her finger on exactly what it was that so bothered her about Liberty's dad. Now, of course, she knew exactly what it was. Even though she and her dad had occasionally rowed massively, there really was no comparison between Martin Slater and Amir Latiffe. No, the latter could be simply terrifying in his sudden rages, his devotion to his daughter behaving in what he perceived to be the "proper" way and above all his deeply unpredictable behaviour.

Her thoughts were interrupted when Liberty's voice took on a suddenly surprised, questioning tone, and Jinx sat up and listened. Even though they'd been chatting pretty amicably for the last ten minutes about Liberty's forthcoming exams and the terrible weather Jinx hoped Amir hadn't phoned to impart bad news of any kind and was only now deciding to impart it.

"What do you mean you think it's Stagmount?" Liberty asked, frowning as she doodled on the cover of the notebook on her lap. "Oh. Well," she continued after a long pause during which Amir talked nonstop, she nodded thoughtfully and Jinx realized thanks to the doodling that nothing much was wrong anyway. "I don't know anything about it, Dad."

Liberty wiggled her fingers at Jinx to indicate Amir was banging on about something or other at length and rolled her eyes at Jinx. Well, thought the latter, even though she'd not heard a word about the fallout yet, at least they seemed to be getting on as well as they used to. She was sure Amir loved his daughter, she just hadn't ever been sure he knew how to show her he did—or not properly anyway. Designer clothes, flash handbags, and bundles of cash were one thing, of course, but honesty, trust, and respect were another entirely.

"Okay Dad," said Liberty, winking at Jinx. "Thanks for calling. Yes, yes," she nodded. "I will. Love you too. Bye Dad. Bye!"

Liberty snapped her phone shut, uncrossed her legs and looked at Jinx. "Well," she said, "that was weird. In more ways than one."

"So, what did he want?" asked Jinx, very relieved indeed to see Liberty looking so happy and pleased at having renewed communication with her father. "Anything interesting?"

"Well," Liberty said, reaching for her own mug and sipping thoughtfully, "he didn't say one single word about the row or me going to America or Mum or anything." She laughed ruefully. "But I didn't really expect he would. Why change the pattern of a lifetime, hey?"

"Hmm," Jinx murmured, not really knowing what to say about this at all.

"He asked me about my school work, how the exams were going, and whether I had enough money. And then," Liberty said, putting down her mug and frowning, "he started banging on about some property plans he'd been sent by a business associate."

"What do you mean?" Jinx asked, looking blank and wondering what the hell Amir had up his sleeve now.

"Well," Liberty went on, "he said he'd been sent the floor plans of some luxury new flats. He said the location was top secret but the planners were trying to ascertain interest or something, and he'd been sent one."

"So what?" a baffled Jinx replied, knowing that Amir never discussed any of his business ventures with his daughter. She'd once asked Liberty what her dad did and Liberty hadn't been able to tell her. "What's it got to do with you?"

"He said he thought the plans looked like Stagmount," Liberty answered. "He said he recognized the formation of the main school houses and said the helipad on the plans is in exactly the same place as the one here."

"I don't get it," Jinx said, standing up and stretching. "What's he saying?"

"He basically said he thought someone might be trying to buy Stagmount and turn it into a property development," Liberty said, looking Jinx in the face. "And that since Mrs. Bennett had visited him in Saudi in December he wanted to see if we knew anything about it."

"Mrs. Bennett went to Saudi?" Jinx asked incredulously, sitting down again. "In December? *This* December?"

"Yep," Liberty nodded. "Apparently she was passing through on her way to a meeting about something and she came round to Dad's for coffee."

"But—" Jinx interjected before Liberty cut her off, knowing what Jinx was thinking pretty much even before she did.

"When I was there," Liberty said, "exactly. He said they talked for two hours and she convinced him to send me to live with Mum. He also said he respected her as a sensible English woman and that I was lucky to have her as my headmistress."

"Bloody hell," Jinx exhaled, truly shocked by all of this. "I knew Mrs. B. was cool but I never realized she was, like, the raddest dude alive. I can't believe she did all that. *Passing* through! My goodness. What a woman! What else did he say about it?"

"Well, he banged on about the plans," Liberty continued, "but then said he might well be wrong. I think he was looking for an excuse to get in touch and used them—it must be a coincidence."

"Who knows," said Jinx, still shocked by the revelations about their headmistress's intervention into Liberty's plight. "And who cares. I'm sure Stagmount can't be sold—the whole idea's ridiculous. It's a charitable trust as well as a listed build-ing—there are rules and regulations about those kinds of things. You can't just knock a place like Stagmount down. I still can't believe Mrs. Bennett went to Saudi and saved your ass and never said a word about it."

"Me neither," Liberty said, shaking her head and shudder-ing at what might have been if Mrs. B. had done nothing. "We owe her so much."

"Yes," agreed Jinx. "We certainly do."

They looked at their watches and realized they had only three and a half minutes in which to make it back to the main school for lunch, and so they grabbed their bags and sprinted back up the drive. For once, the rain had stopped. They turned their faces to the weak March sun trying its best to shine through the clouds and laughed as the puddles splashed around their furiously racing feet. Weak with laughter and exertion, they skipped down the corridor barely daunted by the prospect of a gross lunch and feeling happier than they had for ages.

By the time they hooked up with the others at their usual table they were so intent on telling them about Amir, Mrs. Bennett, and Jamie's text that all thoughts of the plans Liberty's dad mentioned had flown their minds entirely.

22   *Tutor Group*

Jinx and her friends sat in classroom 4b on Thursday morning, waiting for Mrs. Carpenter and their daily tutor group session to commence. All of the lower sixth were positively delirious compared to how low they'd all been feeling a week ago. The weather must have had something to do with it. Whilst it had seemed floods of biblical proportions were scarily imminent for pretty much the whole freaking term, today had dawned cold but sunny, for once, and all of their moods had lightened as a consequence.

Chastity, Jinx, and Liberty, in that order, were sitting in the very center of the back row with Liv next to Chastity and Charlie next to Liberty. The girls were whiling away their waiting time with good-humoured, idle gossip about dear old Mrs. C. Meanwhile Fiona—who sat at the front due to what she claimed was her terrible eyesight but actually had more to do with her terrible fear of missing something one of the teachers might say—was sitting on the side of Liberty's desk, swinging her legs and enjoying joining in the chatter until the teacher arrived. Even Daisy had thrown in a couple of remarks and not been shouted down. Their tutor had, they unanimously agreed, been in the very best of moods all that term.

"Hey," Mimi Tate yelled from her seat at the end of the second row, "it's because she's in *lurve*."

"Yeah," said Chastity, looking round for Igor and not spotting him anywhere. "But where *is* the object of her affection?"

"Masha?" Jinx directed her comment at the three identical backs in front of her. Even though she didn't know which one was Masha, she knew they'd all turn around when she said one of their names.

"Yes?" said Masha, who was wearing, if Jinx had only thought to look, the corresponding green diamond on her finger.

"Where's Igor?" Jinx asked, winking conspiratorially at them, for she liked these girls a lot.

"We don't know," replied Irina with a shrug and an unconcerned glance at both her sisters. "We haven't seen him yet this morning."

"Some bodyguard," muttered Liberty. "My dad would have a fit if his security guys left him alone for even a second."

"Oh, we don't care about that," said Olga, flashing a blue glint around the room as she ran her right hand through her hair and the huge diamond on it caught the light. "We're going to tell our dad we don't need him next term."

"Yes," Masha added with a giggle. "Next term we won't need him at all. But he's here now so it's a bit difficult for us to get rid of him with just a few days still to go."

"What about him and Mrs. C.?" pressed Chastity. "What do you think about that?"

"Oh," Irina said, pausing to glance at her sisters almost as if she wanted confirmation of something before continuing. "We don't know what you're talking about."

"Are you serious?" asked Liv, who found it very hard to believe all three of them had singularly failed to notice the budding romance as it occurred underneath their very noses. "Come off it. We've been talking of nothing else for weeks. You guys can't have missed it, surely!"

Whatever the triplets' response might have been was lost to a gust of cold air as the door flew open. Mrs. Carpenter strode through it and headed straight to the chair behind her desk. Fortunately this term there had been a total sea change in both Mrs. C.'s moods and the way she interacted with the girls in her class. Sweetness and light was very much the order of the day and—very strangely, considering the undiagnosed bipolar disorder the girls were utterly convinced she suffered from—she'd hardly been heard to raise her voice above polite conversational level at all. She'd also not once thrown a lump of chalk at any of their heads.

When she raised her head to look around the room, however, the girls who were arranged in neat rows in front of her immediately realized all was not well in the mad, mad world of Mrs. C. Dressed entirely in black, as usual, accessorized with chunky silver pieces of jewelry, the vibrant flash of block colour the tutor had, of late, been adding to her all-black repertoire on a daily basis was missing. Her red-rimmed, bloodshot eyes provided the only accent on today's outfit. Her swollen face, heaving shoulders and shuddering breaths indicated to all of them that Mrs. C. had rocked up to tutor group fresh from an absolutely mammoth crying fit.

The girls stared at her, beyond appalled. It was one thing to deal with *each other* having a personal crisis of some kind, but quite another to be faced with a member of *staff* going through the same thing. And Mrs. C. was evidently in the midst of a really bad one. None of them knew quite what to do, and they all felt more than a little uncomfortable. At that moment the silence in 4b was completely deafening.

Igor's tall, forbidding form suddenly appeared in the doorway. The expression on his face was unlike anything the girls had seen before. The tension in the room, alongside the sudden drop in temperature, somehow found its way through Mrs. Carpenter's misery, and the tutor raised her head to see what was causing it. When her anguished eyes landed on Igor in the doorway, they instantly welled up with fresh tears and a small moan escaped her lips. Igor's face appeared to have been molded from the hardest granite. So fixed was the stern, forbidding, and above all closed-off look on the bodyguard's face that some of the girls couldn't stop involuntary shivers from shuddering down their spines.

After what seemed like a lifetime of Mrs. C. and Igor staring at each other eye to miserable eye but was in fact only a few seconds, the door slammed shut behind Igor. He strode across the room to his customary seat adjacent to the triplets and next to the classroom's biggest picture window, folded himself down into it, crossed his arms and stared pointedly out of the window. The triplets appeared not to have noticed anything amiss whatsoever. Their blonde heads were bent together over a letter they'd received that morning, and none of them so much as flickered an eyelash at the scene playing out in front of them. The rest of the girls had no idea what was going on, but a couple of things were abundantly clear.

Mrs. Carpenter, whom they were very fond of when she was nice, was absolutely devastated. And the cause of this devastation, obvious from the stricken glances she kept flicking his way whilst desperately trying to pull herself together in front of her girls, was Igor.

"Girls," Mrs. C. said in a voice hoarse from crying, a distant relation indeed from her usual booming tones, after drawing a jerky breath, "I..."

The girls watched, alert to her every shaky move, as Mrs. Carpenter grabbed her coat, bag, and class register from her desk and dashed out of the room as fast as her legs could carry her. They continued to sit there in a state of shocked suspension for a few seconds. All at once and seemingly out of nowhere a buzz of humming chat enveloped classroom 4b. Chairs were scraped back and desks pushed aside as the girls gathered in small groups on the corridor side of the room, away from where Igor was sitting, as if made of stone, by the window.

The triplets still had not looked up and were now, giggling

occasionally, whispering softly to each other in Russian.

The bell sounded for the beginning of morning lessons, and the girls watched, enthralled, as the triplets stood up as one and pushed their chairs underneath their desks. They smiled around the room as if nothing had happened, waved at Jinx and Liberty, who were closest to them, and walked out the door. Igor followed close on their heels, his black coat flapping behind him like a crow's wings. Most of the others followed suit, shooting meaningful glances at each other as they did so and raising their eyebrows in the direction of the dining rooms to indicate that today's morning break was going to be one hell of a gossip fest.

Since she'd finished this term's project the previous week, Jinx bade farewell to Chastity, Liberty, Liv, and Charlie, who were heading off to double art and agreed she'd see them at lunchtime. Left to her own devices in their form room, she took her time in packing up her bags and thought about what had just happened in there. God, she felt sorry for Mrs. C. Although since Igor had looked so completely terrifying this morning she had to admit she was hard-pressed to see the attraction. Either way, thought Jinx, as she turned left down the corridor, she'd never seen anyone as cut up as *that*. That was something else entirely.

Jinx minced along quite happily, studying the notice boards for anything new or interesting—not a chance. She decided to pop into the ladies' loos on the off chance she might locate the trainers she'd misplaced the other day. As soon as she walked in, though, Jinx regretted this decision. Sitting on the very end of one of the low slatted benches that hugged the walls around the small shower area was Mrs. Carpenter. Her face was turned to the wall. She was hugging her knees, rocking slightly and moaning incoherently whilst taking in great, shuddering breaths. She looked, frankly, like a mental patient, and Jinx so did not want to be trapped in this confined space with her for any amount of time at all.

At that moment Mrs. Carpenter looked up, wailed, and held her arms out to Jinx like one of those dolls that wets itself when you pull the string on its back. Oh Christ, thought Jinx in a panic, the bloody woman obviously wants a hug. Yucksville!

Jinx managed to hold it together enough to smile weakly at her lachrymose form tutor before gingerly sitting down next to her, avoiding the outstretched arms at all costs. Jinx patted Mrs. C.'s knee whilst also desperately trying to avoid looking her in the face.

"The thing is, Jinx," wailed Mrs. Carpenter in a shaky, squeaky voice weakened by excessive recent emotion, "I love him so much b-b-b-but I just don't think I know enough about him."

"Um..." Jinx really wasn't sure of the appropriate response to this and was busy thinking on her feet.

"An-an-and if you don't know someone properly," she continued in the same vein, "then can you truly love him?"

"Well—" Jinx was hating this more than she could ever have imagined possible.

"I mean," Mrs. C. interjected, grabbing Jinx's hand and fixing her with a desperate stare, "I obviously KNOW him. But I don't *know* him. Do you understand me?"

Jinx's panicked prayers for intervention were answered by a most unlikely source. Daisy Finnegan strolled round the corner of the washbasins and into view. She pulled up short when she saw her form tutor and Jinx sitting on the bench at the back like that. But since Daisy had witnessed the whole morning scene she wasn't as shocked as she could have been. Daisy, in her role as teacher's pet and chief suck-up, was also a lot more used to "crisis management" than Jinx and her crew. Daisy turned back to a second-year who had come in behind her.

"Betsy," she snapped, after winking surreptitiously at a delighted Jinx, "none of your year seems to have the right number of towels. As head girl, it is one of your duties to make sure every pupil has the right equipment, and I should not have to be checking up on you like this."

"But," Betsy said, staring mutinously at the lockers in front of her—she clearly didn't give two shits whether anyone had the right amount of towels or not—"what am I supposed to do about it?"

"You," Daisy said, twisting round again to block Betsy's view of the shower area, "are going to go back to your house, find the missing towels and bring them to me here."

"But," Betsy said again before Daisy cut her off.

"I'm not interested in buts," snapped the older girl, causing a small wave of mirth to flow through Jinx's veins even in the midst of this undesirable scenario. "I want you to go back to your house and scour the place. When you have done so, and not before you have found at *least* half of the missing amount, I want you to bring them back to me here and we will continue the inventory. Off you go!"

The second-year threw a total death stare in Daisy's direction but raced off to do her bidding nonetheless. Daisy waited until the door had closed behind her before moving over to sit on Mrs. Carpenter's other side. Jinx was as appalled as she was impressed when Daisy put an arm round Mrs. C.'s shoulders and squeezed her tight, but since she'd rarely been so pleased to see anyone in her life she made a mental note to let it go.

The arm seemed to have a soothing effect on Mrs. C., who dropped her head onto Daisy's shoulder. Her breathing certainly appeared a lot calmer than it had a few minutes earlier in Jinx's company, anyway. Jinx and Daisy locked eyes over their teacher's bowed head and Jinx mouthed her extreme thanks for Daisy's excellent save. Daisy blushed slightly at yet more unexpected niceness directed at her from the unlikely Jinx Slater and shook her head to indicate it was nothing. They both raised their eyebrows at the same time, and both smiled when it registered that for once they were on the same wavelength.

Mrs. Carpenter chose that moment to wipe her eyes for the final time in their presence, stand up, and nod her thanks at the pair who'd witnessed her breakdown. She didn't say a word, but smiled weakly as she gathered her things together and headed in the direction of the san. Mrs. C. was no stranger to Mister Sinton's lair, and she knew the matron would give her a couple of strong sleeping pills and the loan of a private room for the rest of the day.

"Bloody hell," said Jinx, staring at Daisy with uncharacteristic gratitude. "Am I glad you came in or what! I honestly don't know what I would have said to her if you hadn't turned up. She was practically babbling."

"Poor thing," Daisy replied, looking sideways at Jinx as she accepted the offer of half a piece of Juicy Fruit. "What did she say? I've got the feeling something very weird is going on at this school."

"Well," said Jinx, chucking the gum wrapper at the bin and missing, "she said a lot of stuff about knowing him, but not *knowing* him. I didn't understand a bloody word of it, Dais, I really didn't. And what do you mean about something weird going on? I mean, it's sad that they broke up and all, but I can't see it being anything more sinister than that. Can you *really*?"

"Yes I can. Something's not right, Jinx," Daisy said, looking at Jinx and willing her to listen for once. "And I'm not sure what it is, but it's definitely something and it's definitely not been right for a while now. And," she continued, warning Jinx with a glance not to interrupt her, "I know you hate it when I say this, but I'm convinced it's something to do with the triplets and Igor."

"What do you mean?" asked Jinx, suddenly exhausted. She wanted nothing more than to be curled up in bed listening to the new mix Chastity had made her, drinking a Diet Coke, thinking about Jamie, and maybe flicking through one of her old Malory Towers books.

"Have you noticed their rings?" Daisy responded, unable to believe any of the others had totally missed them.

"No," said Jinx, who could distinctly feel a headache brewing behind her frontal lobes. "What about them?"

Daisy, whose avaricious eye missed nothing, sighed deeply at such negligence before continuing.

"The triplets all have matching diamond rings," she said, speaking slowly to make sure Jinx was listening. "One stone is blue, one is pink, and one's green, but they're all set in exactly the same ornate gold base."

"So," Jinx pressed, keen to get this chat over with and herself out of the loos as soon as possible. Someone must have left the heating on too high or something; she was beginning to feel a bit queasy. "What about it?"

"Igor has exactly the same ring as they do," Daisy said, her chest puffing up with delight at being the only one to have noticed. "The only difference is the stone in his is a regular white diamond. What kind of so-called bodyguard has exactly the same item of very expensive, unique jewelry as his clients? And," she continued, pleased to see Jinx appeared to be concentrating at last, "what kind of bodyguard is more often than not nowhere to be seen anywhere near his precious cargo? Lastly," she said with an officious shake of her head, delighted at finally getting the chance to expound upon her theory, "I saw him coming out of the bursar's office a few days ago. Whatever it was they'd been talking about was not to Igor's liking—far from it. He was in a proper mood, Jinx; I heard him shouting in the office and he practically kicked the door when he came out. If he hadn't seen me waiting down the corridor I think he would have done it."

"Okay," said Jinx, leaning forward, resting her elbows on her knees and cradling her head in her hands, "so let's say you're right. Let's say there *is* something suspicious or sinister or whatever going on. Let's say the triplets, Igor, and the bursar are all over it. But what the hell are *we* supposed to do about it?"

"I don't know yet," muttered Daisy, "but I do think we need to find out what's going on."

"Join forces you mean?" Jinx asked, not looking up but clutching her head tighter as she spoke.

"Yes," agreed Daisy, smiling for the first time since she'd started talking. "That's exactly what I mean. I think together we'll find out whatever it is a damn sight quicker than if I go it alone. Also, you're much more friendly with the triplets than I am, so it'll be easier for you to hang around them and ask questions without looking suspicious."

Jinx sighed but raised her head and looked Daisy in the eye. She held up her right hand and Daisy's left met it in a weak high five. They were now locked in together, for better or worse, but at least Jinx was now free to go back to Tanner and get into bed for a couple of hours.

Well, she would have been if Betsy Johnson hadn't chosen that moment to come crashing back in through the door of the loos, her face and most of her curly brown hair hidden behind a pile of towels she had clutched in a stack in front of her. In her surprise at seeing Jinx and Daisy in front of her she stumbled and the stack went flying. As they settled around the place in messy heaps, a piece of shiny paper flew out from between two of the unattractive maroon ones. The three of them watched as it came to rest, front side up, on the white tiled floor.

"Oh my God," Daisy gasped, leaping on it and glaring up

at a flame-faced Betsy. "It's my chemistry revision aid. What the hell is it doing here?" She took a menacing step towards the second-year in front of a completely confused Jinx. "Where did you get it?"

"It's nothing to do with me," snapped Betsy, beyond cross at the way these sixth-formers thought they could boss everyone about all the time and get away with it. She had to bite her lip hard in order not to stamp her foot. "You told me to gather up all the Steinem girls' towels and bring them down here and here they *are*, as requested. Whatever that piece of paper is, it must have been stuffed in between a couple and fallen out when I dropped them. Can I go now?"

"You just hold on," Jinx interjected sharply, fixing Betsy with a look that told the junior this particular member of the lower sixth was not at all inclined to put up with any cheek from a member of the lower school, however disgruntled she might currently be feeling. "Is that the thing you were looking for the night we came back in the police van and Mrs. B. opened her door and caught us all?"

"Yes," said Daisy, throwing a by-now terrified Betsy an even scarier look than Jinx just had and pointing at the offending items on the floor. "It is. And I intend to find out exactly where it came from. Come on, Betsy, out with it. Now! Where did you get those maroon towels from?"

"Katie Green's room," said Betsy sulkily, staring at the floor and mentally cursing Katie Green to hell and back. "She'd obviously washed them and shoved them in the back of her wardrobe instead of bringing them down here. She's very lazy, you know," Betsy continued, throwing caution to the wind and deciding she couldn't be bothered to stand up for Katie, whom she didn't like much anyway. "And weird. She's obsessed with you lot for a start."

Jinx and Daisy both frowned at the obvious intended insult, but decided not to pass comment on it at this stage.

"Right," said Jinx, standing up and looking down at Betsy, who was really quite short from this angle. "We've heard all we need to from you. But before you go," she continued, taking a step closer and narrowing her eyes as Betsy shrank back against the wall, "there are a couple of things you *won't* be doing when you leave here. Number one: you will not mention a word to anyone— ANYONE—about what you've seen in here. Number two: you will especially not be saying a word to Katie Green about any of this. And let's have number three for a bonus: if we find out you have said anything, your life will literally not be worth living."

"Capiche?" Daisy added, thrilled with her new role as a *Sopranos*-style enforcer alongside Jinx.

Betsy stared mutinously at the pair of them for a second before dropping her eyes in compliance and muttering her assent. No one said a word as Betsy turned round and walked out the door, but as soon as she'd gone Jinx and Daisy stared at each other in amazement. What a fucking day.

"Let's go back to Tanner, Dais," begged Jinx, who was concerned about what might happen next if they continued to lounge around in here and fearful for her sanity. "Come on, we'll go and thrash the whole thing out if you like, but whatever we do we've got to get out of here."

The two of them walked back to Tanner mostly in a stunned silence, each marching along highly occupied with her own whirling thoughts. Since Daisy had a pressing English essay to write—although Jinx, who was in the same class couldn't for the life of her think which one it might be—they separated once they walked through the front door, agreeing to hook up later on and discuss the whole shebang.

"Well," muttered the head girl of the lower sixth, "I can't remember the last time I had such fun at Stagmount."

23 *You Couldn't Make It Up*

Jinx was sitting on her bed in between Liv and Chastity after dinner that evening. Charlie, whose cello practice sessions kept her over at the main school far later than the others, was sitting on a bean bag she'd brought with her and resting a plate containing four fish fingers alongside a handful of oven chips on her knees. Liberty was sitting on a pile of Jinx's clean bed sheets on the floor next to her and periodically grabbing a chip off the teetering plate. The five of them were arguing good-naturedly about who would go and get the two bottles of Merlot Chastity had stashed at the back of her jumper drawer next door when there was a timid tapping at Jinx's door.

"Come iiiiiin," they chorused, looking up expectantly until the door opened and their faces registered shock at who stood before them.

"Hi Daisy," Jinx said nonchalantly, standing up to greet

her visitor and ignoring the shocked expressions of the others. "Come and have a seat. I'd grab the desk chair if I were you. Hey Lib, you're closest to the door—go and get the wine!"

The others exchanged querying glances as to the head girl's unusual presence at their soiree, but shrugged their shoulders and prepared to be entertained when it became apparent Jinx was giving nothing away.

Daisy settled, Liberty returned and six glasses of wine were poured. A hush fell over the six girls in the small room as they each took their first sip.

"God," Daisy giggled nervously as she accepted her glass of red wine, "I feel like I'm at some kind of initiation ceremony. Like I'm at a meeting of the Inner Elite or something!" She giggled again. "Do you call yourselves the IE for short?"

"Anyway," said Jinx swiftly, keen to bring the discussion back to order, "we're here tonight because a few weird things happened today and, well, Daisy and I think we're on to something. Or rather, Daisy does, but I agree with her. Or something." Jinx looked across the table at her old nemesis and smiled. "Daisy, why don't you explain it? I think you'll do a better job than me; I'm not sure I quite understand most of it myself."

"Okay," said Daisy, thrilled to be treated so respectfully by these girls for once and really rather enjoying drinking her wine in so civilized a manner. "Here goes. Basically, I think there's something fishy going on between Igor and the bursar."

Jinx clocked the various sarcastic looks flying amongst the rest of the girls in the room. "No," she said. "Let her finish."

"Thanks, Jinx," Daisy said, smiling shyly at her in gratitude for the stick up. "So, I've heard all of you guys talking about Mrs. Bennett arguing with the bursar, and I just think it's significant that he and Igor are looking pretty close all of a sudden. These are a couple of things I've noticed," she said, pulling a small notebook out of her cardigan pocket and flipping it open to a page closely covered with her small handwriting. "The triplets and Igor all have matching rings. He's so laissez-faire about his so-called shadowing of them he's practically out of town. He broke up with Mrs. Carpenter this morning and she has no idea why, except I saw him having a huge row with the bursar last night and I just have a hunch it's all connected."

"Oh my God," said Chastity, putting a hand over her mouth as something clicked in her mind. "What about the plans we found in the gym? The plans of the school with *Russian* writing all over them?"

"What plans?" Daisy, Liv, and Charlie asked in unison, having not been privy to the others' discovery during their punishment in the gym.

"Plans of the school," said Jinx, staring at Daisy in amazement and wondering if maybe there was something in what she was saying after all. "We found them stuffed between a couple of the yoga mats when we were cleaning out the gym last week. I'd forgotten all about them. Go and grab them, Chas."

Chastity jumped up again and raced next door. Whilst she was fetching the plans from where she'd handily stored them in her waste-paper bin, Jinx and Liberty quickly filled the others in on the circumstances as to how they were found. During this conversation Daisy went very still and thoughtful. She was obviously thinking deeply about something or other, although the rest had no idea what this might be.

Heads bent over the plans spread out on the end of Jinx's bed, the girls were in total agreement that they were of the school. Charlie, whose father owned a very successful business building and running his own nursing homes, assured them that these were most definitely property-related. At that moment Liberty's head shot up and she put a hand over her mouth in shock.

"Shit, guys," she said, turning to Jinx and smacking her arm for emphasis, "my *dad* said something to me about seeing a plan of what looked like Stagmount turned into luxury flats or something. He said he recognized the shape of the main school and the exact location of the helipad! I thought he was just making up some rubbish as an excuse to call me after such a long time."

"I don't get it though," said Jinx, confused as hell and more than a little alarmed at how fast things seemed to be developing. She'd considered Daisy's theories little more than a series of benign coincidences and only decided to humour her as payback for helping her out with Mrs. C. earlier. "How does it all link up?"

"I think," said Daisy, sitting up and looking round excitedly, "we're all forgetting something very important. Maybe the most important thing yet, in fact."

"What?" screamed Liv, who really could be very impatient and couldn't stand having important information withheld from her for any length of time. "What is it we're all forgetting?"

"The day the fire alarm went off," Daisy said triumphantly. "Don't you remember Dirk coming from the sports hall?"

"Yes," said Liv, who tended to grasp things quicker than the others. "He said he'd heard *foreign voices* coming from the *gym* but that someone had thrown a glass at him and he'd felt so threatened he honestly believed he'd been shot so he ran all the way along to main school before collapsing at Mrs. B.'s feet."

"And," Charlie added, bouncing up and down with excitement, "the bursar didn't appear for ages, even though he's the one who's supposed to be in charge of all the fire regulation stuff."

"And loads of us heard him and Mrs. B. having a massive row about it later on," Liberty finished with relish.

"So what are the facts then?" asked Jinx, wanting to get this bundle of crazy information all neatly tied up in her head. "What does all of this tell us?"

"Well," said Daisy, who had been busily writing lists of everything they were saying on a fresh page of her notebook and connecting things with arrows back and forth, "it reads like this to me. Firstly, we have a meeting of what we can only assume are some kind of Russian businessmen in our gym on the day of the fire alarm some weeks ago. Secondly, we have Dirk disturbing this meeting and whoever was present at it subsequently seeing fit to get rid of him before, presumably, fleeing the scene, but mistakenly leaving some of their plans behind. Thirdly, we have the bursar—alongside generally suspicious behavior and an even more suspicious alliance with some Russian pupils' bodyguard—appearing late at the fire alarm as if he had rushed to the main school from somewhere a lot farther away than his office. For our purposes here tonight I think we must hypothesize that this place was indeed the gym. He did also, I clearly remember it, arrive *after* Dirk did."

"Don't forget the triplets and Igor having matching rings," cut in Liv, who was quietly fuming at Daisy's casual takeover of her normal role as plan formulator and general brain behind the scams of the lower sixth.

"I won't," Daisy replied tightly. "After all, I was the one who thought of it first anyway."

"Okay, okay," said Liv, "keep your wig on, I was only *saying*. What do you suggest we do about all of this then, Ms. Brainbox? How the hell are we supposed to find out whether the triplets' dad is involved with the bursar or whatever? I know we're clever and everything, but we're only schoolgirls, and we've got seriously limited access to the kind of information we'll need to make this thing—whatever *it* is—stand up."

"One of us needs to speak to him," Daisy said. She looked around and felt exasperated by the blank stares that greeted this announcement. "He's obviously in love with Mrs. C. And she's clearly in love with him—we've never seen her look happier than she does this term, and I bet you it's mutual."

"So?" muttered Liberty, concentrating hard on pulling apart one of her split ends.

"So," Daisy said passionately, "that's his Achilles heel. I also bet you he's involved in whatever it is that's going on and suddenly got cold feet because of her. And somehow the bursar found out and forced him to dump her. I have never," she went on, betraying a sensitivity no one could ever have assumed existed inside that geeky, stuck-up, suck-up exterior, "seen anyone quite so lovesick as he was this morning. Did you see his face?"

"So," said Chastity thoughtfully, "who's going to be the one to front him up?"

"Bagsy not me!" yelled Liberty, shaking her head from side to side so wildly half her ponytail came unstuck.

"And me," added Liv. "I'm not doing it. No way!"

"I think," said Daisy, looking as exasperated as she felt by now and keen to get back to her essay, "that Jinx should do it." She held up a hand to indicate they should let her finish and ignored the expression of total horror that passed across Jinx's face. "You were the one who comforted Mrs. Carpenter in the loos this morning, so you can use that to start the conversation off. Also," she added, fixing Jinx with a look not dissimilar to the one she'd given Betsy Johnson in the bathroom that morning, "you've got two brothers, so I assume you know how to deal with men in moods?"

"Well," said Jinx, "yes, but..."

"And," finished Daisy, standing up as if this were the end of the matter, "you love the school and you'd do anything for Mrs. Bennett. If anyone can find out what's going on, you can."

"Hear hear," said Chastity. "I think Fingers has got it bang on the nose."

"Me too," agreed Charlie. "You're our man, Jinx!"

"You *are* good at stuff like this," Liberty said, tapping Jinx's knee. "You know you are."

"I'm NOT though," yelled Jinx, feeling truly horrified at the task that lay in front of her. "I'm bloody crap at it. I couldn't think of a single comforting thing to say to Mrs. C. this morning—I just stared at her in mute horror until you came along, Dais. And as far as Igor goes, he and my brothers are, like, *exact* opposites. I can't do it."

"You can," said Liv. "Come on, Jinx. Think of what Mrs. Bennett did for Liberty. This is nothing compared to what she did."

Jinx sighed. Really, when Liv put it like that she knew she didn't have any choice in the matter. However awkward, embarrassed, and terrible this cringeworthy scene was going to make her feel, she owed it to Mrs. B. to at least try and find out if anything was threatening the school.

"Okay. I'll do it tomorrow morning and I don't want to hear another word about it from any of you until afterwards. Hey," she said to Daisy, suddenly remembering something and wanting to change the subject before they all started banging on and confusing her anyway, "did you ever speak to that second-year? The girl who stole your chemistry revision thing or whatever it was?"

"Oh," replied Daisy as all the others gaped at them in astonishment—since when had *these* two become so freaking friendly? "No, not yet. I'm going to tackle her about it tomorrow morning. I just can't see a second-year banging on Mrs. Bennett's door in the middle of the night to purposefully get us into trouble. The more I think about it, the more I think she must have just found the thing lying in the grounds somewhere and kept it. I'm going to speak to her after chapel, though, and tell her she should have given it straight back to me."

"That other one this morning was bloody rude as well," Jinx muttered, shaking her head in disgust at the wanton bad manners of the youth of today. "She reminded me of my cousin Cassie—whom I can't *stand* and who, my dear mother incidentally informed me last time we went home, might be coming here to Stagmount next term."

"Oh yes," said Liberty with a giggle, "she sounds awful!"

"She is. Anyway," Jinx said, standing up and stretching her arms above her head as she yawned, "I know Daisy's desperate to get back to her books, and I've got to bank some serious Zs tonight so I'm on form for my torture session in the morning."

Lying on her bed, staring at the ceiling after they'd all bundled out, Jinx was wondering how the hell she'd gotten herself sucked into the middle of yet another fine mess. This term, she thought with a scowl as she flicked her digital radio on, was supposed to be nothing but fun—and a lot of it. Well, she had to admit, there *had* been some but nowhere near enough of late and she really was not looking forward to buttonholing the scary Igor. That was an understatement. She was, in fact, beyond terrified about the impending encounter and decided she needed to work out exactly what she was going to say and how she was going to say it.

However, always one for looking on the bright side, Jinx quickly decided that if she *did* manage to figure this whole thing out she'd get back on Mrs. B.'s good side before it was too late. She still hadn't heard a word about what her extra punishment was going to be, and the longer the headmistress left it the more anxious Jinx became. No doubt that was the point, but still—she needed to know! Since Jinx had a tried and tested theory that Diet Coke is the best thing in the world for sharpening one's brain power, she rummaged around in the bottom of her bag for a fifty-pence piece and headed out of her room towards the vending machine just outside the ground floor common room.

It was half past eleven and the house was in darkness. Jinx crept silently along the wall of her corridor with only the green glow of the emergency exit lights to help her on her way. She reached her destination without seeing a soul. The weather had been so bad of late and the nights so miserable that everyone had started going to bed way earlier than usual and it seemed the habit had stuck, for now anyway.

Jinx fed her coin into the slot and leant slightly against the front of the machine to make sure the can fell properly from its slot. She was straightening up from collecting it from the tray below as she felt the air change around her. She had the distinct feeling someone was watching her. She instinctively knew that whoever it was wasn't one of her friends and that this person was not far away. She gulped and turned around, telling herself to get a grip. Who the hell did she expect to be lurking by the Diet Coke machine in Tanner House anyway?

"Oh," Jinx gasped, covering her hand with her mouth as her eyes lit on a shadowy figure behind her. "It's you."

Igor stood on the other side of the glass door that led into the common room. He wore a black shirt underneath a black jumper with black trousers and shoes, but the first thing Jinx noticed was the preponderance of silver jewelry he wore about his person. In the greenish gleam of the emergency light the massive ring on his finger glimmered as he raked a hand through his jet-black hair. At his white throat a pair of chunky silver chains jangled together as he silently opened the door and motioned for Jinx to walk past him into the room beyond. She did so without a word. Standing by one of the chairs at the table by the window, Jinx gripped her ice-cold refreshment as if it were a weapon and turned to face the bodyguard.

The bank of dark cloud moved past the moon at that point, and Igor's face was lit with a ghostly pallor. Daisy, Jinx thought, was right. That something was seriously bothering Igor was evidenced with one single glance at the deep hollows underneath his sad eyes, the more-sunken-than-usual cheekbones, the not-so-designer stubble covering his jutting jaw and the deep lines recent pain had left etched across his forehead.

"Igor," she said, putting her drink down on the table and moving towards him without a thought for her personal safety, "you look terrible. Maybe if you tell me about it you'll feel better. What's *wrong*?"

"I can't discuss it, Jinx," said Igor, clutching her icy hand in his own, so out of it he didn't even register the drop in temperature. "I wish I could, but I cannot."

Jinx gritted her teeth. Not only was she now doing this for Mrs. Bennett—as long as she lived she'd never be able to pay her back for rescuing Liberty like that—she also felt genuinely moved by Igor's plight, whatever it was.

"I think it's got something to do with Mrs. Carpenter," Jinx said, squeezing his hand and sitting down at the table without letting go, thereby forcing him to do the same. "And I had a very interesting talk with her this morning that you might want to hear."

"Cathy?" asked Igor avidly, leaning forward, "You spoke to Cathy about me today?"

"Yes," Jinx said, looking away as she fought an urgent desire to laugh, "I did speak to…um…Cathy, and she said a lot of things I think you'll want to know." She looked at him intently. "But Igor, I also think there a few things you might want to tell me. Like what's going on with you and the bursar for example. And why you and the triplets have matching diamond rings."

"Ha!" Igor let out a short bark of amazed laughter. "So you *have* noticed. I wondered whether someone would. Well, Jinx, with all due respect, I didn't realize you were so on the ball. You're more clever than I thought you were."

"Well," Jinx replied, having instantly decided it would be *far* too complicated to bring Fingers into the game at this late stage, "I am, I'm afraid. Guilty as charged! So come on then, what's going on with you and…um…Cathy?"

"Oh, Jinx," Igor said, putting his head in his hands and shaking his head roughly, "I have never been so in love with a woman. This passion inside me is unlike anything I have ever known before." He lifted his head and stared at Jinx like a broken man. "But there is nothing I can do. We are star-crossed lovers, the real deal. I can't see any way for us to be together that does not involve lying either to my family or to her. And true love such as ours should not be tainted by deception, deceit, and disloyalty. I love her too much for that. If I can't be with her in the proper way then I won't be with her at all."

"I don't understand," Jinx faltered. "She said this morning that she loved you, and if you love *her* then I can't see what the problem is. You're not," she said quickly as an idea floated into her mind from a Jilly Cooper novel she'd been reading earlier, "married already or anything, are you?"

"No," Igor said crossly, fixing Jinx with a black look. "Of course I do not already have a wife. Have you not listened to a word I have said to you? I am in love with Cathy! I want to marry Cathy!" He paused to bang his head on the table with what Jinx considered unnecessary force. "But I can't."

"But why not?" Jinx pressed. Christ, this little chat had only been going on for ten minutes, but she was already beginning to feel a tension headache starting up behind her eyes. "I just don't get it. If you love her and want to marry her then for God's sake tell her so. You'll be doing all of *us* a huge favor if nothing else, I promise you."

"My father would—" Igor stopped suddenly and banged his head against the wooden tabletop once more.

"What would he do?" asked Jinx, exasperated beyond belief by all these dramatics. She just wanted to know what the hell was going on, once and for all. "Come on, tell me. Mrs. Carpenter, um, Cathy, said she *knew* you, but she didn't KNOW you. What did she mean?"

"Oh, Cathy," Igor wailed, clutching his breast and staring at the moon, painful longing etched across his strong face, "what have I done? What am I doing? What will I do?"

"Right." Jinx reached for her drink and flipped back the ring pull. It was time to regain some semblance of control over the situation. "That's it. I've had enough. You've got one minute exactly and if you don't start speaking sense then I'm afraid I can't help you anymore."

"Okay, okay," Igor said, looking impossibly hurt at the callous way he was being treated. "Hold on. I was getting to it." He twisted himself around in his chair and stared moodily out the window towards the sea. "So you have already seen the rings. I suppose you have already worked out that Olga, Masha, and Irina are my sisters? I am not their bodyguard anymore than you are."

"Of course." Jinx nodded encouragingly, not giving away an inch of how completely blindsided she'd been by this information and pretending she'd known all along. "That much was obvious."

"My father has been planning this for ages, since at least the time he sent off for the Stagmount brochure four years ago and fell in love with the beautiful picture of the building on the front cover," Igor said. "He thought the girls could have a lovely time studying here and that when they were finished with school he could move in and buy the place. He had a vision of Stagmount as the most exclusive gated community in the world, an icon of modern property development and a sure-fire winner of the coveted design awards. He wanted me to join the family business and thought sorting this out would be the perfect test. He decided he wanted me to be his man on the ground, so he arranged with the bursar that I could stay here with the girls under the guise of being their official bodyguard. Then he thought I could arrange the whole sale for him and slip away unnoticed at the end of term."

"But," Jinx interjected, "I don't understand how he imagined he could do that, that he thought it was even possible? Stagmount is not for *sale*."

"To my father," Igor responded sadly, "everything is for sale, as you call it. To someone like him, he can get whatever he wants if he pays enough people off. Some things are just harder to organize than others, but nothing is impossible. That's the mentality, and normally, I must admit, it is true." He shook his head. "But this case is proving very difficult indeed."

"So the bursar..." Jinx said, trying hard to follow the incredible story she was hearing.

"The bursar is a very bad man indeed," Igor said, "He doesn't care about this school at all. Not like Cathy. She loves it here, and seeing it through her eyes I have grown to love it too. He is being paid a vast fixer's fee by my father to put pressure on the members of the school board and the governors to find a way around things."

"What about the triplets?" Jinx asked suddenly, leaning forward. "What do they think about all of this? They seem really happy here. Surely *they* don't want to see the place turned into a series of luxury flats, even if they are the most luxurious ones in the world?"

"My sisters," Igor replied gravely, "do not really understand what is going on. They pay no attention to the business, nor do I imagine they ever will. They think the whole thing is hilarious and have delighted in tormenting me ever since I arrived with them. It was they who told my father I had fallen in love with Cathy. They thought it was funny, but he then instructed the bursar to tell me to break up with her or be cut off and cast aside. I don't even want to be a property developer, but if Cathy found out I was involved in this plot against Stagmount she would hate me anyway. So what could I do, Jinx?"

"Well," Jinx said, thinking that Igor really was a bit of an idiot, "the way I see it, the whole thing is very simple."

"It is?" he asked disbelievingly, before throwing his packet of cigarettes across the room in anger at her insouciance.

"Yes," she said, standing up to better make her point, for there was no way in the world she was going to be intimidated by him now. "You just need to make some decisions and then stick with them. Here's what I think you should do. Firstly, if you truly do love, you know, Cathy, then you need to tell her so, the sooner the better I'd say. Secondly, you need to phone your father and tell him that you don't want to be a property developer. Thirdly," Jinx said, resting her hands on the back of the chair and leaning forward to press her point home, "you need to start doing things for yourself. If you want to be a…"

"Poet," Igor supplied sulkily. "I mostly write poems about Siberia in the winter."

"Okay, so if you want to be a, um, poet," Jinx continued, fighting a desperate urge to snort with laughter but beating it once again, "then just be one. Write some poems, or, like, go to

Siberia or whatever. And tell Cathy you love her and then tell your father you love her. You can't predict his responses," Jinx carried on sagely, wondering where on Earth all this stuff was coming from, "but you can tell him the truth so all the facts are out there. Honesty *is* the best policy…um…in most cases. But moving on, what can your father do that's so bad? So he cuts you off—who cares! Write some decent poems and you won't need his money. And as far as I'*m* concerned," she continued, looking warily at him for the first time since she'd entered the common room, "I'm going to tell the truth too. Tomorrow morning I'm going to see Mrs. Bennett and I'm going to tell her everything we've talked about here tonight. And I'm telling *you* that's what I'm going to do so you can speak to Mrs. C. beforehand and sort everything out with her. Okay?"

"It is more than okay," Igor said, gripping Jinx's hand in his and holding it to his chest. "I don't know how to thank you, Jinx, I really don't. Is there anything, anything at all, I can do for you?"

"Just be nice to Cathy," Jinx said, a small giggle escaping her lips at this unlikely statement. "And then she'll be nice to us. We love her too, when she's in a good mood."

"I will be nice to Cathy forever," Igor said solemnly. "I promise you that."

"Good," said Jinx, releasing herself from Igor's strong grip and making for the door. "I'm beyond thrilled we had this little chat, and I'm so pleased you've got everything sorted out, and I can't wait to hear how Cathy takes the news, but right now I really must go to bed. Good night, Igor. God bless."

"Good night, Jinx," he replied, staring out the window once more, an expression of dazed relief on his face this time. "I will never forget this."

A few minutes later a wide-eyed Jinx lay on her bed and marveled at the sheer insanity of everything she'd just learnt. She had never known Mrs. Carpenter's name was Cathy. Cathy Carpenter, bloody hell. She could hardly have made it up. She could also hardly believe she had to go and inform Mrs. Bennett of yet another dastardly plot so soon after last term's debacle. She knew her friends would find it hard to believe, so she just hoped the headmistress would take this undoubtedly tall tale seriously.

24 *Coming Clean*

Jinx sat on a bench in the very same lock-up bike shed she'd caught Mrs. Gunn and The Dick doing unspeakable things to each other at the end of last term. She took a deep drag on her Marlboro Light. She'd had a key to this place for as long as she could remember and she often shut herself away in here for a bolstering cigarette before a tricky meeting or a nasty test. Although this running to Mrs. B. with shocking news at the end of term business, she thought with a frown as she ground the fag end underneath her heel and slung her oversized tan leather Simultane bag over her shoulder, was becoming just as much of a bloody tradition. And it wasn't one she liked much, either.

She hadn't seen Liberty or Chastity or any of them when she'd emerged from her bedroom, but it was half past eight at the time and she presumed they'd all gone off to lessons or chapel happy in the assumption she was busy dealing with Igor. None of them knew she'd seen him the previous evening and she decided she preferred flying this mission solo. This way, she could take her time thinking about what she should say to Mrs. B. without factoring what anyone else thought into the equation. Although, to be honest, the only thing she'd decided was to tell the truth. And she intended to tell it in as clear, sane, and unexcitable a way as possible.

At the same time Jinx was standing next to Jo's desk outside Mrs. Bennett's office, halfway down the main school corridor, Daisy Finnegan was standing by the entrance to the chapel, waiting to buttonhole Katie Green and take her off for a little chat about things. Daisy craned her neck to better peer over the top of the crowd at the stragglers crawling along behind, fast becoming frustrated by a sea of lower school girls cracking gum and hitching up their skirts right in front of her and before they were hardly out the chapel door.

Jinx, meanwhile, was becoming frustrated by Jo's relentless questions as to what, exactly, Jinx wanted to see her boss about, and Jo was becoming frustrated with the lack of information.

"I just want an appointment as soon as possible please, Jo," Jinx said firmly. "It's, um, personal. Sorry."

"Katie Green?" Daisy asked imperiously as she spied her quarry a few feet in front of her, stunning Katie and all the second-years around her into a shocked silence.

None of them could possibly imagine what a lower-sixth would want with one of their humble lot.

"If I could just have a word," she continued, gripping Katie's arm and ushering her towards the courtyard. "This way."

"What on Earth *is* it, Jinx?" Mrs. Bennett pushed open her door and stuck her head through the gap. "I can hear you haranguing poor Jo from all the way inside! Come in, come in, I've not got a huge amount of time but I can spare you ten minutes before my meeting."

Jinx retrieved her book bag from where she'd casually flung it on the floor, smiled apologetically at Jo and dashed after her headmistress. Mrs. B.'s office was usually a peaceful place, but as she seated herself in one of the red velvet hard-backed chairs opposite the vast mahogany desk, Jinx felt a lot less than calm. Mrs. Bennett leant her elbows on the desk and linked her fingers, her forearms making a pyramid shape in front of her. This was Jinx's cue to swallow, take a deep breath and start talking. And talk she did, without stopping, for the next ten minutes. Mrs. Bennett's spectacles slipped practically to her jaw, but she was too entranced by what Jinx was telling her to even notice.

"So the thing is," Daisy said to a dazed Katie, "all you had to do was write me a note and put it in my pigeonhole and I wouldn't have had to go to all the trouble of making a new one. Do you understand that?"

"But…" it was slowly filtering into Katie's befuddled, panicky mind that Daisy was not accusing her of having anything to do with knocking on Mrs. Bennett's door that fateful night. Eventually, a good few minutes after most people would have cottoned on, it became clear the older girl just assumed she had found the revision aid and pocketed it. Katie had no idea, of course, but she was currently experiencing a classic "fingering." Daisy was adept at moving between anger and sorrow during an uncomfortable encounter, therefore negating the need to go into any situation with more of one than the other and invariably confusing her opposing number to her own advantage.

Mrs. Bennett stared at Jinx, marveling at how on *Earth* the girls had managed to find out all this information, why the hell she herself had heard not even a whisper of anything, and the bursar's amazingly treacherous duplicity.

All finished now, Jinx regarded her headmistress somewhat warily across the gleaming expanse of desk. As Jinx talked she had watched Mrs. B.'s face register a huge variety of expressions and still had no idea what the end result would be. Initial shock at what Jinx was telling her had given way to bemused disbelief, which in turn—and as Jinx had expounded on Daisy's theories and what Igor had told her—gave way to a grudging acceptance. Now, however, was the turn of pure rage.

"Right," Mrs. Bennett said eventually, standing up and pacing back and forth behind her desk. "Right."

Jinx didn't say a word. She felt beyond relieved just to have shared the information with her headmistress. Keeping things to oneself was a most tiresome business indeed, it really was. She hoped Mrs. Bennett believed her and would do something to sort the whole damn mess out.

"Jinx Slater," Mrs. Bennett said, one hand on the back

of the desk chair she had stopped behind, the other pushing her glasses back up her nose, fixing Jinx with a very serious look indeed. "I told you last term that you were a credit to this school, and once again you have proved me absolutely correct. You might," she continued in a much softer voice, smiling warmly at the squirming girl in front of her, "just have saved the school from a fate worse than death."

Jinx blushed and looked down at the toes of her silver Top Shop pumps. She absolutely adored Mrs. Bennett, but she found all this gushing both unnatural and hard to deal with. Her blush swiftly became a magnificent magenta when Mrs. B. enveloped her in a huge hug and whispered "thank you" in her ear.

"So you see, Katie," Daisy was saying to the second-year, "it's *okay* to be a geek. I mean, look at me. I've never been involved in the so-called popular crowd, but I'm still having the best time of my life at Stagmount. I've got plenty of friends who are just like me and I'm getting the best education in the world."

"But…" Katie mumbled, still not quite able to believe Daisy Finnegan was giving her an unasked for pep talk like this and deeply wishing she was anywhere in the world but sitting here on this bench in the cloisters.

"No, don't interrupt." Daisy cut across her imperiously, quite taken with her current agony aunt pose. "As I was saying, Katie, it's only natural to be fascinated with us older girls when you're in the second year. I can remember being quite obsessed with a girl called Annette Walker when I was your age. You can't let it take over your life though, Katie, or the other people in your year might make fun of you."

Daisy scowled as she remembered Jinx making her life an absolute misery by sending her a load of faked letters purporting to be from the aforementioned Ms. Walker, a beautiful blonde American-cheerleader-type who'd been in the lower sixth when they first arrived. Daisy had made a right fool of herself when she'd lovingly, innocently replied to them on a despicable pink, heart-shaped notelet and the others had laughed long and hard at her about it for ages—oh, until the end of the bloody third year at least.

Katie was feeling so pole-axed, appalled, and furiously embarrassed by the whole goddamned thing, so freaked out by Daisy's speech and so longing to get the hell out of there that all her crushes on the older girls died an immediate, irre-versible, and largely painless death on that surprisingly sunny March morning. As long as she lived she never wanted to have a single other thing to do with any of them. It would be a long time before she could even see one of them passing in the corridor and not squirm involuntarily, remembering the hell of Daisy Finnegan telling her they were alike. Sparks practically flew out from under her Clarks brown lace-up shoes, in such a hurry was she to get away when Daisy indicated their cozy chat was at an end.

Daisy, meanwhile, sat on the bench a few seconds longer. So many interesting things had happened to her this term, and she'd forged alliances she'd never even dreamed about. As she ran through the events of the term in her mind, Daisy realized she'd never even come close to discovering the door-knocking-in-the-middle-of-the-night saboteur. She turned her face to the winter sun and decided to give that one up as a bad job.

Jinx watched in awe as Mrs. Bennett buzzed Jo and told her to get the bursar in to see her as soon as possible, *like yesterday* her steely tone implied, and wondered what would happen to the triplets.

"And let's not forget, Jinx," Mrs. Bennett said, "none of this has anything to do with the triplets. If their father wants them to continue their education at Stagmount—as I hope he will—then of course they must. I know I can count on you girls to keep this episode as quiet as possible and not to treat them any differently because of it. Igor, of course, will have to leave, but I'm sure he'll be absolutely fine." Her eyes twinkled as she said this—she'd found it very hard indeed not to laugh when Jinx was breathlessly recounting the love story of Cathy and Igor earlier that morning. "And Jinx, I think we should forget the vodka business. I won't mention it again and neither will you."

Finally released, Jinx smiled at Jo and began walking slowly, thoughtfully, in the direction of the modern languages department, blissfully unaware of the nasty French vocabulary pop quiz that awaited her. Mr. Christie had finally decided to toughen up and sort his act out. She was pondering Mrs. B.'s promise to call a meeting of the school governors, investigate—and immediately get rid of—the bursar, and wondering how Igor's romance mission was going when she heard some-one running up behind her and yelling her name.

"Hi, Dais," she said, turning round to see Daisy, ginger pigtails flying behind her, pink with exertion and gaining on her fast. "What's up?"

"Did you speak to Igor?" demanded Daisy as the pair fell into step and paused at the foot of the DOWN stairs. "What happened?"

Jinx immediately recounted everything that had happened the night before, naturally hamming up the bits about Cathy, and finished with leaving Mrs. B.'s office a few minutes before. Daisy stared at her open-mouthed. She'd known something was up but, super sleuth as she was, she could never have predicted all of *this*. Jinx held up her hand and the pair of them awkwardly high-fived before beginning the trudge to French. Daisy had never knowingly walked up the DOWN stairs before, and the thrill it gave her caused her to throw caution to the wind and ask Jinx if she had anything planned for the weekend.

"Um," Jinx muttered, thinking it was one thing to talk to Daisy on school property but quite another to take her out on the freaking town, "we're going to, like, this skateboarding con-test on the seafront on Saturday. Do you, um, want to come?"

"That's really kind of you, Jinx," Daisy replied with a sur-prised smile. She could hardly believe the great Jinx Slater had actually just invited her to a social event and for a moment she did consider accepting. After another second, however, she decided against it. Calling a halt to hostilities was one thing. Spending their weekends together was another entirely. Daisy wasn't sure they'd quite reached that stage, or indeed if they ever would. It was best all round, she decided, to keep things on an even keel.

"I can't, I'm afraid," she finished decisively. "But thanks anyway."

"S'all right," Jinx said as they stood outside the classroom door, feeling relieved as hell that Daisy had declined and liking her all the more because of it. "Thanks to *you*. If you hadn't realized anything was up God knows what might have happened to Stagmount."

The pair of them smiled sheepishly at each other, locked for a second in a mutual understanding, before Mr. Christie threw open his door and ushered them inside, loudly wondering what on Earth had kept them for so long. They took their seats amidst a chorus of winks, raised eyebrows, and hissed questions. They gave nothing away, but smiled at each other once more before turning to their books.

25 Hanging Ten

Staurday morning dawned bright and sunny, although a biting wind blowing off the sea meant it was still business very much as usual as far as fluffy-hooded parkas, overlong scarves, mittens and the occasional beanie hat. The girls, milling about waiting for a *Days of Our Lives* rerun to start in their common room, had witnessed the bursar's quiet exit from Stagmount life yesterday lunchtime. He climbed into his Volvo Estate, put a cardboard box filled with the contents of his desk on the passenger seat, started the engine and quietly drove off, never to be seen again. Needless to say, nobody was there to wave him off.

Not a great deal had been seen of the triplets, but Liberty said they'd assured her they would meet up with the rest of them on the seafront later that day for the Skate Fest. The others were pleased—the triplets were a hell of a lot of fun and anyway, it wasn't *their* fault their dad was a grasping asshole who'd tried to turn the school into the world's most exclusive gated community, was it?

As far as Igor's conversation with Mrs. C. went, she appeared at lunch on Thursday sporting a massive smile plastered across her face and an even bigger diamond ring on the fourth finger of her left hand. Mimi Tate had seen her skipping—yes, skipping—out of Mrs. Bennett's office yesterday morning. None of them had seen her since, and they could only assume she and Igor were already en route to Gretna Green. Mimi also swore blind she'd been wearing a silver lame skirt and a hot pink jumper. This was simply way too hard to envision, a step too freaking far for sure.

Katie Green, although none of them had noticed of course, was being much more assertive since her little chat with Daisy. She'd discovered a couple of the girls in her own year were not as boring as she'd imagined them, and had even started a surprise alliance with Betsy Johnson. The pair of them bonded over a petition Betsy had started to extend their weekend curfew, and they became thick as thieves as they planned to hand it to Mrs. Bennett at the end of term.

Liv and Charlie had hardly been seen at all recently, but they'd been surprisingly enthusiastic about the Skate Fest. Although they were nowhere to be seen when the others were getting ready that morning, they told Chastity they'd wanted to go all along and were very insistent about them all meeting dead on two o'clock by the main ramp. Wandering along the seafront in a throng of dudes and rudes, Jinx, Liberty, and

Chastity were in a state of high excitement as they pushed through the jostling crowds, keeping one eye on the huge setup about a hundred metres ahead of them, just across from the volleyball court, and the other eye out for their friends and various love interests.

"Fucking hell." Chastity gripped Jinx's arm as they passed one of the ubiquitous Redbull stands and pointed towards the top of the ramp, where all the competitors were massed around a list and a man with a can of Red Stripe in one hand and a loudhailer in the other. "Is that who I *think* it is?"

The three of them stopped where they stood, nearly causing a pileup with the people behind them, and shaded their eyes from the winter sun as they peered over to where Chastity was pointing.

"Oh my God," Jinx exclaimed, covering her hand with her mouth she'd suddenly turned rather pale. "I think you're right. Fucking hell!"

"What?" demanded Liberty, who couldn't see a freaking thing from this angle. "Is it Jamie?"

"No," Chastity replied, folding her arms and leaning back in amazement. "It's Liv and Charlie. Look!"

The three of them, by now pushed to the side of the path by the insistent crowds coming in both directions, stood where they were and stared at their friends in shock. Liv was wearing the baggiest jeans they'd ever seen, teamed with huge pink and grey Etnie trainers with a pale pink T-shirt with a white fairy on the front. Charlie was wearing what looked like green board-shorts with equally huge trainers in bright white and a black

T-shirt. Around her waist was looped a tough-looking chain belt; her knees and elbows were covered with protective pads just like all the boys hovering around them, and she was clutching a bright pink helmet with a black chin strap in her hand. Liv's short hair was gelled close to her head and Charlie's bright blonde hair was pulled back into a sporty-looking ponytail. They looked fresh-faced, cool as hell, and ready for anything.

"Bloody hell," Liberty whistled admiringly. "I've never seen them wearing any of that skate shit before, but it really suits them. What are they *doing* up there, though?"

"I don't know," said Jinx, gripping Liberty with one hand and Chastity with the other as the crowd along the top of the ramp thinned out and it became apparent someone was about to throw themselves off the side of it into the bowl beneath. "But I think we're about to find out."

At that moment the man with the loudhailer pushed a button on the sound system next to him and Avril Lavigne's "sk8ter boi" blasted out into the sea air. They watched agog as Charlie turned to Liv, clasped her left hand to her chest and raised her right arm in a salute before she placed the tip of her board at the edge of the bowl, rocked back and forth as if thinking about something very mundane and then shot off at great speed into the center of it. The crowd held its collective breath for a couple of agonized seconds until Charlie's jubilant face appeared above the parapet of the other side. The girls gasped as she landed on the rim and jumped up, spinning her board beneath her feet to great applause from the male competitors, until she launched herself off the side once again. She did this about five or six times more, each more impressive than the last, until she performed a perfect somersault to rapturous applause from the crowds of hot boys watching.

Impressed hardly does justice to how Jinx, Liberty, and Chastity were feeling as they finally reached the side of the bleachers and managed to get Liv's attention above the roar of whopping and cheering in Charlie's honour.

"I thought one of you dumb bitches would eventually put two and two together, but you're dumber than we thought," Liv yelled rather impolitely over the heads of about fifteen people in between them.

"The bruises!" Jinx screamed, punching Chastity's arm in excitement as she realized they must have been training in secret all term. No wonder they'd hardly been around and when they had they'd suffered all those suspicious injuries. It was *such* a cool thing to do, the three on the sidelines couldn't help but feel slightly envious. What a freaking achievement.

Before they could scream and yell at each other any more, Charlie's round finished and it became obvious Liv was next. Charlie barely had time to pull her helmet off and wave at her school friends before she was surrounded by a crowd of skater boys, all of whom were clearly madly in love with her and showering her with more praise and attention than the others had ever seen at one time. This was an actual master class in how to make guys dig your action going on right in front of them right here.

The others looked on, laughing. The music was so loud they could hardly hear themselves think, but they caught occasional glimpses of Liv leaping into the air above the heads of

Charlie and the myriad boys gathering round to pat her on the back, kiss her cheek, and stuff their phone numbers into her deep pockets. Jinx, Liberty, and Chastity were transfixed by the spectacle, madly impressed, and very proud of their friends.

Liberty spun around as the dark-haired boy from the party appeared from nowhere, tapped her on the arm, leant forward and whispered something in her ear. Whatever it was, it was clearly to her liking, for she beamed and leaned in close to hear the rest. His extremely tall, dark, and very handsome friend stared at Chastity for a second before instantly starting to chat her up. Jinx smiled at them both, moved away and turned round to scour the crowd, looking for Jamie. Her attention was momentarily diverted by a man clutching some delicious-looking sticky hot wings.

Jinx stared at him and wondered if she was hungry. She was aware of something going on behind his head, but it took her a second to realize what she was seeing...

There, to the side of the lowest tier of the silver bleachers, was Jamie. And he wasn't alone, oh no, far from it. Attached to his face like a giant squid was a tall, leggy, very familiar blonde. Jinx turned round to check that Liberty and Chastity were still occupied before moving to the side to get a closer look.

Yes, there was no mistaking it. Jamie and one of the triplets were engaged in a serious snogging session. The pair of them were sucking each other's faces practically off down there, and they didn't seem to care who saw them at it.

Jinx stood there and stared at them. So many things flashed through her mind and she wondered if she'd been an absolute idiot about the whole Jamie thing. The two parties where he'd dumped her as if she had a severe case of nits when George had turned up; the way he'd always involved her friends in things, especially the night Chastity and Paul broke up; how it had taken him eight days to contact her after she'd last been seen leaving his premises in the back of a police van. Realizing Liberty and Chastity were engrossed in conversation and that Liv and Charlie were unlikely to emerge from the midst of their adoring throng anytime soon, Jinx got a fast grip on herself. She made the executive decision to remove herself from the scene ASAP, before Jamie looked up or she bumped into her brother— George was forever turning up where he wasn't wanted; it was one of his special skills.

Jinx turned on her heel and started marching determinedly up the steps to the main road opposite East Street. She was getting the hell out of here and she was getting out fast. The main thing bothering her was how foolish she felt. Not to mention how embarrassed she'd be when her friends found out. She needed a coffee and she needed to have a think, away from the hustle and bustle and the suddenly too-many dudes.

Jinx paused on the esplanade and turned round to survey the scene on the beach beneath her. Jamie—the fucking snake—was still lip-to-lip with the triplet. Jinx gasped as she looked slightly to the right of them. There, as bold as you like, was another triplet, also busily kissing a boy who looked, on closer inspection, very familiar indeed. Shading her eyes with one hand against the bright March sun reflecting off the sea and almost blinding her in its intensity, Jinx used the other to steady herself against the railings and leant forward to get a closer look.

"No way," she muttered under her breath, hardly able to trust the incontrovertible evidence laid out right there in front of her eyes.

"*Way*," she said to herself, disbelievingly, as the boy relinquished his stranglehold on the triplet's neck and turned his face towards Jinx's general direction. She'd thought it was him, but Jinx was still shocked as hell to realize the second snogger was most definitely Paul. Chastity's most recent ex-boyfriend was clearly as over their relationship as she was. Jinx giggled. She couldn't help herself. She was *pleased* Paul wasn't weeping over Chastity somewhere, but really—the whole scene was just too unexpected, too goddamn radical, and too freaking unlikely.

Jinx stood by the traffic lights, waiting to cross the road. However much she tried to force herself back into a state of emotional devastation—what she imagined was appropriate when one has just seen the supposed love of one's life kissing someone else by the bandstand—every time she thought about Jamie, Paul, and the triplets, a massive grin completely ruined the effect. Whichever way you looked at it, Jinx decided as she strode towards town, you had to hand it to the triplets—those girls really didn't let anyone or anything get in the way of what they wanted. And what they wanted—and what they got—was fun, great big bucket loads of it.

Jinx wended her way slowly through the back streets, thinking about how random and weird things were. She was just congratulating herself on how well she was holding herself together, and pondering her most recent realization that a girl could waste her whole life worrying yet still have no idea what was round the corner, when she heard a volley of beeps from a car horn. Jinx turned round ready to give the perpetrator the finger, or at the very least a bad death stare, when she clutched her hand to her mouth in shock at what she saw.

Driving erratically down a thin alley to her left was a very familiar-looking battered black Volkswagen. As the car skidded to a halt, a tall, leggy blonde—unmistakably a triplet—moved out of the shadowy doorway she'd evidently been loitering in whilst waiting for her paramour, threw open the passenger door, sat down, and treated the driver to a tender kiss. Jinx snorted with a mix of glee and horror as she saw the driver's profile. Although George was right there in front of her, she still had a hard time believing her own eyes. Those girls really *didn't* care about what they did. But her crush *and* her brother? This was a hat trick of the first class. The car sped off up the hill and disappeared from view, but Jinx stayed rooted to her spot on the pavement. It really was, she decided, best to take life in a simplistic way; to deal with things as they came up, and not spend too much time endlessly agonizing, analyzing, and obsessing.

She almost—just for a *second*—felt sorry for Lydia. "Nah," she muttered to herself, "that bitch deserves everything she gets and worse."

Although Jinx herself would never dream of going any-where near any of the boys her friends had had dealings with, however small, she almost admired the triplets' insouciance. They'd never let a little thing like an unwritten rule about not going after your friends' crushes get in their way. But Jinx's female friendships were way more important to her than any stupid crush. Even the remembered pain of nearly losing Liberty at the end of last term was far more acute than the current mélange of squeamishness, embarrassment, and bemused anger she was now feeling thanks to Jamie's performance on the seafront.

After a ten-minute, mostly uphill march, Jinx sat at one of the tables clustered together outside Café Nero in town and disconsolately stirred two lumps of crystallized brown sugar into her soy latte. As she contemplated the sad fact that dressing all in black like a suicidal French poet was never going to be a good look for her, even if she *had* just been kind of dumped in the most publicly humiliating fashion, she wondered why people never had sugar like this in their houses?

It was fair to say she was rallying admirably when she bent down and saw the cutest, tiniest Boxer puppy with the wrinkliest face and softest nose she'd ever seen nudging her leg under the table. She held onto his collar and looked around for his owner. It being a biting cold Wednesday afternoon in March, the square was pretty much deserted.

Jinx pulled him onto her lap and searched for an identity tag. Bingo—there it was, attached to the circular join on his collar.

Jamie was the last thing on her mind as she held the pup close to her chest and reached for her phone. Punching out the digits she wondered what kind of retard would let the cutest little dude in the world roam around the streets of Brighton on his own like this. She resolved to give the owner a piece of her mind as the ringing tone started. The voice that answered the phone, however, was beside itself with worry. Jinx found herself reassuring a woman who sounded about the same age as her mum that her puppy was fine. She told her where they were sitting and settled back to wait, delighted beyond reason to have this cutie to herself for a few minutes.

She hardly noticed the man who appeared in front of her until he coughed and said her name.

"Yes?" said Jinx, looking up and blushing instantly at the vision of masculinity she was confronted with. Tall, bronzed, about her age, and with thick, shoulder-length, dark brown hair, this guy was seriously stacked and very good-looking. His green eyes bored into her own as he pulled up a chair and reached over to tenderly stroke the side of the squirming puppy's little nose.

"My mum said you were sitting here," he said to her, laughing as the boxer caught his finger in its mouth and started nibbling it furiously. "I was furious with her for leaving the back door open, but I had no idea this one was clever enough to seek out such a gorgeous rescuer."

Jinx blushed and reflected that, on balance, she really was over Jamie. He was so spring term. And since that was nearly over, it seemed fitting her crush should be, too.

"I don't suppose," he said, leaning forward and smiling at her, "you're doing anything on Tuesday, are you?"

Jinx smiled beatifically and mentally gave Irina, Masha, and Olga the biggest high five. Thanks to them, kind of, Mrs. Bennett had rescinded their Tuesday punishment cleaning and the girls had one free Tuesday afternoon left.

"Nothing," she said, stroking the puppy's back as he fell asleep between her thighs, looking up at him. "And I'd love to."